SENTINELS: LYNX DESTINY

DORANNA DURGIN

Published in Great Britain 2014
by Mills & Boon, an imprint of Harlequin (UK) Limited,
Eton House, 18-24 Paradise Road, Richmond, Surrey, TW9 1SR

© 2014 Doranna Durgin

ISBN: 978 0 263 91384 2

89-0214

Harlequin (UK) Limited's policy is to use papers that are natural, renewable and recyclable products and made from wood grown in sustainable forests. The logging and manufacturing processes conform to the legal environmental regulations of the country of origin.

Printed and bound in Spain
by Blackprint CPI, Barcelona

Doranna Durgin spent her childhood filling notebooks first with stories and art, and then with novels. After obtaining a degree in wild-life illustration and environmental education, she spent a number of years deep in the Appalachian Mountains. When she emerged, it was as a writer irrevocably tied to the natural world and its creatures.

Doranna received the 1995 Compton Crook/Stephen Tall Award for best first book in the fantasy, science-fiction and horror genres; she now has over fifteen novels spanning an array of eclectic genres, including paranormal romance, on the shelves. When she's not writing, Doranna builds web pages, enjoys photography and works with horses and dogs. You can find a complete list of her titles at www.doranna.net.

This book is for sweet Belle Cardigan Corgi:
PACH Cheysuli's Silver Belle, CD RE MXP5 MXPS
MJP6 MJPS PAX2 XFP EAC EJC CGC.
Run fast, run clean and take all my love with you.

Chapter 1

You may have driven my mother mad, but you won't do it to me.

Regan Adler gazed out at the intensely rugged vista of the Sacramento Mountains—vast slopes of ponderosa pine, towering cliffs and deep blue sky, all nearly nine thousand feet high. It should have been inspiring; it should have been invigorating.

Regan scowled out over that beauty. "Don't you dare talk back to me," she muttered at it.

The land said nothing back. After a moment, her sturdy blue roan gelding snorted impatience, and Regan released a breath she hadn't realized she'd been holding. The gelding's winter hair curled damply under her hand as she patted his neck; he'd shed out in another month or so, but the April noonday sun already beat down hard, and they'd covered only half the generous acreage attached to the Adler family cabin.

For now, Regan Adler focused on getting reacquainted with this place to which she'd vowed she'd never return.

"Yeah," she said, when the horse snorted again, bobbing his head in suggestion. "It's not your fault that Dad's away, is it?" Or that Regan was trapped here, caretaking the place for some unknown length of time while her father recuperated from a back injury with his brother in El Paso. Although he was still a man in his prime, this was no place for a man—or woman—who couldn't hold his own against winter snow, the woodstove or the long hike off the mountain if the truck didn't start.

Another shift of her weight, and the horse moved forward again, placing his feet carefully in spite of the spirit in his movement. She'd already come to appreciate this canny little mustang and his responsive nature; his good judgment left her free to hunt the boundary markers on a land that hardly seemed changed since she'd been here last.

The horse snorted again, but it held a different sound; it came with a head raised and small ears pricked forward. Regan sat deliberately still in the saddle, quiet and balanced and waiting.

Plenty of bear up in these parts. Plenty of tree trunks and shadows and juts of land to hide a bear even nearby.

"Shh," Regan said softly as the horse trembled briefly beneath her. "It's not exactly safe to go bolting off through the woods, either."

Neither ear swiveled back to acknowledge her. Not good. "I was thinking admiring thoughts about you a moment ago," she told the horse, laying one hand on that sweaty neck—feeling the tension there. "I'm trusting you to keep me safe."

Safe...

The word eased through her mind, an unwelcome susurrus in her thoughts. *Oh, just perfect.*

Safe...

"I heard you the first time," she snapped. "Stay out of my head!"

Even silent, the whisper crawled across her skin.

Regan gritted her teeth. *You may have driven my mother mad, but you won't get me.*

And the horse exploded into bucking beneath her.

Kai hadn't meant to intrude. He hadn't meant to alert the horse, never mind spook it.

The woman had been sitting the blue roan with a comfortable grace, well mounted on the compact creature. The sun beat down on a battered straw cowboy hat, glinting off the amazing pale gold of her hair as it trailed down her back in a single braid. She stayed quiet when the horse detected Kai, alarmed at the unfamiliar lynx-and-human mix of scents; she'd scanned the woods, as aware as the horse—and as aware as Kai—of the dangers that lurked in this natural beauty.

And Kai responded instinctively, as he did nearly everything. He imbued his thoughts into the land, making it an offering…a reassurance. An intent to stay silent and unseen, here where he tracked the other recent intruders in this place.

He hadn't expected her to hear the ripple of his message so clearly.

He *really* hadn't expected her to react so strongly.

It put the horse over the edge into bucking, right there on the slant of the earth, a tangle of deadwood to one side and a tight, scrubby cluster of knee-high oak to the other. Not wild bucking, but without footing and without space.

Kai didn't expect it when the woman came off, either.

The horse didn't hesitate for an instant. Reins flying, stirrup leathers flapping, it whirled and bolted away.

But the woman didn't move.

Kai crouched to the earth, appalled…his broad lynx

paws spread over humus and twig, his claws flexing momentarily deep, and his concern rippling out as loudly as his reassurance a moment earlier.

Her voice rose from amidst the scrub oak. "I'm *fine*," she said, with sharp annoyance. "Now butt *out*." The words slapped back at him through the land, a light smack of retribution, and Kai crouched even lower, his ears slanting back and his mouth opened to a silent snarl of protest... and surprise.

He pulled back into himself and did the only thing he could—the thing he'd wanted to avoid in the first place. He reached for the human within himself—stretching out into his shoulders, straightening long legs. He put noise into his feet so she would hear him coming with his human stride, and moved through the woods as though he had no habitual cause for silence—and as he reached her, he pretended he hadn't heard her earlier words, or felt that stinging slap. "Are you all right?"

His voice came out rough with disuse, a voice with a rasp at the best of times. She seemed to understand him regardless, though she didn't respond directly, and she didn't yet get up. She lay tangled in the oak, one bent knee upright and casual. "He was sure there was a bear. You must be it."

"Lynx," he responded, before he could think not to, and winced.

She gave him a sharp look from the corner of her eye, but she did as so many others in the outside world did— she ignored that which didn't make sense. "You know, if you weren't trespassing, you might not have spooked my horse."

"I didn't expect you to fall," he admitted. "But I'm not trespassing."

"The hell you aren't." That brought her upright, indignation on her face. "And I didn't fall. I *bailed*." She had the fair skin to go with her bright hair, her face flushed from her fall and her ire. "It didn't seem like the place to go mano a mano with the mustang. Especially not when he was *right*. There *was* something creeping around out there." She fixed him with a blaming glare, her eyes a pale blue in the sun, before she snatched her straw hat from the brush and crammed it back over her head.

Kai rose to that glare in ways he hadn't expected—a notch of his own temper, the hint of a growl in his throat as he nodded over her shoulder. "The boundary is behind you. Frank knew this."

"My father?" Something crossed her features, then—a brief inner conflict revealed and dismissed. "He's not here. But I know our land." She climbed to her feet, brushing off her jeans—twisting to check her posterior and in the process revealing a glimpse of toned belly and the wink of a stone in her navel.

The shiny flicker woke the cat in him—but more so, the man in him, laying over his protective nature with a new alertness.

She gave him an odd look—and then another, clearly taking him in for the first time. "Seriously?" she said. "You're out in the middle of nowhere with no shirt and no water and Daniel Boone pants and *no shoes?*"

This was why he hadn't wanted to take the human, or to approach her—why he rarely spoke to others at all. What was right for them? What was normal? At least when he slipped into the Cloudview general store, they knew him. He thought they liked him. Outsiders even occasionally hired him as a guide, which was money enough for his scant needs.

So he responded in the way that so often worked—ignoring the question and the implications that he might just be crazy, and pretending to ignore the glint of jeweled fire nestled at her belly button. "Let me help you find the horse."

She laughed shortly. "He's probably back at the hay feeder by now. I just hope he doesn't step on a rein along the way."

"Then let me walk you back to safety."

"I'm safe enough," she said pointedly, and reached a hand for the small sheath on her hip, a weapon of some sort.

But she had no idea. She couldn't possibly, this woman who didn't know what he was and yet had still somehow heard him through the land.

This woman who had no idea the Atrum Core recently lingered nearby, encroaching on her world in the wake of increasing activity along the edges of it. Playing with their workings and amulets up here where it was easy to hide, searching for illicit advantage and power, searching for a foothold against all that was right with the world.

Maybe even searching for *him*.

"Let me walk you home," he said again. He put some voice behind it this time, letting it resonate in the land between them. Her eyes widened just enough so he knew she'd felt it, if not identified it.

She put her hand back on the sheath…a message. "Let's go, then," she said, even as she eyed him with obvious doubt. "It's a long way back, and I'm getting hungry."

But she wouldn't have turned her back to him if she'd truly understood what he was.

What Regan hadn't said was "No shirt and no water and Daniel Boone pants and that body?" But it had been a close thing. And in the moments during which this man led the way back to her home—obviously familiar with the land between here and there—she watched not her own path but the expanse of his shoulders, the fine taper of his back and the unique nature of his movement. There lay a primal strength behind his completely unselfconscious grace, and it drew her eye whether she willed it or not.

She spotted the boundary line on the way back in, chagrined to realize he'd been right—she'd wandered over into Lincoln National Forest. But he said nothing, and it felt natural enough to walk in silence.

She stopped them when she glimpsed solar panels gleaming in the sun—her family's cabin, as self-sufficient and tucked away as any house could be in this modern world. "I'm home," she said. "It wasn't necessary to come with me, but I appreciate the gesture."

He studied her a moment. "I don't know what that means."

She almost laughed—until she realized he'd meant it. Then she floundered, glancing toward the snug cabin in which she'd grown up—the careful combination of old-time sensibility and modern tech, so far off the grid and so self-sustaining. "It means I still don't think you needed to come with me, but I understand that you meant well by it. And now I would like to be left alone."

"Ah." He flashed her an unexpected grin, all Black Irish coloring with dark hair and deep blue eyes and features cut with hard precision, an unexpected smudge of kohl around his eyes. "*That,* I understand."

He moved away, bare feet confident on the spring-damp ground with its unique and primitive mix of fern and desert thistles, and she felt an instant of regret—but she still took a step back when he turned again, not so much wary of him as *aware* of him.

"My name is Kai," he said. "Call me if you need me again. Because you have been away too long, Regan Adler—or you would know why I needed to walk you here."

And what was *that* supposed to mean? She frowned, and she would have asked him—but he'd taken her dismissive words to heart and he had the long casual strides to act on them. By the time she might have opened her mouth, he was into the woods and gone, and she was left awash with conflicting impulses—and with the sudden realization that he'd called her by name, when she'd never given it to him at all.

And then she stared into the apparently empty woods just a little bit longer, her eyes catching on a flicker of there-and-gone-again light—tumbling blue-white shards of energy that made no sense in this day of bright sky and clear spring sunshine overhead.

Safe...

"Oh, I don't think so," she said out loud. "There wasn't anything safe about him. Not a single damned thing."

No one had anything to say about that.

By the time she'd located the mustang grabbing hay from the wrong side of the paddock's corral panels, unsaddled him and groomed him and inspected both horse and tack for damage, Regan's stomach growled with ferocity and she ached with stiffening bruises.

She'd told Kai the truth—she'd bailed from the sturdy little horse. Bailing was better than waiting for him to hit a tree or catch a hoof in the uneven ground, and it was better than falling—it meant controlling the circumstances... controlling the landing.

But there had still been a landing out there on the side of the mountain. *Ow.*

She finally slipped in through the tiny mudroom and through the kitchen to the bright splash of sunshine in the great room, thinking about the big homemade cookies her father had left in the freezer. But when she saw through the picture windows to where the mountain fell away from the front of the house, she didn't withhold her groan at the unfamiliar car sitting behind her father's old pickup.

Her father's cat responded with a flick of his tail from

his sprawling perch in the sunny bay window; outside, her father's old dog waited for his master's return, maintaining his station on the worn wooden porch.

She took her cue from the dog, who would have greeted a friend. A glance showed her the shotgun leaning quietly in the corner closest to the door; she left it there as she headed outside, but she kept it in mind.

The people here on this mountain were good people. But she wasn't expecting anyone, and the man exiting the car hardly had the look of a local. Not with the expensive cut and perfect fall of his suit coat and slacks, or the heavy silver at his ear and wrist—or the affectation of his tightly slicked back hair and the short gather of it at the nape of his neck.

Bob the Dog regarded the man's approach with disapproval, his tail stiff, his gaze flat and staring—and a little growl rising in his throat.

Maybe it was the dog's reaction that made Regan cross her arms as she waited on the porch, a less than friendly demeanor. Maybe it was the little whisper of unease she felt, not knowing if it came as an irrational little inheritance from her mother or her own common sense.

Maybe it was Kai's words—*You've been away too long*—or his insistence on walking her home.

Maybe she was just cranky, and not expecting company.

The man smiled, stopping a few feet before the open porch, his eye on the dog even as he pretended not to be concerned. "You must be Frank's daughter."

It wasn't an introduction; it wasn't a reason for visiting this remote little home without the courtesy of a call.

Beware...

Right, she thought back at that insidious little voice. *Because I needed your help to tell me that.*

"I'm sorry," she said. "My father isn't here. If you'd

like to leave your contact information, I'll let him know you stopped by."

"Regan," he said as if it wasn't a guess. "Frank said I might find you here. Is that dog safe?"

"How did you say you knew my father?" *Because if you'd been here before, you'd be familiar with the dog. You'd know he won't let you on this porch unless I tell him to stand down.* Once it had been the entire yard—but like her father, the dog had aged.

"I'm sorry. I didn't say." He didn't look sorry. He looked aggrieved that she hadn't simply welcomed him inside. "I'm with Primary Pine Realty. My name is Matt Arshun." He pulled a business card from his inside suit pocket, holding it out between his first and second fingers. "Your father contacted me about listing this property."

The shock of it made her chest feel empty; she found herself momentarily speechless. She hadn't wanted to come back to this place—but she hadn't realized until that moment how much it was still part of her. Deep in her mind she heard a wail of denial…and she didn't think it was hers.

I am not my mother.

She caught a flash of satisfaction on the man's face, as if she'd told him something he hadn't been sure of until this moment. "I was hoping to take a look around."

She shook her head; hidden by her crossed arms, her nails bit briefly into her palms. "I wish you'd called first. You could have saved yourself a trip. This isn't a convenient time."

"When should I come back?"

Never. But she managed to not say it out loud. "Leave your card in the delivery box at the end of the drive," she told him. "I'll call you when I'm ready."

He'd been ready to hand her the card. He gave the glowering dog between them a second glance and shifted his weight back. "I was hoping to move on this property," he said. "Vacation property in the high country has only a seasonal interest."

"Leave your card," she told him again. "Or don't, if the delay is a problem for you. It's all the same to me."

"Maybe you should call your father," Arshun said, tipping the card between his two fingers and finally dropping it to the porch. She stood behind the dog until Arshun got into his luxury car, slamming the door even as he started the powerful engine. There wasn't much gravel left on the driveway surface, but he managed to spit some out behind his wheels anyway.

Bob the Dog looked over his shoulder at her, his tail wagging faintly in question. Part cattle dog, part Labrador, part huge…a good friend to her father, and still unfamiliar to Regan. She patted his broad head. "Good boy," she said, and her legs suddenly felt just a little bit wobbly. She sat down beside him, letting her feet hang over the edge of the porch. He didn't lick her or demand attention; he just *was*—a stolid old dog sitting beside her.

It would have been presumptuous to lean on him, in his aloof dignity. She settled for leaving her hand on his back.

She'd call her father; she'd find out about the Realtor, and her father's intentions. But that was the least of her wobbly reaction—and he couldn't truly tell her what she needed to know.

For if her father could offer her answers about the whispers, if he could offer reassurance…she never would have left this place. And if he'd had any true idea how deeply the land and its whispers gripped her, how insidiously it threaded its way back into her being, he never would have asked her back.

She had an unbidden flash of an image in her mind— Kai, moving through the woods. Kai in his rough deerskin leggings and barefoot confidences, his quietly primal intensity, his sinuous strength.

And she suddenly thought he was the one who might understand.

She has no idea.

Kai sat on an outcrop between Regan's land and his own territory, scowling inside. *She has no idea.*

Then again, neither did he. Not really. He'd never dealt directly with the Core; he only knew of them—just as he knew of the Sentinels and their Southwest Brevis to which he might well have belonged as a full-blooded field Sentinel. Within the past year he'd felt several periods of activity—a swell of Core workings affecting distant Sentinels and reaching him even here; a cry of grief that had resonated through the land, fading by the time he recovered from it well enough to go looking for clues. A thing of weeping and nightmare intensity that had left remarkably little trace but had left him increasingly wary.

The Core had changed the game somehow, and even in his isolation, Kai knew it.

He knew more of their mutual history: that the Sentinels had started two thousand years earlier with a single druid, a man who had channeled earth energies into the discovery of his inner self. His animal form.

The druid's half brother—a man sired by a Roman soldier, utterly without power—began an immediate quest for ways to control his sibling. That quest had been fueled by fear and jealousy…and these millennia later, had resulted in two worldwide organizations locked in an endless cold war. The Sentinels protected the land, as they always had—just as Kai did. The Atrum Core coated their activities in a righteous manifesto—*keep the Sentinels in check*—and used it to justify stolen power and corrupted energies. The need for secrecy kept both factions running silent, but lately...

Lately Kai had felt the Core pushing at his world. More activity from their workings, more touches of their presence. His lynx had become uneasy; his human knew to listen.

For they were *here*.

His family had brought him to this high, remote place because of his innate ability to detect even the faintest Core workings and presence. They'd hidden him here, trained him here...kept him apart from both Sentinels and Core.

That sensitivity was the reason they had finally left him here, drawing away the danger while he plunged into a life alone, always remembering their words. *One day...*

One day, you'll be the one who can make the difference. Until then, they can't know of you.

Kai had been satisfied with his life. By guiding people through these forests, he made sure they treated the land properly along the way. He knew which elk herds needed to be thinned; he knew where the coyote population had tipped out of balance. He knew where people were stupid enough to leave food out for bears, and how to discourage them.

Here, where the world still ran high and wild, he kept things right.

But maybe that wasn't enough any longer.

If the Core had any true clue of him—of what he could do, or that he was unique in his ability to do it—its minions wouldn't be tramping so freely on his chosen turf. He'd stayed silent, circling quietly around their insidious invasion—seeking to understand what they were doing in a way that no one else could. Once he did, it would be time to reach out to the Sentinel regional headquarters at Southwest Brevis. To let them know, finally, that he was here...and so was the Core.

But then Regan Adler had come back to the Adler cabin.

She reverberated through her land, whether she knew it or not…. She reverberated through *him*. She had an awareness that wouldn't allow her to go unnoticed by the Core—or for them to go unnoticed by her. She had a vibrancy and determination, bouncing up from the ground to challenge him while the sturdy little horse bolted away—perfectly aware that she faced something not quite tame. And she had no idea how dangerous it would be to interfere with him…with the Core.

Yes, Regan Adler changed everything.

For one thing, she had already changed *him*.

Chapter 2

The day after she ran into the mysterious Kai, Regan stuffed her pockets full of surveyor's tape, added a water bottle to her belt, jammed her feet into her riding sneakers and headed out to walk woods full of spring warblers and morning song, stout walking stick in hand.

He'd been right, Kai had. She'd been over the boundary of their acreage. And if she didn't know where those lines ran, then she needed to find out—especially if the word had gotten out to real estate agents that her father might sell.

After all, she needed to know just where she could kick them off the land. At least until she confirmed what Matt Arshun had said—and so far, all she'd found was a business card identical to the one he'd given her, tucked away in her father's desk.

Arshun was, she thought, overstating his case.

She poked the walking stick in between some downhill roots and used it to steady her descent, heading for the first boundary tree. A rare dew soaked her high-top riding sneakers, adding to the chill of the morning.

Rae...

"You must be kidding," she muttered, more incredulous than she liked. Ten years away from the cabin, illustrating Southwest specialty guidebooks and selling fanciful little paintings on the side, and she'd lived in blessed silence. But less than a week after her return, that silence had broken. And not with the little nudges and intuitions she'd denied having as a child—denied hard, in the wake of her mother's breakdown—but with actual whispers.

Less than a week after her return. But even then, she'd had silence until the previous day.

Until Kai.

As if that made any sense at all. She steadied herself on the rugged bark of a ponderosa, scraping through the prickly, hollylike leaves of a scrub oak. *Kai.* A man who knew the land—better than she did at this point. A man who dressed the part—who surely had resources nearby, to have come out bare-chested and without a canteen. *Barefooted.*

Primal.

And she'd first heard those whispers only moments before her horse dumped her—*I bailed, dammit!*—and then he'd appeared, full of apology.

Since when did the savvy little mustang spook at a man in the woods?

Too many questions.

Rae...

God, was that her mother's voice, using her childhood pet name? Whispering into her head? Or had this place simply stolen so much from her mother that now it sounded like her?

"You can't have my life," she told it, a snarl of defiance—and didn't know if she was talking to the land, or to herself. To whatever had started inside her that would slowly erode her sense of self until she didn't know where she started or where she ended.

Beware...

Regan stopped, cocking her head to the sudden change. That had *certainly* not come from within—that sense of alarm and foreboding. It hadn't been part of her morning so far at all, no matter the unsettled nature of her ruminations.

She turned from it, just as she had turned from the affectionate greeting—she did what she'd always done in these unsettled moments, reaching out to the artist within herself. Her practiced eye found the beauty in the stark lines of a fallen tree, the sharp shadows of the morning and the contrast of the orange-brown pine bark against the ferns splashed across the rugged slope. She picked out shape and detail, and her hand twitched, reflexively reaching for watercolors, for oils...for a smear of pastel in a wild, expressive movement.

By the time she saw the boundary tree, she'd almost forgotten why she'd come out here in the first place.

But as she pulled the flutter of stretchy, orange tape from her pocket, ready to take another wrap around the tree, the warning sensation hit her again. Stronger.

BEWARE...

She didn't snap back at it this time, or wonder at it or even resent it. She simply reeled in it, alarm twisting the pit of her stomach, and her fingers tightening over the tape.

It didn't matter that it wasn't her alarm. It was still *real*. And it felt like...

A cry for help.

Beware...

The whisper of warning slapped within Kai, reverberating...and bounced back out to the land. With it came a twist of pain, and a still unfamiliar but unmistakable taint.

The Atrum Core.

After a moment there came a faint echo of awareness—one that would have been imminently welcome had it not been for the Core presence. *Regan Adler,* not far away.

Kai moved out as lynx, broad paws stepping through dew, a luxury in the desert. *Ration your lynx,* his family had often told him. *Keep your balance.*

But that had been long years earlier, before his family had left him here to survive with a home carved out of the mountains, a bank account rarely touched and the weepy enjoinder that neither the Core nor the Sentinels could ever know what he could do. What he was.

If the Sentinels knew, the Core would know. And if the Core knew, they would stop at nothing to kill him.

That didn't mean Kai would let them slink in here to poison the land. He moved through the shadows of the morning, staying on the cool north slope where the vegetation ran thicker, the dew lingered longer and the ground sank beneath his feet. The sickening vapor of Core workings swirled around them all, skimming the ground like a living fog. Kai lifted his lips in a silent snarl, flattening whiskers—cursing, as he could while lynx. The ugly energy held no structure, no directive, and Kai could discern no purpose behind it.

But by the time he'd circled along the slope and curved into the sparser cover of the southeast exposure, he had a good idea where it came from. He planned his steps accordingly—and his temper rose with each.

They weren't quite over the boundary and onto Adler land. But they were close. They'd found the spot where the dry creek spilled out near the dirt Forest Service access road; like many before them, they'd followed that rocky path uphill to the spot where it spread wide—where rainwater and snowmelt sometimes pooled and where Kai himself often slaked his thirst as both human and lynx.

Kai had been patrolling that spot for years. Careful hikers—those who packed out what they brought in—he left
alone. Careless hikers...

One way or another they didn't stay.

Kai didn't plan for the Core to stay.

He found them arrayed around the dry pool, the ground
scuffed around them and rocks carelessly overturned.
There were three of them—the first of the Core he'd ever
seen. He watched them for some moments, paws spread
wide over the ground, short tail restless—lashing as it
could.

It surprised him that they were so recognizable. Big,
beefy men, one of them in a suit with an expensive sheen
and fall of cloth, the other two in serviceable black slacks
and dark gray short-sleeved shirts under identical black
jackets. They all bore silver at their ears, silver on their
wrists and fingers, and dark olive skin tones that owed
nothing to the sun. The suited man had his dark hair pulled
back in a short club at his nape; the other two wore utilitarian styles, long enough to lick at their ears and collars.

And while the suited man watched, the others were
hard at work. Two large metal cases lay by the side of
the dry pool, open to reveal padded, sectioned interiors.
One case still held its original contents—gleaming piles
of dark metal, glinting dully in the uneven trickle of light
through the overhead pines. Kai narrowed his eyes, finding it painful to focus on those metal disks for reasons he
couldn't discern; his lynx's vision preferred motion to stillness and muted colors into smears of similarity, but never
had it simply slid away from an object under examination.

He quit trying and focused on what they were doing,
instead.

Not that it made any more sense. Loose piles of the
metal disks sat one off to the side in the dry pool, and Kai

couldn't see so much as *feel* it steaming with the same dark and desultory emissions that now crept over the land.

The men gave it a wide berth, murmuring to one another as they moved efficiently around a second pile, placing additional disks to make four enclosing corners while the suited man uttered short directives.

Kai growled into the morning. Deep in his chest. Deep in his heart. The suited man's head jerked up; he'd heard it. He heard it again when the land picked up the sound, rolling it along the slopes and down the dry creek bed. The other two heard it as well, stopping their work to look around.

The suited man spoke sharply to them, his manner peremptory. But as they returned to work, he also pulled out a gun, scanning the woods above and around them.

Kai growled again. He imbued it with threat and intent and sent it out through the living forest, letting the trees thrum with it.

You are not welcome here.

The two men stood, backing away from their work to join the third in searching the woods—and distracting him in the process. Kai took advantage to slink closer, paws spread wide and silent on the ground, long legs coiled beneath him.

"There aren't supposed to be any Sentinels in this area!" one of the men argued. He was stouter than the other and held himself with stiff awareness that they weren't alone— and a wariness of the woods that bespoke his utter lack of familiarity. "That's why we're *here*."

The suited man offered no sympathy. "And that's exactly why we'll stay. Now finish cleansing those amulets— we need the blanks."

Cleansing those amulets... Core pollution. The very equivalent of dumping toxic waste.

"It's a trick of the terrain!" the suited man snapped at

the extended hesitation from his minions. "Sound carries out here. Now get back to work!"

Kai's tufted ear twitched with satisfaction and no little derision. Sound did carry in these woods—but it carried uphill, not down. If these men knew no better than that, it didn't matter that they were three to his one. He could deal with them as he had to.

Never had he taken on a human before—never had he used his quick strength to overcome another. But he'd spent a lifetime on the hunt…on his own, whether fighting off aggressive, hungry coyotes or bringing down his own prey. And he'd spent a lifetime studying human disciplines— running the miles to the tiny town of Cloudview and its tiny Tae Kwon Do dojang, where the students accepted him even if they didn't quite know what to do with someone they clearly thought of as a modern-day mountain man.

But Kai enjoyed the run, and he enjoyed the discipline—and besides, he had to return his library books.

All these men had to know of him was that he would— and could—stop them. *Core minions,* his father had called such men, with a wry twist of his mouth that told Kai he might well be disrespectful of them, but he was nonetheless wary.

Kai let his growl roll across the land, a twist of threatening yowl in the undertones. Not quite big cat…but big enough. He didn't want them here…the land didn't want them here. Surely, together they could—

Concern. Resistance. Intent.

But that wasn't the land whispering to him now. It was Regan.

He'd grown too used to the undertones of the voice she didn't seem to know she had…he'd let her grow near without paying heed.

And she had no idea who these men were. If they had

active amulets, they could sicken her and she wouldn't even know what was happening.

If they were looking for trouble, they could do worse.

They hadn't yet seen her, but she wasn't far. Her bandanna-print shirt flashed brightly between the tree trunks; her walking stick seemed a token thing.

She looked, for that moment, a wild thing—just as at home in the woods as he was. The shadows muted the bright gold of her pale hair; she moved easily down the rugged hill, barely touching the trees for balance on the way past. And for that moment, Kai was lost in her—her presence, her free movement, her resonance on the land.

But only for that moment. For the corruption of new Core poison crept out along the land, and Regan came on. And Kai couldn't stop her without giving himself away to the Core—not as lynx, not as human. They knew Sentinel as well as he knew Core, even on first sight.

If he gave himself away as Sentinel, it would be the beginning of his end.

Chapter 3

Regan couldn't believe it. Not on any count.

I did not just follow impulse and voices in my head to find these men.

She *hadn't*. Because if she had...

It didn't bear thinking about.

And what were they doing anyway?

Not burning, although her eyes stung as if smoke hung in the air. But it was something more than mere littering, even if it made no visual sense.

Nor did that undertone of a deep feline growl, something she heard not with her ears at all.

She adjusted her grip on the walking stick—a stout, twisting maple stick, polished by time and handling—and stuck her chin in the air, coming on out of the woods as if she owned them.

Even if she knew better than to get close.

"This is national forest," she told them, speaking before they'd even noticed her. Whatever they did with their inexplicable piles of crude metal disks, it demanded most of their attention. The remainder of it had gone to scowling up at the dry creek bed.

As if maybe they, too, had heard that threat of a growl.

"Mind your own business." The man in the suit gestured at the others to continue, pocketing something she hadn't quite seen. Dark hair, olive skin tones, silver at his ears, and an expensive suit altogether incongruous to his presence in the woods... He looked unexpectedly familiar.

The other two...

What had she been thinking, to brace these men alone?

For the other two were pure muscle, a matching set. And they held twin expressions of scorn while they were at it.

She stayed uphill, standing on a jut of root and rock at the base of a massive ponderosa. Not within reach, as she slipped a hand into her backpack pocket and closed her hand around her phone.

Not that she was likely to have any signal bars in this area. She certainly didn't have them in the cabin.

"I *am* minding my business," she said. "This land belongs to everyone. It's not yours to spoil."

The growl sounded not so much in her ears as in her chest, the rumble of it vibrating within her.

Beware...

Right. As if she didn't already know.

The man in the suit gave her all of his attention for the first time. With some exasperation he said, "Are we going to have a problem here?"

"Marat, do you want—?" one of the muscle twins asked.

But the suited man shook his head. "I'm sure we can come to a quieter understanding," he said.

She understood, then. They might not care about her, but they did care about being caught. Although, since they'd have plenty of time to get away from this place, maybe they cared just as much about having official attention drawn to whatever strange thing they'd done—them with their ominous disks, inexplicable glyphs digging into tarnished bronze.

She pulled out the phone.

Marat's expression darkened. "You stupid cunt," he said, his crude language a shocking contrast to his urbane appearance but not to the malice on his face.

"Take your garbage and go," she suggested, but her voice didn't come out quite right—it lacked any ringing strength, mostly because she'd forgotten how to breathe. She'd expected thoughtlessness, not malevolence—and she knew she'd made a big mistake. That these woods, these roads, this town…it had changed more than she'd ever expected.

Kai was right. She'd been away too long.

"Seriously," she said, trying to hide her uncertainty in a conciliatory tone. "It's not a big deal. There's a bear-safe garbage bin just down the—"

"If we'd wanted a *bear-safe bin,*" Marat said, cruel anger licking his words, "we'd have found one in the first place. Hantz, find a memory wiper. Aeli, grab her."

Memory wiper? What the—?

One of the muscle twins regarded the open case with dismay. "But these are all damaged workings, or we wouldn't be—"

"Do it!" Marat snapped, and the other muscle twin unlimbered himself to move.

Beware them!

"Don't you dare—!" Regan said, the words a gasp of combined fear and outrage as she stepped back up the hill. "Don't you—!" She stabbed at the phone pad. "Nine-one-one!"

The suited man only looked at her with scorn. "Reception," he said, a single-word response that called her bluff.

Deep in her mind the world growled. If the men heard it, they showed no sign.

The one called Aeli strode across the dry pool—and instead of scrambling back up the hill, she stood fast, struggling to take it all in. Because how could they really care so much about old metal disks? How did any of this *make sense?*

So she couldn't quite believe it, and her hesitation left her perfectly positioned to see the strobing flash and flicker of light from the woods behind the men, to feel the burst of relief that certainly wasn't hers.

And then Kai emerged from those woods.

He ran hard and barefoot, not in those Daniel Boone pants but in a damned breechclout and leggings, his torso bare to the morning spring and gleaming with health, muscles flowing.

Her astonishment must have warned the men. The muscle twins turned; Marat jerked around, his hand dipping into his pocket to pull out that which he'd slipped away upon her approach.

"Gun!" Regan cried wildly, gripping the walking stick like a bat, unable to reach Aeli from her perch. "He's got a *gun!*"

Not that it slowed Kai for an instant, even as the gun went off—a thin, sharp report that barely echoed against the slopes. He ducked the incoming blow from Hantz and left the man staggering to regain his balance; rather than charging around to grab Marat's gun, he somehow flipped his body around and slammed his heel into the man's chest. Another bullet dug into the thin, hard dirt of the dry pool; Marat sprawled on his back, and the gun went flying.

Kai landed in a crouch—impossibly upright if on all fours, and already facing Hantz again.

"No!" Regan cried again as Aeli jerked around to take Kai from behind. She threw the useless phone aside and slid off her platform of rock and root, surfing the slope down to the dry pool with the walking stick in hand.

Aeli reached for Kai's vulnerable back—a move of brute force, to yank him away and toss him down—but suddenly Kai wasn't there any longer. He dropped down to a crouch and along the way his leg whipped out, his low shin catching Hantz just above the knee. Hantz shouted in pain as the leg gave way—and Kai twisted like a cat, back in a crouch and facing Aeli, ready to drive up from below.

But Regan had reached Aeli, too, and she'd found her temper somewhere along the way. "I said *no!*" she cried and slammed the walking stick down across the meat of his shoulder, close to the base of his neck. Kai leaped out of the way as Aeli fell—and when he landed and rolled, he came up with the gun in hand.

"Sentinel!" Marat spat at him.

"No," Kai told him, crouching easily, one knee on the ground and the gun not pointing at anything in particular. Regan backed uneasily away, the stick still held like a bat, aware that Kai hadn't truly needed her and that she might, in fact, just get in his way. "Just myself. But this is my home, and this is my friend. I won't let you get hurt, either."

The man narrowed his eyes and climbed to his feet, dusting himself off. "There were rumors of a family here many years ago," he said, and gestured peremptorily at the muscle twins—a command to stand down, not that either of them had actually regained their feet. "But not for some time. Just as we became interested in them, it seems they left."

Kai said nothing.

The man smiled grimly at him. "We always wondered why a family would stay apart that way. And why Southwest Brevis allowed them to do it."

Kai said nothing. Nor did he move. For the first time

Regan realized he'd been shot—that blood sheeted along the outside of his arm.

Finally, the man said softly, "My name is Marat. Remember it. You'll be needing it in the near future." He jerked his head at his muscle twins, who hauled themselves upright. Hantz limped; Aeli seemed dazed. But they gathered the metal disks and returned them to their partitioned and padded cases, while Marat stood off to the side and Kai waited, still silent.

Regan tried to pretend she wasn't there at all.

Marat lingered as the men headed unsteadily down the narrow cut of the dry creek leading out from the pool. He eyed Kai with a deliberate gaze, taking in his remarkable nature, making obvious note of the breechclout and leggings and even of his preternaturally quiet strength in waiting. "It would have been better for you," he said, "if you had not interfered."

Kai still said nothing. Regan understood it to be not reticence, but that Kai had already said what he'd had to say.

Then Marat looked at her, and she flinched from it, suddenly exposed. She and her stick. He said, "It would have been better for you, too. What lies between us is nothing of yours."

Her hands tightened around the stick. "I'm here because you were dumping on the forest." It had been more than that, she was sure of it—but let him think she hadn't heard that cry of pain in her head. She certainly wished she hadn't. She wished herself sane and sound and sequestered back at the cabin, her paintbrush smearing deep color across canvas. "Maybe *you* shouldn't have been doing *that*."

He smiled, and it wasn't at all nice. "Oh, no," he said. "I'm delighted at the results of this day so far. And to think, it's just getting started."

Only after he'd left did Regan let herself truly breathe

again. She wanted to stagger back to the bank she'd slid down and sit against it, waiting out the shakes—but there was Kai.

He rose. If the encounter had affected him, it didn't show. Nor could she read his expression, though it made her shiver. "You're hurt," she said, and then wanted to smack her forehead. *Just in case you didn't know.*

"It's nothing," he told her, and looked at the gun in his hand as if he wasn't quite sure how it had gotten there and definitely didn't know what to do with it. "I heal fast."

She looked at the dark gouge of the wound and the generous flow of the blood and something in her temper snapped. "It's not *nothing*," she said sharply. "It's not even *close* to nothing! And what was that all about—all that stuff about your family and *Sentinels* and *what lies between us*—"

Kai said nothing—but he grinned, suddenly and completely, and damned if it didn't snatch her breath away.

Damned if it didn't snap her straight from irate to furious.

"It's not funny! It's *not*—"

He took a step closer and she lost her words—she lost her glare, too, her eyes widening with belated understanding. By the time he cupped one hand behind her neck and bent to kiss her, she'd pretty much lost everything but the sense of him standing so close. Clean sweat and strength and the sweet tang of blood—it surrounded her. His mouth was warm and firm on hers, and his hand full of gentle strength behind her head, her body full of quickly rising heat. Somewhere in the back of her mind, the deepest of purrs resonated with satisfaction.

When he took a distinct bite at her lower lip and withdrew, she followed—until she realized suddenly that her lungs burned for air. She pulled back to fill them deeply, staring at him with utter loss to define what had just happened here—from the moment she'd found herself drawn to this dry pool, to the moment she'd so completely given herself to the touch of a stranger.

A stranger who had just fought off three goons and a gun, taking them down with a casual, violent competence. Taking them down with remorseless intent, his every move one of feral potency.

A stranger who stared back at her from a darkened blue gaze and now looked every bit as stunned as she felt.

Chapter 4

The fight had left him less staggered. Being *shot* had left him less staggered.

Kai Faulkes, thirty years old and never been kissed.

Never like that.

He made himself step back, made his expression rueful and his body still. Because he'd never known such *want,* and he'd never taken such liberties, and he didn't begin to trust himself not to take more. He *knew* not to trust himself—not to trust the lynx that rode so close to the surface.

He'd been warned hard enough.

Regan touched her mouth, her cheeks full of flush, her brows drawn together in a faint frown. "I—" she started, while he was still far from able to find words. *"You—"* She started again, and then shook her head, impatient with her own struggle. Then she shook herself off, pushing a wayward strand of gold away from her face. "Later," she said. "I'll deal with that kiss later. Right now, I've got too many questions."

For this, he met her gaze without flinching; he found words. "I might not answer them."

"We'll see about that." But she scowled suddenly and turned to glare up the hill. "Will you just be *quiet?*"

He hadn't heard it—not with his body still immersed in the feel of soft hair beneath his hand and soft lips beneath his mouth—but he understood. She'd heard some mutter from the land, some reverberation of what had happened here. And she not only didn't understand…it distressed her.

She turned back to him with the conflict of it on her features. "Oh—damn! I didn't mean you."

"It's all right." But he left it at that, because he didn't know how to explain his own connections, his own nature, to the first person who might possibly understand.

It wasn't something he'd ever done before.

Guard yourself. Guard others against who you are.

Lessons once impressed hard on a vulnerable youth soon to be on his own.

Her obvious chagrin at reacting to the land passed, submerged in everything else that had happened here. "That needs care," she said, latching onto the most obvious need—looking at where the Core bullet had furrowed along the curve of his biceps.

But the arm would wait; it would heal faster than she could imagine. Other things wouldn't wait at all. For he needed to sweep through this area and make sure Marat had truly gone. No matter what his family had told him about staying out of sight—about what the Core would do if they ever learned of him.

They cannot suffer you to live, his father had said, his arm around his mother's shoulders, his younger sister, Holly, lingering at his mother's side, sniffling and confused—their things packed as they prepared to leave him. *Never forget.*

He hadn't forgotten. But he was the only one here. The only one who knew the Core had finally infiltrated this remote and pristine area.

"Kai," Regan said, aiming a pale blue gaze his way with intent, regaining some of her composure—but not without the hint of remaining uncertainty.

Self-retribution slapped home. This woman wasn't Sentinel; she wasn't lynx. She wasn't born to be a protector. She'd been threatened and she'd fought back—but that didn't mean she wasn't still frightened.

She didn't need to walk back to the cabin alone.

She lifted one honey-gold brow, striking a note of asperity. "In case you haven't noticed, you're bleeding everywhere."

It would stop soon. He'd been hot, his system in high gear from the change. Already he'd cooled down, his injury throbbing sharply. Healing quickly didn't mean not hurting.

Sometimes, he thought, it meant the opposite.

"I'll come," he told her. "But first I need to make sure they haven't left anything behind."

She climbed up the slope just far enough to reach the root and rock upon which she'd originally taken her stand and sat there, long legs thrust over the side, heels digging into the dirt.

"All right, then," she said, grasping for an equanimity she couldn't quite pull off. "But if you faint from blood loss, I'm going to find my phone—" she glanced around, already looking "—and find a signal and call for help. That'll mean cops and an ambulance ride down the mountain to Alamogordo and the nearest hospital. And somehow I get the feeling that's exactly what you're trying to avoid."

And Kai said nothing. Because Regan Adler saw—and heard—a lot more than she wanted to admit.

Even to herself.

* * *

Regan rested the walking stick against the porch railing, breathing a sigh of relief to realize she'd regained her internal balance on the way home. She was here—she was safe. The encounter in the woods was already fading, tinged with the absurdity of it all, diminished by the physical memory of Kai's touch still tingling at her mouth, at her nape, at every single spot he'd so much as breathed on.

"So," she said, as if it had been a casual hike on an average day, "what's with the breechclout anyway?"

She turned to look at Kai and discovered him no longer just behind her. Discovered him, in fact, at the edge of the woods—waiting in patience and silence, as seemed to be his norm.

Discovered, too, that Bob the Dog had risen to his feet, his hackles a stiff brush down his spine and over his rump. Since when did Bob have hackles on his rump? And though he stared at Kai as he might assess any intruder, she saw no true challenge there—just concern and puzzlement. "What's up with you?"

His low tail wagged once in acknowledgment, but he didn't look at her. He didn't turn his massive head from Kai's direction, his nostrils twitching as he lifted his head slightly, hunting scent.

"It's fine," Kai said. "He's figuring me out."

"What's there to figure? Bob, he's a guest. Deal with it."

Kai shook his head. "He's probably scented me around. He needs to put the pieces together."

Suddenly Regan understood. "Good grief—Bob, you're *afraid* of him!" The hackles weren't a threat…they were a sign of *fear*.

"Cautious," Kai said, by way of both agreement and correction. And he sat, cross-legged, in the straggly grass of the clearing.

Regan reached for the door. "You two figure things out.

I'll be back in a moment." She headed inside—and though she hadn't locked the door that morning anymore than they ever locked the door in this remote place, she wondered if that had been a mistake.

She found herself glancing around the cozy living area, checking that the shotgun leaned where she'd left it, that the papers on her father's desk had gone undisturbed, that the catchall drawers in the little dresser hadn't been left ajar. And she thought not of the morning as she did it, but of the Realtor from the day before.

Huh.

It didn't stop her from moving briskly through the house to the bathroom, where she rummaged through the built-in cabinet for first-aid supplies. She pushed aside the earthy ceramic teapot and set bottles and bandages on the tiny, wooden kitchen table before she went to the sink, washing up while she peered out the biggest window in the back of the house to spot the horse in the paddock.

He heard her and called out a suggestion of carrots, completely unconcerned with the oddities this day had wrought so far. Regan toweled her hands dry with a smile and returned to the porch.

She found Bob half in Kai's lap, leaning that big head against Kai's bare chest and...

Crooning.

Kai rubbed the dog's ear with an expert hand, eliciting a moan of canine delight. "Either they love me or they won't get near me."

"Well," she muttered, "he loves that old cat, too."

And Kai smiled and patted the dog. He pushed to his feet, replete in his breechclout and buckskins, and stood there looking more wild and more masculine than Regan would have thought possible.

Mine...

She started at that—the insidious murmur in her head,

offering not just the intrusive, but the unexpected. How did *that* make sense?

No more sense than the way he'd kissed her—or the way she'd kissed him back, this man she barely knew. Or that she'd responded to his touch as if she'd been waiting for it.

"Regan?"

She spoke a little more abruptly than she'd meant to. "Come inside. Let's get you cleaned up." And led the way.

He entered more warily than she expected, hesitating at the door just long enough so she looked back with impatience—and then, once inside, looking as though he might just step out again. His gaze flicked around the room to absorb the homey space, the unpretentious and utilitarian nature of her father's small desk, the little chest of drawers, the couch and the small television. His expression lit up at the sight of the bookshelves that held not only books, but her mother's ceramics, and the stark, engaging nature of his features reminded her all over again that he'd reached for her in the woods.

She squirmed away from the thought. She wasn't ready for that honesty. She still had too many things to hide. From him...from herself.

"In the kitchen," she told him, and watched while he again hesitated in the doorway, his gaze skimming the appliances, lingering at the window and finally landing on the barely big-enough-for-one table. There'd been more activity here during her childhood—a busy kitchen, cozy with the scents of homemade bread and baking casseroles, freshly washed canning jars gleaming in neat rows on the table....

When her mother was still alive.

Regan pulled ice water from the refrigerator and poured them tall mugs—also from her mother's pottery throwing wheel—without asking if he wanted it. This might be a high desert with melting snowpack and tall trees and even dew, but it was still the desert. One offered water; one drank it.

Kai took the mug without hesitation, his throat moving and water gleaming at the corner of his mouth. Regan sipped, her gaze drawn again to the play of muscle over his chest and arms, still amazed at the definition there, the casually loose rest of his belt over hips and obliques. Up close—and with the time to think about it—she could see that the breechclout was of a soft, woven cloth, darker brown than the leggings and carefully edged. Buckskin leggings tied off to the belt, leaving a generous portion of his thighs free to the air.

Right.

"Seriously," she said, clearing her throat as she turned away to the sink. She ran water over a clean washcloth and wrung it out. "What's with the getup?"

"I didn't expect to see anyone today." Kai set the mug aside on the table, wiping the corner of his mouth with the back of his hand.

She gestured at the old wooden chair, trying to decide if he'd been deliberately evasive or simply offered the best truth he had. He sat, unaccountably awkward for a moment, and rested his elbow on the table to offer her access to the arm.

"Right," she said. "But, you know…why *ever?*"

He sat silent for a moment, while she smoothed the cloth over the dried blood, dribbling water over the deep gouge in his biceps to soften the clotted areas. Finally, he shrugged. "It suits me."

Yes. Yes, it suits you very well indeed.

He eyed her, absorbing the curiosity she couldn't hide, ignoring the press of washcloth over raw flesh to soften dried blood. "You have questions."

"I definitely have questions." She pulled the cloth away,

and this time he winced. "Ugh," she said, looking at the ugliness of the wound.

"I heal quickly," he told her again, but she saw a certain tension in his jaw, and she moved more quickly—flushing the wound, disinfecting it…slathering it with antibiotic ointment.

Rather than wrap an absurd amount of tape over the gauze pads she pressed over the ointment, she produced a faded red bandanna and snugged it around his arm, tying off the corners in a tight and tiny knot. "There," she said, sitting down opposite him, and didn't think she imagined his relief.

He might feel differently once she'd fired off her questions.

And she had plenty. "Who were those men? How did you know them? What did Marat mean when he talked about your family? Where *is* your family? Where do you live? What do you do?"

The gauze packaging sat between them, crumpled and crisp. He rolled the pieces in his fingers, tumbled them onto the table like dice, and flicked them absently from one hand to the other and back again. "I thought," he said, glancing up at her and then back to the packaging, "you might ask why I kissed you like that."

She flushed, an instant reaction—not flustered, not regret, but pure visceral reaction. It put a certain amount of self-aware humor into her words. "I'm pretty sure I know why you kissed me like that." She put a hand over his, stopping the motion—surprising him, as if he hadn't quite realized he'd been playing with the crackling paper in the first place. "I'll go so far as to say that if we keep running into each other, it's probably going to happen again."

The look he gave her then—all his attention, all his intensity—pretty much melted her to the chair. She managed to say, "But that doesn't answer any of my questions."

He held her gaze just as captive as she still held his hand. "I don't know those men. I do know what they were doing. I live nearby. I don't *do*—I *am*. But people hire me to guide them. Hikers and sometimes hunters. Bow hunters."

Regan jerked her hand away and sat back, crossing her arms. "That's the biggest bunch of *non*answers I've ever heard."

It didn't seem to ruffle him. "Why have you come back?" he asked. "Where has your father gone? What do you do? What happened to your family years ago, and what drove you away from this place? Who are you talking to when you hold your head just so and look far away in your eyes?"

Bull's-eye. The questions hit harder than she expected they could—maybe because of her instant impulse to respond to this complete stranger with whom she'd fought, who she'd kissed, and whose bloody arm she'd just tended. *I left because my mother went mad here and I thought it was happening to me. And now that I'm back, I'm pretty sure that it is.*

Wisdom overrode impulse. She huffed out a breath, and chose the only easy answer. "I paint," she said. "I draw. I illustrate regional wildlife guides and publications." She looked at her hands and abruptly stood to scoop up the detritus of her first-aid work, including the scraps with which he'd been playing. "Okay, I get it. Sometimes the big picture is too big. But those men…" She shook her head, rinsing the washcloth at the sink and watching the red tint of the water swirl down the drain. "I guess I'll call the cops. Or the rangers. Or both."

He stood with a scrape of chair, coming up behind her at the sink. For an instant she held her breath, waiting to feel his hands on her waist or shoulders. And then tried to squash her disappointment when it didn't happen—because really, what was she thinking?

This man was dangerous in all ways. It struck her anew, clear in her mind's eye—how he'd moved, how he'd fought—not just capable, but entirely amazing, using his body with a stunning effectiveness. Moving like she hadn't known any man—any *human*—could. Not in real life.

Somehow she wasn't surprised when he responded to her intent to report the men with a simple, "I wish you wouldn't." Not when he'd already declined help for a wound that would have sent her mewling to the closest urgent care center.

She realized the water still trickled over her hands and twisted the faucet with annoyed force—one did not waste water here. "Those men are dangerous," she said sharply. "They threatened me, and they meant it. And they *shot* at you! Over a little bit of *trash!*"

"They shot at me because they fear me," Kai said, and added in a low afterthought, "As they should." Then, as she took a breath to argue, his hand finally settled on her shoulder. "The police will find nothing in that spot. They will find nothing of those men anywhere." His hand squeezed gently. She supposed it was reassurance.

She didn't feel reassurance.

Or if she did, it was entirely tangled up in other things.

Fear. Disbelief. Response. And somewhere, a whisper deep in her mind—one that came from without, and purred with possession and pride.

The whisper believed in this man.

Regan had no idea if that was a good thing.

Kai said, "They will not return to that spot. And they will not come here."

She turned to him. She should have known he wouldn't step away—that he still stood just that close to her, although his hand trailed down her arm to catch her hand. "And how, exactly, can you be so sure of that?"

He toyed briefly with her fingers, tracing them, running his thumb across her knuckles—touching her, until she suddenly realized he played with them just as he'd played with the crumpled paper—naturally and utterly without awareness. Her bemusement at it left her completely unprepared for his words.

"Because," he said, "now they will come for me."

Chapter 5

Regan hadn't been convinced.

Kai knew as much, moving along the mountain on broad paws—pausing to inspect the dry pool, his head reeling with the intensity of the energies that had been released there, corrupting the ground, the air…the very essence of the land.

He knew she was right, too, about calling the police. From her point of view, it was the only response to dangerous and inexplicable behavior; he could still hear the impact of her incredulous words. *They shot at you!*

They had. But worse, they'd gone for her, too. Rather than quietly disengaging and returning to do their work another day, the men had defied the one single principle shared by both Sentinels and Core—that above all, they would bring no outside attention to themselves.

Not that he truly called himself Sentinel. He had not lied to them about that. He might have the blood, but he had no affiliation. No connections. No way even to get in touch.

The voice of the land stirred uneasily in his mind, as aware of the incursion as he, in its way.

Now they will come for me.

And they would. But they still didn't truly know what he was—that they couldn't hide from him, no matter how quietly they moved. That the merest whisper of a Core working would reverberate through his senses, alerting him.

If they knew, they would never suffer him to live, no matter that the ostensible détente between the two factions forbade such killing.

Kai left the dry pool to wend his way home, slipping into the subterranean structure he called home. More than a bunker, less than a house, it backed up to a tight cave system into which he rarely ventured. Once it had housed his family; now it was his alone—a strange dwelling of pioneer ways and modern innovations, of human needs and lynx habits.

So he walked barefoot past the scuffed hollow near the entrance where he napped when a lynx, and onto the barely raised wood-plank floor, grabbing a pair of clean jeans from a molded, military-grade footlocker and a plain dark blue T-shirt to layer over them. He stuffed socks into a pair of lightweight Merrell hiking boots and snagged a thin khaki jacket with a slim fit and an urban look to layer over the T-shirt.

Camouflage for a lynx in the human world.

After dressing, he walked still barefoot to the road, satchel over his shoulder, and struck out along the narrow shoulder until Greg Harris pulled his old pickup over to offer a ride.

It hadn't always been like that. He'd walked the full distance to town many a time—but they'd grown used to him here and trusted him; they'd understood him to be safe if strange. Whether they saw him as a rugged individual or a crazy hermit, he wasn't sure.... He suspected a little of both. And if they'd made a game of trying to figure out exactly where he lived, it was a gentle game that meant no harm. He was far from the only recluse in this area.

Greg Harris made small talk about his sheep and his orchards, offered the obligatory comments about the weather, the upcoming Apple Blossom Festival and the likelihood of a good season after the winter's snowpack, then dropped Kai off in the center of Cloudview. With tourist season around the corner and a beautiful spring day of bright sky and brisk air, the entire town seemed to be out putting a shine on windows, trimming back brush and fixing the little things that always gave way before winter ended.

Kai had come into Cloudview for the library, another half mile and one steep hill away. But if he didn't stop by the general store—an eclectic collection of goods housed inside an old barn—then they'd give him affectionate grief the next time he did.

"Kai!" said the stout woman behind the cash register, all gray frizzy curls and stumpy features in a padded face. "Hey, you guys! Kai crawled out of the woods today!"

"How's business?" he asked her, having learned the safest ways not to talk about himself.

She snorted, waving a pudgy hand in a broad gesture. "What you'd expect this time of year. We should get 'em in soon, though. The valleys are already heating up. Hey, we just got in a big batch of that dried fruit you like."

He held out his satchel in query. Mary Wells knew his ways—and she knew the question.

She nodded. "Fill it up then, Mr. Granola. We'll get your tab started."

He grinned at her. "The hunters kept me busy. I'll pay my way."

She narrowed her eyes at him. "You just be sure to keep some set aside. You can't live day-to-day forever."

Mary's husband, Bill, made a throat-grumbling noise

from where he and his wheelchair currently occupied the back corner of the store, a lap desk spread with papers and a calculator. "Don't mother the man to death!"

"Someone needs to," she said with sharp asperity. "Especially if he's going to go around bleeding through his jacket like that."

But for the cant of his numb legs beneath the desk, Bill looked the part of a hale mountain man—more so than Kai ever had. Grizzled hair, grizzled beard in need of shaping, grizzled voice and hardworking hands. He gave Kai his own sharp look, then relaxed. "Long way from the heart," he said. "Ain't that the truth, son?"

Kai twisted his arm for a look, surprised. As he'd told Regan, Sentinels healed quickly as a matter of course—far too quickly to pass off as normal. He'd accepted her bandaging in part so he could leave it in place, obscuring the fact that he no longer needed it at all. Now, looking at the spreading stain, he admitted, "I wasn't expecting that."

"Pull that jacket off," Mary said. "Leave it with me while you're in town and I'll get it clean. Otherwise you'll be too long getting around to it, and a perfectly good jacket will go to ruin."

Kai hesitated, glancing out into the sunshine of the crisp day.

"Better do as she says, son," Bill advised him. "That sun will keep you warm until you're ready to go back to your woods. And you *are* going to the library, I take it?"

Kai set the satchel on worn floorboards and shrugged out of the jacket, handing it over with an obedience that, to judge by Bill's sly look, fooled no one.

Mary eyed the red bandanna. "Someone did a nice job for you."

"Regan," Kai said, and Mary's eyebrows shot up. Kai added, "Regan Adler."

"That's right," Bill said, snapping his fingers a few

times as if scaring up memory. "Frank headed into Texas for some big therapy work on his back—he's staying with his brother. He said something about his daughter coming back…. I'd forgotten all about it. Surprised she'd have anything to do with the place."

Kai quit frowning at the stained bandanna. "Why?"

Bill opened his mouth to reply, but Mary cut him off with a brisk cluck of her tongue. "That's Regan's business, you old busybody. She'll tell him if she feels like it." She aimed admonishment toward Kai. "And *you*—you have her look at that arm again, won't you?"

"I guess I'd better," he admitted. The gauze had been all cotton; the bandanna had been all cotton. That meant both had been preserved during the change to lynx and back—just as with the buckskin leggings and breechclout, and just exactly why he wore them. But the wound should have stopped bleeding long ago. Maybe he'd done something to it while he was in his lynx form.

The lynx tended to get caught up in other things while on the move.

"Oh!" Mary said, apparently satisfied on that score. "We got a letter for you!"

"A *what?*" Kai said, unable to help himself.

"Sure, a couple of weeks ago." She glanced up from her rummaging under the counter and gave him a pointed look. "You should come in more often, Kai."

"That's right," Bill grunted, making a notation on his papers. "Whether you need to or not. Just so Mary knows you're all right."

Quick as that, Mary turned and gave him a faux slap. "Wasn't me that was asking after him a couple days ago," she said, and Bill met Kai's gaze and shrugged, a "What're you gonna do?" expression behind Mary's back as she bent to look deeper on the shelves. "Here we go," she said, and straightened with a business-size envelope in hand. "Probably one of your happy hunters, don't you think?"

The hunters usually came to him through Martin Sperry—who handled the finances, checked the permits and vetted the hunters—but sometimes they did try to bypass Martin in hopes of lower rates.

Kai reached for the letter and stiffened.

He knew those stark block letters. He'd always know those stark block letters.

His father.

After fifteen long years? After making it so clear that they could never—*would* never—connect again?

Not after the Core had found Aeron Faulkes those years earlier—not when he'd barely been able to shake them before returning home to gather up his wife, Lily, and his young daughter, and to say goodbye to his son—a day they'd all known was coming. "Kai?" Mary gestured with the letter, concern on her face.

He shook off his reaction and took the envelope. "You're probably right," he said, unconvincing even to his own ears. "A hunter." He scooped up his satchel and tucked it over his shoulder. "I'll look for the dried fruit. Thank you."

Mary exchanged a glance with Bill, who hadn't bothered to hide his concern. But she said only, "Don't forget to come back for your jacket after the library."

"No," Kai said, the letter stuffed into his back pocket only through the dint of greatest willpower. "I won't."

His father. His family.

And the Core, back in his world.

Regan tossed the washcloth in the laundry and ran a quick load, hanging it out to dry and watching the blue roan pretend to have antics over the mild flap of cloth in the breeze. She pondered the garden—should she plant? Would she be here long enough? Would her father be back?—and pulled out her easel, setting it precisely in the best light in her small bedroom studio space.

And then she gave up pretending that the morning hadn't happened, that she hadn't attacked a man with her walking stick, that Kai hadn't been skimmed by a bullet or that her hands weren't still shaking now and then. She stood by the living-room window to look out at Bob, dozing in the sun, and spoke to the old cat.

"I could head down the hill and take in a movie," she told the cat, who didn't care. "I could drive out and get some touristy pistachio products."

The cat made squinty eyes at her.

"Could check out the garden center."

The cat yawned and stretched hugely—suddenly a long, flexible thing with claws extruded at almost every appendage. At great risk, she gave its belly an admiring pat. "Nothing stretches like a cat," she said. "Nice job, there." She couldn't help but join it, stretching out some of the lingering shivers of the morning, regretting that she'd agreed not to call the police…thinking it not too late.

Her gaze fell on her father's desk—on the business cards she'd left out, side by side. *Matt Arshun.*

She'd almost forgotten.

Not that she had any intention of calling him. But she'd certainly check him out. She had the feeling he'd be back—and she didn't want to be caught flat-footed a second time.

She tossed a light jacket into the passenger seat of her bright yellow FJ Cruiser—nothing but four-wheel drive for this area—and headed into town.

Their dirt road took a curving path down to the heavily graveled dirt connector, which took her past the occasional driveway to tucked-away summer homes. A couple of miles out she hit the asphalt, a winding road that ran the edge of this slope face, and which quickly took her into town.

The road had changed since her last visit here, years earlier. More guardrails…mesh screening to the inside of the curves where the rock loomed high and close, and always threatened to trickle down on the unwary. And Cloudview, as she grew closer, held an obvious little cluster of new conveniences—a single mega gas station almost obscuring the old block mechanic's garage, a mini movie rental place tucked in behind and new improvements to the long, narrow park where the summer festivals squatted, one after the other, during the tourist season.

But the town was essentially what it had always been—a long, narrow crossroads built on sheep farming, orchards and hunting, with topologically terraced layers of activity. Along the south street front the original old buildings—heavy log and overhung raised porches, most of them connecting—hosted Realtors and banks and artisans. Rising up on the next level behind them, vacation cabins pushed back into the rising ground, tucked in behind trees and perched on sharp angles. Twisty stairs, stone-paved paths, and wraparound porches ruled the day…and the decades.

The north side of the street held a layer of more practical things—the elementary school, a bank, a handful of brick and block construction. A steep walk and long, narrow parking lot behind it, the long boardwalk of original buildings offered a historic hotel, an ice cream shop…a hangout for cyclists and climbers.

Home.

The murmur behind her thoughts—the one that wasn't hers—stayed silent. Regan breathed a sigh of relief and pulled the Cruiser over in front of the general store, where the parking lot hardly bothered to differentiate itself from the road.

Her footsteps echoed hollowly on the boardwalk; the door jingled wildly in her wake.

"Regan Adler," said a voice familiar across years. "How

about that?" And there was Bill, with more gray in his beard and a little more belly in his lap, his ubiquitous clipboard in hand and a pencil stuck not behind his ear, but in his beard. On the other side of the shelves, a toddler burbled laughter and ran with flat, slapping feet across the boards at the murmur of a maternal command.

"How about that?" Regan agreed. Another glance and she found the old cash register counter—and Mary behind it, fussing with a sign for some sort of festival, the life-blood of the town, those festivals. "Mary. How are you?"

"'Bout the same as I was when you left in such a hurry," Mary told her. "Didn't anyone tell you that going away to school included coming back home now and then to do your laundry?"

Regan sighed. "Found a launderette," she said as neutrally as possible, and realized quite suddenly that if this old family friend brought up her mother, she'd simply turn around and walk out.

Bill must have seen it in her. "Well," he said, preempting Mary's next and obvious words, "we missed you."

"Thanks," Regan told him. "I missed you, too." And she had—she always had. She'd just known better than to come back.

*Home...*said the murmur in her head, and she winced.

Mary chortled. "Still getting used to the altitude, eh?"

"Boulder is high," Regan admitted, "but it's not nearly like this. What I want now is some of that elk jerky I can only get *here*. You still making it?"

Bill's expression brightened. "Yes, ma'am! Let me get some for you."

Mary leaned on the counter, her round face watching Bill with satisfaction. "Don't suppose you could have made him much happier, remembering that jerky. But don't tell me—you're really looking for Kai. You'll find him at the library." She turned aside, grabbing up the khaki jacket draped over the chair behind her. "You can return this to him, if you'd like."

Regan stood rooted. *"Kai?"* she said stupidly.

"Of course, Kai. Nice job you did on his arm, but it's not holding. I don't suppose he was willing to visit the clinic."

"No," Regan said numbly, aware that this conversation, like so many others since she'd returned home, had gotten completely away from her.

Mary smiled, a knowing thing. "Thought not. I'm surprised he sat still long enough for you to get that bandanna on him."

"You know him well?" It was an inane thing to say, but her mouth had done it for her.

"As well as anyone." Mary gestured with the jacket, and this time Regan took it. "He's a special one. Not a crazy old coot in the making, just…takes things on his own terms. Always seems to be where we need him to be when things come up."

Regan felt the dampness of the jacket and realized that Mary had washed it for him. She realized, too, that Mary's words held an underlying message. Warning?

"Regan," Mary said, casting an eye to the back of the store where Bill would emerge, his homemade elk jerky in hand, "you staying?"

That, too, seemed to have a message behind it, but Regan could only respond to the words themselves. "As long as my father needs me to," she said. "But I hadn't planned to stay beyond that." *I have another home now. A life. My work.*

Mary nodded shortly, her wiry curls bobbing. "I thought not. Not after the way you ran from this place." Regan winced, but Mary paid no mind. "Take care with Kai Faulkes, Regan."

Regan took a step closer, suddenly aware that she didn't want the toddler's mom hearing this conversation, either.

"But he's perfectly…" *Safe,* she was going to say, and then thought better of it. If there was one thing Kai Faulkes *wasn't,* it was perfectly safe. Instead, she said, "I trust him," and that felt right. Solid.

It came with a purr in her mind, and she squelched the impulse to swat at it—swatting empty air would not help this conversation.

Mary raised a meaningful eyebrow. "As well you can," she said. "But you won't change him. We know better than to try, those of us who have been here all along. No good will coming of trying—not for you, and not for him."

Regan understood, then. Mary wasn't worried about Regan and her safety—Mary was worried for Kai. She shook her head in befuddled protest. "I only just *met* him—"

And Mary snorted. "He wears your favor."

"The *bandanna?*" Regan could only stare at her. "Mary, that's just the only thing I had on hand, and he was *bleeding*—"

"He still is," Mary said shortly. "But you can bet he'd have lost that thing as soon as he was out of your sight if he didn't want it there."

Regan couldn't process it—not what Mary was saying, and not all the things she wasn't. Finally, she threw her hands in the air. "I honestly don't know what to say."

"Of course you don't," Mary told her matter-of-factly. "But it'll all make sense eventually." Then she lifted her chin, looking behind Regan—and Regan knew that she'd find Bill wheeling up the aisle behind her. "Anything else we can grab for you today?"

Regan took a deep breath, reordering her thoughts. "As a matter of fact…" She dug Arshun's business card from her back pocket. "You heard of this fellow? Or the office?"

Mary glanced at it, shook her head and handed the card over the counter to Bill, who stretched to trade it off with a gallon-size zipper bag of jerky. As he shook his head, Mary slapped her hand down on the newspapers stacked up on the counter and thumbed one off the top for Regan. "Check in here," she said. "If they're trying to pick up business in this area, there'll be an ad." She gave Regan a wry and knowing look. "Along with all the others."

Bill grunted. "If your dad is trying to sell the cabin, he'd best go with someone who's been here awhile." But there was a question layered beneath his advice, and concern.

"As far as I know, he's not," Regan reassured him. "But I'll give him a call tonight."

"And let us know," Mary said firmly.

"And let you know," Regan repeated dutifully, and then couldn't help but smile. For all she'd run from this place, there had been things to miss, too.

"Fine. Now go off and find Kai. From the look on his face when he left, he might just need someone's ear to bend. Either way, he definitely needs that jacket. Soon as the sun starts down, it's going to chill up out there."

"The library?"

Bill grunted again. "Or Phillip's dojo thing, or with Martin Sperry if he's in town, or off doing something, somewhere, that needs to be done. But the library is always your first bet. If he's not still there, Miss Laura will know where he's gone."

Laura, the librarian. She'd been a vibrant young woman a decade ago, pouring over art and illustration books with an awkward teenager who couldn't wait to get out of this town.

Mary shoved the jerky an inch toward Regan, bringing her out of the past. "Now, take this, and welcome back. You can pay for the next batch." And then, when Regan blinked against the sudden sting of tears, startled into emotion by the gesture, Mary smiled. "Welcome home, girl. Maybe you'll stay a bit, eh?"

Chapter 6

Regan found the library as it had been a decade earlier—terraced up from the street, bordered by massive local boulders, and set apart from the smattering of homes by its redbrick and white trim.

Kai sat on one of the boulders, legs crossed, a book in his lap and an envelope in his hand. Pensive and looking out over the town below them. She was surprised to see him in jeans—in *shoes*—and to find that glorious torso tucked away into a dark blue T-shirt. And though she thought at first that he was too immersed in his ponderings to notice her presence, she should have known better. As soon as she was close enough for casual conversation, he glanced her way, the smudge of darkness around his eyes making his deep blue eyes sharp and...

Don't stare, Regan.

But she thought herself a lost cause.

And she thought again that he wasn't the kind of man who would smear kohl along his lids, and that somehow, in spite of his otherwise tanned but fair skin, that smoky effect was natural.

She thought she'd probably never quite figure him out.

Then she noticed the book in his lap. *"Things that Sting,"* she said. "You're checking me out."

"The library has internet," he said, as if that explained it all. In a way, it did. A simple search on her name would turn up her website, her gallery affiliations, her bibliography. Her paintings.

She sat beside him, touching a finger to the glossy pages of the book. He'd been studying a full-page image in the middle-school book, a depiction of a cool desert morning with every possible stinging insect slyly inserted to be found by curious young eyes. Rich earth colors, subtle shifts of color, the luxurious smears of blues and reds so often hidden away in a desertscape, so seldom seen. And each creature, perched on cholla or hidden beside rock or climbing a pale prickly pear flower, subtly limned to make the search easier.

She remembered painting this one—remembered what had been going on in her life at the moment, just as she always did. The ex-boyfriend who'd just learned she wouldn't tolerate the emergence of his inner bully, the caress of wood flute piping in her ear while she wielded the brush, the pleasure of signing the contract to do the work...the faint feeling of familiar isolation as she buried herself in it.

She remembered feeling young and free and just beginning to believe she would escape what had happened to her mother after all. Realizing that it hadn't followed her north to Colorado.

"Why painting?" Kai said, shifting the book slightly to share with her.

She took a sharp breath, pulling herself out of those past

moments. "Why do I paint?" she asked him. "Or why use paintings instead of photographs?"

"The first is who you are," Kai said, startlingly sure of himself. "I mean instead of photographs."

Safe ground. "Because of its illustrative nature." She flipped to the next page, an Arizona giant hairy scorpion. "It would be hard to take a photo that shows the setae— those bristly hairs along the legs and tail—this clearly. And because we wanted to show the differences between this scorpion and the bark scorpion, I chose some key spots to exaggerate them. Not to be misleading, but to make it more obvious what to look for."

Kai ran his finger over the printed image—a big, bulky scorpion with a dark body and blunt head, stiff individual hairs bristling along its appendages. "It's beautiful," he said.

She started slightly. "That's not what I expect to hear when people look at this one."

He glanced at her. "The care you put into it makes it beautiful. It shows respect."

She hugged her arms, surprised at the tingle that ran along her shoulders and spine. "I think…that's one of the nicest things anyone's ever said about my work. Thank you."

"You're cold?" He set the book aside, tugged his jacket from her grasp and shook it out to put over her shoulders. "Now I know how you found me."

"I haven't been gone so long that I don't still know the gossip hub for this town," Regan agreed. She pulled another of her father's bandannas from the jacket pocket, unrolling it to pick out a piece of thick, spiced jerky and offering it to him.

He grinned and took it, biting off a chunk with efficiency. Regan had to work harder on hers, and for a moment they simply savored the burst of flavor, the spring air growing cooler as the low sun settled farther, the quiet steps on the library walk behind them and the squeak and scuff of the door.

When Regan swallowed, she said, "There was a Realtor out nosing around the house yesterday."

"He bothered you?" Kai went still in a way that felt more dangerous than quiet.

"Not like that," Regan said hastily, divining his thoughts from that expression. "But yes. Just a feeling…thought I'd see what I could learn about him."

Kai's silence was as good as a question.

"Nothing so far. But I'm just getting started. I'm afraid I'll have to bother my dad about it."

"Say hello to him for me." Kai closed the *Things that Sting* book and smoothed a hand over the protected cover.

Regan couldn't hide her jolt of surprise. "You really know my dad?"

Kai grinned. "Frank? Yes. Do you think you're the only one who walks out into the woods from your home?"

Regan wanted to blurt "Yes!" because when she'd left this place, Frank had done most of his appreciating from the porch with a young Bob. And before that, her mother had walked the land. And Regan herself, but less so as her mother grew ill, and—

Kai closed his eyes, and for the moment his face was full of pain. His breath caught, his body stilled—for an instant, he was everything that was quiet, his striking face turned slightly to the mountain, his body beneath its camouflage of blue T-shirt and jeans a thing of wild beauty.

For a dumbstruck instant, she stared. And as she opened her mouth for a concerned question, she heard it. Deep inside her head, nearly subliminal…the faintest ponderous moan, a sound that carried all the weight of the world.

She closed her mouth on her question. She wasn't sure she wanted to know. And Kai now looked at her as if nothing had happened at all—as if the extra cast of pale strain around his eyes was only an effect of the light.

And while she tried to discern if he'd been in discomfort from his arm or if he'd felt what she'd felt—sooner and deeper, for this man who lived in the land that spoke to her—he asked her, "What happened to your mother, Regan?"

In an intuitive rush, she understood too many things. That her father had never answered this question for Kai, if indeed Kai had asked it. That Kai had come here not to look at *Things that Sting,* but to check the news archives for background information.

She didn't quite get up, but the space between them had grown less companionable and more like the stiffness of strangers.

"Look it up," she told him shortly. "Isn't that why you're here?"

"I'm here because this is a place that I come." Kai set the book aside and lifted his arms in a startling stretch, one that took her by surprise both because of its casual nature in the middle of a conversation suddenly turned tense, and because of its utter unself-conscious completeness. His chest expanded; his shirt lifted, revealing a narrow line of unexpectedly pale, crisp hair. When he finally lowered his arms and tugged his shirt back into place, he looked at her. "And I got distracted by your paintings."

Somewhat savagely, she stuffed her father's bandanna back into the jacket pocket. "What does it matter what happened to my mother?"

Kai made as though to lean back on his arms, winced, and stayed as he'd been. "It matters to you," he observed. "Maybe it matters to others."

She snorted and abruptly got to her feet, shedding his jacket along the way and holding it out to him. "That's no answer at all."

"It's an honest answer," he told her, scooping up the book and rising in one fluid motion that somehow didn't involve uncrossing his legs until he was already up. "It's just not the one you wanted to hear."

She found herself full of glare and bereft of words—of *sensible* words. So she held her silence and held the jacket out to him again.

"Just a minute," he said as if she wasn't angry at all. Perfectly civilized, this version of Kai Faulkes, as he jogged to the library, briefly disappeared inside and reemerged to join her again. "No ID," he said upon returning. "No library card. Sometimes Miss Laura uses her own card for me, but I try not to ask too often."

The enigma of Kai. She told herself she didn't care, and tried to believe it. She had a righteous anger, by golly, and she wasn't through with it.

"Take the damned jacket," she said, holding it out a third time. "I've got work to do at home. I need to go." She'd intended to stay longer—to nose around further. To reacquaint herself with the town and look harder for Arshun's realty offices. But now she thought she'd call her father first.

Her father, who had known of Kai and not warned her.

Kai might have taken the garment, if he hadn't stumbled—if he hadn't nearly gone down, no warning of it on his face and none of his usual lethal grace in his staggering attempt to catch himself.

Regan caught him instead—a quick step, a shift of her hip against his, and it was enough so he found himself again, looking vague and baffled beneath the strain. Before he could object, she reached across his body and took his wrist, tugging enough to turn him—to see what she hadn't noticed until now. "This should have stopped bleeding hours ago."

He looked down on it. "Yes," he said distantly. "But it's not that bad."

She glared at him. "One stupid man thing after another. You're losing all the points you earned this morning, Kai Faulkes. Did you or did you not almost just pass out?"

He seemed to come back to himself. "Stupid man thing?" he said, and not without humor.

"Don't even try to change the subject. *Yes,* stupid man thing—refusing to see a doctor, checking me out behind my back, pretending you're *not* really hurt."

"Regan," he said, "just because a bullet made that scrape doesn't—" But he stopped, and his gaze jerked back out to the mountain—back toward home. For the briefest moment his jaw tightened; his nostrils flared. When he spoke, it sounded like more of an effort to keep his voice even, and she would have given anything to understand where his thoughts had gone. "That doesn't make it worse than it really is."

With reluctance, she had to concede that point. It had been a deep gouge and ugly, but she'd done as much to herself in childhood falling out of a tree. She released his arm—noting with some absent part of her mind that he'd given it to her without resistance, that he'd allowed her to keep it.

She thought perhaps that particular surrender had been a gift on his part.

Now she didn't wait for him to take the damned jacket— she pressed it into his hand. "Fine," she said. "But humor me. Don't drive yourself home—let me take you."

"I walked," he informed her. "And Greg Harris picked me up on the way."

She wanted to give herself a head slap. "Of *course* you walked," she muttered, and then glared at him more directly. "And now you're going to ride back with me."

He hesitated, standing there atop one of the library terracing boulders as though it had been made for his personal use. Regan slid down from the one on which she'd been standing, and held out her hand for him to follow. He said, "This would be another stupid man thing."

She couldn't help the smile that twitched the corner of her mouth. "Right. If you don't come."

He sighed in another obvious surrender, and joined her on the road—no sidewalks here—and even gently slid his hand into hers, so they walked together toward the old hotel and its boardwalk shops. And if once she thought he faltered—and if shortly after that she felt that deep, grating perception of something else's pain, neither of them spoke of it.

At least, not out loud.

You can't have me, Regan told that voice in her head. *You will never, ever have me!*

Even if it meant forever leaving behind this world that had once been hers.

Chapter 7

Kai woke the next morning with the feel of Regan's hand lingering in his and his head full of cotton. His arm ached sharply, which still took him by surprise. But after drawing water from the hand-bored well at the back of the dugout and scrubbing himself down, he flipped the hair out of his eyes and looked at the inflamed wound. Significant injuries healed preternaturally fast—but only to a point. Such healing exacted its own price, and his body knew when it wasn't worth the trade-off.

Like now.

He glopped on the herbal unguent—prickly pear, sage, and juniper in bear grease and jojoba—that he'd learned to make in his family's first days here, and wrapped the arm with cotton, tying it off with split ends and the help of his teeth. After that came Regan's second bandanna, the one she'd left in his jacket.

Simply because he wanted to wear it. And because he thought she'd like to see it.

Not that he had any true clue what women liked or wanted. Only instinct, and a day with the lady Sentinel who had brought him through initiation at the age of fifteen.

You're strong, she'd said. *You're unrelentingly lynx. You really need more time than this to learn control or you'll end up hurting someone. Be careful. Never forget.*

As if he could.

And then she'd left…and shortly after that, his family had followed.

His gaze strayed to his father's unopened letter. Some small part of him cursed himself as a coward, but the lynx knew differently. The lynx lived in a world where things came in their own time—where Kai did what was necessary, when it was necessary.

Yesterday, ghosting along the mountain ridge from Regan's driveway, he'd been distracted and ill. He'd slipped into this home, shed his clothes and rolled up in the nest of a bed to sleep hard and right on through the night.

This morning, the home set to rights and a breakfast of dried fruit behind him, he'd go see if he could make sense of what had happened the day before—heading for the dry pool with the letter tucked away for a later moment.

He should have known Regan would be there and on the same mission.

Maybe some part of him did. For he'd dressed not only in breechclout and leggings—the all-natural materials that would shift with him if he took the lynx—but had also covered his torso with the loose, long-tailed cotton shirt sewn to pioneer patterns and belted with flat, plain leather. He approached the dry pool as a gliding lynx, but Regan—when she finally realized he was there—found only the fully clothed human.

She wore work jeans that fit loosely enough for active movement and yet somehow rode across her hips in the perfect spot to draw his eye—to make his heart beat just a little bit faster, before he even knew he'd responded to the sight of her at all. Her shirt was red again—red with a field of tiny blue flowers—and it only brought out the bright gold of her braid, the pleasant flush of exertion across fair skin. In her hand she held not the walking stick, but a shotgun.

"Kai," she said, as if seeing him here had been inevitable.

As maybe it had. Given her deep connection to this land, whether she understood and acknowledged it or not.

She said, "You left that handgun at my place."

"I have no use for it." He'd carried it as far as her house and left it there with the vague thought that it was a thing of the human world; it did not belong in his. Now, if he couldn't find what he needed here, he might ask to see it again.

She sat on the throne of roots that had served her so well the day before and looked down on the dry pool, laying the shotgun across her knees. "I guess I had to come make sure they hadn't come back. Or to clean up after their mess if they had."

"You would have felt it if they'd come back," he told her, easing around the base of the pool until the butt of the shotgun, not the muzzle, pointed his way.

She didn't fail to notice. "Nothing in the chamber," she said. "You think my dad let me grow up with a long gun in the house, and no gun safety?"

"I think every gun is loaded," Kai said—not speaking from the perspective of a Sentinel who'd been shot by a Core minion the day before, or from that of a human who'd also been taught gun safety on the way to adulthood, but from the perspective of a lynx who never assumed on the safety of his skin in the woods.

But Regan winced, and he knew she'd taken it the serious way. The *day before* way. "How's your arm?"

"Healing," he said. He crouched by the side of the dry pool, letting his splayed fingers push through crackling leaves to feel the faint dampness below—moisture left from the spring melt. He let his awareness filter outward, a whisper of a question.

He pretended not to notice when Regan stiffened, lifting her head—searching for what she'd heard without quite understanding from where it came.

"Here," he murmured, and lifted his head in invitation.

She frowned, not quite certain. He gestured again, and she set the shotgun aside, sliding off the roots to land at the edge of the dry pool.

Kai beckoned her closer and nodded at his hand. "Like this."

She crouched beside him, slowly imitating his reach for the land—stiff and wary and closed away.

Not from him—Kai understood that right away. From fear of hearing again that faint whisper.

But it wasn't something to fear. It was something to celebrate. It was something to breathe in and exhale and feel *alive* about.

He eased closer, his arm reaching out beside hers, his hand covering hers, his fingers gently reaching between hers to touch the ground. "Easy," he said. "Quiet." He brushed his thumb over her hand, soothing her.

"What—" she said, her voice at normal volume—and then cut herself off, chagrined. When she spoke again, she did so quietly. "What are we doing?"

"Listening," he told her.

"Why? To what?"

"Shh," he said, close to her ear and barely putting sound behind the words. "To learn."

"I don't—"

"Shh. Learn." He stroked her hand with his thumb again, and went back to the land.

Gentle burble of precious water soaking deep, feeding roots, damping ground. Hints of icy cold below, the touch of warmth above. The great, thrumming heartbeat of networked life, scampering little nails...the crunch of a seed, the hull left behind...

And the dark blot of the spot that felt nothing at all. Cold metal, a whiff of corruption—

Hurts...

Regan's hand jerked beneath his.

"Shh," he said, coming back to himself. "You're safe. You're..." He trailed off, suddenly aware that his head tipped forward against hers, that her pale gold hair tickled his face and the beguiling scent of it tickled his nose. His hand had slipped around her waist to press across her stomach, now suddenly aware of the flutter in her breathing. "Regan," he murmured and nuzzled behind her ear.

"Not," she whispered, freezing under his touch. "Not safe at all." And she turned in his arms, her hand coming up to cup his cheek. He leaned into it as she leaned into him, mouth closing in on his.

Instantly, he tugged her closer, bringing them together so she suddenly straddled his thigh; she gasped into his mouth and twined her fingers through his hair, holding him so she could tilt her head to touch his lips with her tongue, a flirt that led to ferocity and his shudder of response.

He hadn't planned to tuck one hand under the firm muscle of her bottom and tip her so she could have received him, but his body made that choice for him. He hadn't planned to tumble over on his back so she sprawled across him—but *she* made that choice for him, levering him over and freeing herself to roam her touch across his chest and down his ribs and right down to rest where he strained for her. He pushed against her, and his eyes rolled back as sweet, fiery warmth gathered deep within him, beckoning a growl from his throat.

He flipped them around, his hand cushioning her head before it could hit the ground. He stalked her from there, showing tooth and showing prowl and showing the power of the lynx. Her eyes widened and her hands stilled, and suddenly they were two people aware of themselves again, breath gusting against each other's faces and bodies trembling.

"Oh," Regan said, as taken aback as Kai felt. "My."

Remorse hit him—and concern. The sudden awareness that he'd let the lynx in—that he'd been just exactly what he could never be.

But she wouldn't understand that, either—so he made himself grin, easing back to give her space as he struggled with the fact that in spite of the remorse, in spite of the concern…there was no regret. Only a kind of glory in how much he'd wanted this woman.

He couldn't reconcile the two.

Regan gave her shirt a futile tug, twisting it back into place. "This is the part where I say I'm not this kind of girl," she told him, brushing a stick from her hair. "And that I've never done this before."

"This?"

She looked slightly taken aback. "You're not following the script. Now you say 'Yeah, yeah, we shouldn't have done that.'"

He removed a final twig, caught just behind her ear. "Why would I do that?"

Because he didn't regret a moment of it. What he'd let slip through to her, yes. What they'd done, no.

After a moment, she snorted gently. "Right," she said. "Why would you? Truth is, I've done *this* plenty. But never just *like* this."

Kai wasn't sure how to untangle that one. "I don't really understand."

He understood one thing well enough: never—*ever*—had he felt what Regan brought out in him. Not as a teen; not in his early years alone. Not when brazen female tourists brushed against him on the town boardwalk, or when the hunters' lonely wives opened their blouses down one more button.

Not when the Sentinel woman quietly hired for his initiation took him for the first time, unlocking all that was lynx within him—and then stayed for days, teaching him control, teaching him responsibility...teaching him how to please. Mia, staying for an extra several days to do the impossible—trying to show him everything she thought an isolated youth should know about being a man, and about being a man with a Sentinel's strength.

But not how to love. Now he sat with Regan in the dry pool and caught his breath, his body stuck in relentless and unfamiliar turmoil. This was response; this was pure physical yearning. It was beyond anything he'd learned with that fleeting encounter.

It just possibly was everything she'd ever warned him against.

Of course Kai didn't understand. Of *course* Regan would have to spell it out.

Or else pretend she hadn't heard him.

But looking at Kai's lightly furrowed brow, she could hardly do that to him. And still trembling as she was from his touch, she could hardly do it to herself.

"Like this," she said, "means that I'm feeling overwhelmed. There's a difference between kissing a guy I've only recently met and...what just happened. How *much* it happened."

He watched her with a quiet intensity that made her

want to squirm away—even as her body cried, *Yes! That's what I want!* He asked, with more caution than she expected, "Is that good or bad?"

"It means I don't know what to do." She shook her head, climbing to her feet. "You are a strange man, Kai Faulkes."

He lifted one shoulder in what looked like concession, still sitting—more comfortably now, she thought—as he drew his knees up, hung his arms around them and looked up at her. "About yesterday," he said. "I didn't mean to upset you."

Yesterday. At the library, when she'd been so busy enjoying being with him that his prying had felt like a slap. "It was nosy."

"Maybe. But it's important."

She gave him a cross look. It seemed altogether unfair that this gorgeous and entirely out-of-place man could stir her up so when she had so many other things to think about. "I don't see how it could possibly be *important.*"

"Because it's still with you. Because there is a thing between the two of us, and I want—" He shook his head, looking at a frustrated loss for words.

She knew the feeling. "That's no excuse."

He didn't argue it. "You felt it, too, just now."

Yes. She had.

Much as she wanted to deny it, as much as it frightened her, she had. And there he was, watching her…and understanding. Comfortable with it, comfortable with himself. Comfortable *here.*

Not out of place at all. More *in* place than anyone she'd ever known. Including herself.

Regan knew she should run from this man. She knew he wouldn't stop pushing. Or asking.

She knew she didn't want to answer.

Only moments since that kiss—that *encounter*—and

she sat back up on the roots, looking over the dry pool. Looking at Kai.

He crouched, one knee to the ground and his fingers pushed against the silty, packed soil, just as he'd knelt beside her—*around* her—but in a different location. *Triangulating.*

What and how—*that,* she didn't want to know. She let herself watch, and let her mind roam.

He remained motionless—his eyes closed and head slightly tilted—for so long that when he finally stood, she came to sharp attention. He took three certain steps into the rock-strewn detritus and bent to prod the ground.

When he straightened, turning to her, he held a small lump between his thumb and forefinger, his distaste palpable as he displayed it for her. She squinted. "What—?"

"The reason I kept bleeding," he said.

The bullet. She said carefully, "That's what bullets *do.* Make people bleed."

A few long strides and he stood below her—reaching up for her hand and to tuck the bullet away there, closing her fingers around it. "Do you feel it?"

She gave him a look. "Of course I feel it." Cool hard metal, a misshapen lump that could have been lethal.

"No," he said, looking up at her with meaning in his gaze, one she couldn't comprehend. Just clear, dark blue eyes searching hers. "Do you *feel* it? *Hear* it?"

She understood, then—knew he alluded to that sensation of being swallowed by someone else's thoughts. She opened her hand; the spent bullet tipped off her fingers to hit the ground, rolling down between his bare feet. "No," she said. "It's a *bullet.*"

Disappointment flickered in his eyes—not that she'd failed to feel anything, but that she'd rejected the chance to try. As if she *wanted* to invite the madness. He plucked the bullet from between long-dead twigs and pine needles. "It is more. Much more."

She opened her mouth, not quite sure what to say. Wanting to tell him to stop pushing, wanting to ask him what was going on. But in the end she asked him nothing.

The problem was—he might tell her.

Chapter 8

"Dad, it's me." Regan rolled her eyes at her father's gruff voice mail message, but not too hard. He'd had eyes in the back of his head when she'd been young and he could no doubt still perceive an eye roll across the miles and over the state line into Texas.

El Paso, it turned out, not only held her uncle's home—it had a fantastic physical therapy facility. And if there was one thing she and her father both understood, it was the critical nature of his recovery from injury. In order for him to continue his life here—alone—he had to put himself back together right. Better than right.

He'd been twenty-five when she was born. Now she was pushing thirty and he was still a man in his prime, but this was no place for a man—or woman—who couldn't hold his own against winter snow, the woodstove, or the long hike off the mountain if the truck didn't start.

Somewhere along the way, her father had discovered cell phones and voice mail. But he still clearly wasn't entirely comfortable with either. "Leave a message!" he'd barked as a recording, making his dare.

Regan just might have rolled her eyes after all. "Everything's fine here, so stop worrying. I'm going to guess everything's fine there, too, but if I don't hear back from you I'm going to call Uncle Cal and we're going to talk about you behind your back. Your choice. Meanwhile, I need to know if you've talked to a Realtor named Matt Arshun. I found his card on your desk, but surely if you were thinking of selling this place, you'd mention it to me?"

If only as a kind of blackmail to get her back down here, very much as this trip to Texas had been.

"Call me," she added quickly before the voice mail cut her off. "Love you!"

He'd pretend not to hear that. He'd never quite forgiven her for leaving. *You can paint anywhere,* he'd told her. *What happened to your mother won't happen to you.*

After her mother had died, her father had finally stopped asking. But never stopped wanting.

Regan supposed that if she'd moved back home—had done so for good—then maybe her father could convince himself that he was right all along. That he hadn't waited too long to get her mother help.

That this mountain had nothing to do with her mother's death after all.

Regan might have been convinced, too. If only she couldn't hear the whispers in her head.

Kai sat at the top of the ridge, well over nine thousand feet high…not quite the high point in the Sacramento range, but close to it. He crossed his legs on his blocky limestone perch and turned his face to the sun, soaking in the warmth—still uneasily sensitive from what Regan had stirred in him earlier.

From here he could see the world. *His* world. From

here, the air was clear, without scent of Core or even of human. Cloudview lay tucked away several ridges over; those few who lived between were so ensconced beneath the trees as to be invisible. Off to the northeast, the Mescalero Apache reservation resonated with its own unique energy—a boundary Kai respected too well to breach, even from a distance.

He once again ran his fingers over the stiff paper of his father's letter.

Yes, Kai, it's me. It was the first line in his father's letter, as if Aeron Faulkes had anticipated Kai's disbelief—the thick natural paper beneath his fingers, the firm press of the pen into flax fibers, the lingering scent of his family, as if Aeron had had them each hold this letter in turn before sending it. Kai as human could barely perceive it—but the lynx had had no trouble.

> *I've had a friend mail this. We live nowhere near the postmark. Neither does our friend.*

That much came as no surprise. He'd noticed the postmark, but had immediately discarded the notion that his family—his mother, who also took the lynx; his father, who showed his wolf strongly even if he didn't take the change; his sister, Holly, who hadn't been old enough to know, but whose black hair and blue eyes and playful nature had mirrored Kai's at that age—had somehow ended up in the heart of Detroit.

> *I hope you're well, son. I can't tell you how much we miss you.*

And Kai put the letter aside again, blinking fiercely into the sun—wishing he had as much skill with distance and time and interpersonal connection as he did with the land. Trying to make it so, with that moment of welling grief and intensity of purpose.

I love you, too.

Unlike Regan, he hadn't chosen to separate from the only family he knew. And now, in his prime, he felt the weight of unfulfilled responsibility. The need to keep his mother safe, his father supported…his sister free of attention her beauty would bring.

Not that he even knew what she looked like anymore. Or that he wasn't aware of the irony of their situation— that just as he was safer here, on his own, they were safer without him.

I wouldn't break our silence without good reason, so let me just say that we're all well.

Of course he wouldn't say more. If the letter had been intercepted…every detail would be a clue.

We still live apart, but that doesn't mean I don't hear things. You need to know that the others have developed something new.

He had no trouble interpreting those words. His family hadn't officially joined with the Sentinels of their brevis region, but his father must have a contact. Risky enough at that. And *the others* could only refer to the Atrum Core.

They consider their development to be virtually undetectable. Silent.

And this was the reason his father had broken silence. This one sentence, impregnated with so much meaning.

The Core had a new weapon—something important enough to make them bold. Bold enough so they were branching out, pushing boundaries…moving into new territory. Willing to push around the civilians they encountered in the process, in direct defiance of the single directive shared by both Core and Sentinels—*don't be seen; don't risk exposure.*

And the new weapon was something the Sentinels couldn't find. Not readily. After millennia of tracking Core activity by the distinct stench of their unnatural workings, the effluvia they left behind…when it came to this development, the Sentinels were blind.

The Core would stop at nothing to keep them that way.

But Kai wasn't blind. And when it came to the Core, Kai would never be blind.

He was the one who could detect whatever the Core had created—the *only* one. The one who could make the difference.

His father didn't say as much. But this letter…this letter was giving him a choice. This letter was giving him permission.

Do what you have to do. We support you, whatever the consequences.

Including those to his family.

Kai folded the letter, tucking it carefully inside the envelope. He already knew the rest of it by heart—the brief sign-off, the faint dab of his mother's airy perfume, the spot where his sister had touched the corner. They'd all reached out to him in ways only the lynx would know. When he turned back to the sun, he felt the dry trail of a tear down his cheek and knew this had been as hard for them as it was for him.

Do what you have to do.

How could he even know what had to be done, isolated as he was? Tucked away from the Sentinels and from the Core, protecting his land in the most quiet of ways.

But with the sun on his face, he considered the uproar from the year past—the evidence that the Core was pushing its boundaries, breaking through the ongoing détente to act against the Sentinels.

Exactly what they'd done, he didn't know. But they'd created a turmoil of activity so extensive, so far-reaching, that it had reached him even here, along with the wave of Sentinel grief that had followed. It had left him gasping and wrung out and without answers—and at the time, had only convinced him that he could never venture down into the more populated parts of the world, where underlying Core activity would simply poison him as a matter of course.

He'd felt, too, the impulse to respond, to stop the Core as he could…to *help*. But by the time he'd been well enough to think rationally about it, the noise had faded. He'd had no other clues, no information…and he tucked it away to ponder until something came along to make it make sense.

One day, you'll be the one who can make the difference.

His father's parting words, resonating in his memory more strongly than ever.

The others have developed something new.

It made sense now—what he had felt then, what he felt now.

Do what you have to do.

It made far, far too much sense.

Chapter 9

Regan had been here a bare week and already the mountains had changed around her, reaching for true spring—though they'd been silent around her for days. Ever since she'd last seen Kai, and while she waited for her father to return her call.

Tomorrow, she'd start to worry. Today, she'd just call them both typical men, not quite tuned in to the passage of time after so many years alone.

But while she waited to hear back from her father, while she struggled to understand her response to the absent Kai, while she realized there were things—and people—about her life here that she had indeed missed, Regan needed activity. So she'd taken the mustang along the dirt road to hunt for signs of egress.

Now the horse stretched his neck, playing against the bit, and she gave him a pat of apology on a shoulder damp with sweat. "Sorry," she told him. "I didn't know it would be so warm today."

She'd already tied her jacket off behind the saddle to ride in shirtsleeves, her morning gloves stuffed in the pockets. She'd brought a snack and water in the saddlebags, and—on impulse—the gun Kai had left at her house. Not that it would do more than make her feel better to have it, no matter how she'd familiarized herself with its workings. Not only was it tucked away in the saddlebags, but she'd only ever handled long guns—the .22, the 12-gauge, the occasional thirty-aught.

And still, she'd brought it. A sign of just how spooked she'd grown in the past week.

She wasn't sure who or what she expected to find, only that she no longer assumed there would be nothing. And that if someone had taken advantage of her father's injury to establish activity in these woods—whether on their property, bordering neighbors or the surrounding national forest—she wanted to know about it.

She wanted it stopped.

So far she'd seen nothing here of concern, in spite of her compulsion to look. She waited for the downhill road to level out and let the mustang canter and, as she felt the sturdy strength of the horse beneath her and the breeze against her face, she wondered what it would be like to run with Kai—and she wondered again at the ongoing silence of the land, its juxtaposition with Kai's days of absence.

Not that he owed her anything. But she'd thought…

She thought there'd been connection. And promise.

Maybe he'd simply realized that this was no longer her home. Maybe he hadn't been willing to give of himself to a fling.

"I don't see why it has to be so complicated," she complained to the horse, turning him aside to enter the woods and reach the snow seep where she could water him. After a few moments of brisk walking on the game trail she swung out of the saddle to trail a rein behind her, letting the horse snuffle against her back as she approached the changing foliage of the damp area.

But there she stopped short.

Tracks.

Unfamiliar tracks, at that. *Big cat?* She put her hand beside one, found it narrower than the track. *Big* some*thing.* But the toes weren't quite right—the spread between the outside toe and its neighbor, the murky nature of the track edges. She'd seen mountain lion tracks aplenty, and they pressed into the ground clear and firm. Bobcat tracks did the same—and they weren't nearly this large.

She sat back, baffled. *What?* What other wildcat even lived in these woods?

The mustang nudged her shoulder, and she swatted idly in his direction. "Hold on. I'm committing these tracks to my outstanding visual memory." And she did, sliding into her artist's headspace...feeling the memory sink in.

Greeting welcome...

"Stop it!" she cried, coming to her feet in a fury—and then had to manage the mustang who so wisely wanted to spook away from the crazy woman. "Stay out!"

The woods fell into silence. The mustang snorted on her neck. Regan took a deep breath, led him around to the other side of the seep so they wouldn't sully the mystery tracks, and used a rock to scrape at the damp dirt while water filled the hole. She stood aside, her movements stiff and tense, and the mustang fluttered his nostrils, double-checking for danger before he dipped his head to sip water.

Regan moved along his side, rein draped over her elbow, and jerked on the buckle of the saddlebags to grab her water bottle, drinking deeply before briskly screwing the top closed. She touched the gun as she replaced the bottle, and her fingers lingered there. After a moment, she left it. False security was worse than no security.

But she left the saddlebag flap loosely fastened.

The mustang lifted his head, water beading his lips and whiskers—and before she saw it coming, slyly cranked his nose around to swipe down her sleeve, leaving a damp and dirt-streaked trail. "Great," she told him. "A horse who thinks he has a sense of humor. Does my father let you get away with that one?"

The horse wrinkled his nostrils and flicked his ears, pretending to think.

"You got me once," she said. "Next time I'll know." She checked his girth and mounted up, picking their way back out of the woods to stop short at the edge of the road— and only in afterthought realizing the hesitation had been a mutual decision, she and this trail-wise little horse.

Something had changed.

Except...

Nothing had changed.

No clouds between her and the sun to make things suddenly seem darker. No sudden change of humidity to make the details of the woods suddenly sharper.

Except the mustang was leery, too.

Doesn't mean anything. The mustang was an alert little horse, primed by his early years in the wild. He'd certainly react to her tension.

Beware...

"Shut up!" she said more fiercely than she meant to. As the mustang stepped onto the road, he snorted challenge—a resounding blast of alarm and suspicion. She felt the spring in his step, patted his neck with a hand that pretended to be casual. *Just...one step at a time...*

The woods groaned; they shifted with a grinding, wrenching sound that reverberated deeply within her. The tree trunks gleamed dark and sinister; the scent of corruption suddenly misted around the roan's hooves in a sticky fog and crawled up along Regan's leg. She made a noise deep in her throat—unthinking, gut-level fear. The horse bunched up beneath her, dynamite barely contained.

Something belched nearby, a sucking expulsion in growly bass.

Regan broke. The horse broke.

Even in the depths of her fear, she knew to channel the mustang's reaction *forward*, and she quivered her calves against his sides, releasing him with her seat, raising the ends of the reins—

There was no need to touch him with leather. He burst into an explosive gallop, charging up the slope with a speed that slapped air against her face, in no way under control.

Then again, neither was she.

She crouched over his neck, one stirrup lost and banging against his side, her hands and reins and his mane all a wicked tangle in her grip. *"Go,"* she sobbed at him, barely able to breathe in terror released. *"Go, go, GO!"*

The hill grew steeper; the horse barely slacked his pace. They ran together, leaving a growl of dark laughter in the air—and although Regan didn't see the driveway entrance, the horse did, leaning tightly into the curve to lunge upward.

Regan choked on new fear—on the barely rational thought that slipped into her mindless flight. *Never run a horse toward the barn.* Not only because it was bad training and dangerous habit, but—

Because the horse had to *stop.*

And sometimes they didn't. Or sometimes they skidded to a halt at the last moment, and the *rider* didn't.

Regan wrestled with the reins, unable to disentangle fingers from that black mane and finally, wildly, shifting her grip up close to the bit, clamping one hand against the foamed neck and lifting high with the other, working against the thrust of the horse's jaw on the bit.

The roan flung his head against the pressure, jerking at

her—but his gallop stuttered, and as he released his jaw and softened his neck, they fell into a jarring trot. From there the horse stumbled and seemed to realize how blown he was. He staggered to a dazed stop.

Regan all but fell out of the saddle, fumbling at the paddock gate with shaking hands and blurred vision, tears spilling out onto her cheeks—the fear still clinging to her, and the strangeness, and the deep terror at knowing just how quickly she'd lost herself.

She pulled the horse into the pipe-panel corral and slammed the latch home, making it only that far before she put her back to the nearest panel junction and slid down to sit there, trembling with tears and leftover panic. And she reached blindly, instinctively, for comfort, aching for strength to lean on.

To make it stop.

Kai froze in midstep, one broad paw reaching, the angular slopes of pine and aspen marching down before him. *Something was wrong...*

Something dark, something corruptive, something *Regan.*

The trickle burst into a flood, twisting sensations of ugliness and pain washing through all his senses—pressing him to the ground with his ears flat and his stub tail lashing, eyes squinting closed against it.

Kai had never tasted Core in these rare heights and he had never tasted it so strongly at all. He reeled from it, from its implications—from the returning throb of it in his lynx's foreleg, where the tainted bullet had left him so slow to heal.

The burst of sensation faded, trailing away into a lingering sickness—and above it rose that voice he'd heard first. *Regan.*

She probably didn't mean to cry out to him—full of

tremulous fear, of gasping panic…a wild golden spirit fluttering against the onslaught of Core workings. But she had. One deep, strong thread of longing, thrumming through the land with all the clear, healthy connection of one born to it. *Hold me. Help me. Oh, please help me—*

His ears flicked; he found himself on his feet, oriented unerringly toward her call. The forest stretched out between them, full of rugged terrain and secret places and no physical way to get from here to there without hours on the run.

He put his whiskers to the ground—gently brushing the flaking rock of his perch, hunting detail that was slow to come…sending out his own message. Wordless reassurance, understanding, a calming subliminal and raspy purr.

After a moment, he thought her internal trembling eased. He shook himself off and started down the mountain. *I'm coming, Regan.*

No lynx was a long-distance sprinter.

But Kai ran.

Chapter 10

Regan eventually pulled herself together...or as together as she was going to get. She jerked the mustang's girth loose and flung the saddle over the top pipe of the corral panel, saddlebags and all—perfectly aware that she was babbling and helpless to stop herself.

"I'm sorry, I'm sorry," she told the horse, excruciatingly aware of his steaming body, his soaking and foaming coat. She pulled the bridle off his lowered head, easing it past his teeth and tossing it over the saddle. "I am so sorry."

She should walk him dry; she should sponge his flanks and shoulders and towel him off. Instead, she grabbed the cooler from the barn, shook off the dust with a motion that was more jerky than it was effective, and slung it over him, tying it under his neck and fastening a stretchy surcingle around his body. "I'm sorry—"

Only when she reached the gate did she realize she had no idea what she still ran from, or what she ran *to*. Her stomach roiled; emotion filled her to stretching, too big to

hold within mere flesh—the sensation of the woods closing around her, of the stench curling around her feet and
legs. And then, when she'd thought herself safe—at home,
curled up outside the paddock with the woods blessedly
quiescent around her—the crystal clarity of a new voice
had reached out to touch her.

It didn't matter that the voice had held comfort, or that
it had held compassion, or even that it felt familiar. Because it shouldn't have been there at all.

She stumbled for the house and promptly fell over Bob
the Dog. To judge by his heavy panting, he'd paced them
along the driveway, a burst of speed and effort no longer
familiar to his aging bones. Now he looked to her for ex-
planation and she had none.

"I'm sorry," she told him. "I'm sorry. I can't stay. I'll
find someone to take care of you. Maybe Kai—"

Bob stopped looking at her and looked at the house instead, his panting stopped to listen. She heard it then—
the phone. She ran to answer it, slamming through the
screen—expecting only one call, knowing so few people
who even had this number. She grabbed the handset of
the ancient rotary phone fast enough to fumble it. "Dad?
Dad? Where have you been!"

The hesitation alone told her how frantic she sounded—
made her realize, suddenly, that this might not be her father at all.

In fact, a smooth voice said, "Having second thoughts
about staying there?" and she realized it was Matt
Arshun—and before she even thought about it, she
slammed the phone down, hard enough to rattle the fanciful little table on which it sat.

When it rang again, she almost didn't pick it up. But
after days of waiting to hear from her father...

"Hello?" Her voice came out thick and teary...and cautious.

"Rae?" Her father sounded wary in return—and more protective than she expected. "What's wrong?"

"Dad!" she said, and it was all she could do to keep from bursting into tears all over again. She recognized the wavering adrenaline. So instead of asking after him or mentioning Arshun, she blurted out, "What happened to Mom?"

His silence held a different kind of wariness before he said, "What's going on?"

It wasn't an answer. But then, she didn't expect to get an answer without a fight. Not after all this time.

"Mom," she said, a little steadier. She hooked her fingers behind the handset cradle and plunked the phone on the kitchen table, nudging the chair out with her foot so she could sit. "What happened to her?"

"You know what happened to her. Rae, you know I hate this cell phone. I'd rather not talk about this now."

"Then maybe you should have talked about it earlier," she shot back at him—then covered her mouth in surprise at herself, making a strangled noise of dismay. She'd never braced him about this before—never much braced him about anything. After her mother had died, the house had turned into a quiet, somber place—and her father a quiet, somber man. They'd lived here together, but not truly *together*.

And then Regan had left. As soon as she could.

"Well, I'm doing fine. Thanks for asking," her father said drily. "So is your uncle Cal."

"I expect you are," Regan told him, finding her feet again—understanding that something ineffable had changed between them. That something in the past week had changed in *her*. "And we'll get to that. Along with why you never mentioned Kai."

In true surprise, Frank Adler said, "I didn't think you'd ever see him." And then his voice became more resigned than implacable. "Rae, you know what happened to her. As much as anyone does."

Regan didn't hesitate. "I don't know how she died."

He replied with silence.

"I know I was twelve years old, and she went away— and she never came back. I know *why* she went away— that she didn't trust herself any longer and she wanted to get help. She wanted to make sure we were safe with her. I know everything was fine before I said too much to my friend Kathleen, and then she said too much to everyone else." *And I never spoke to Kathleen again....*

She hadn't heard him sound subdued before. She heard it now. "I didn't realize you understood so much."

"What do you think I've been afraid of all this time?"

"There's no reason to think it'll happen to you," Frank said sharply. "Not a single doctor thought it was something to be passed along."

Regan took the plunge—without thinking, which was a mercy. Maybe that meant it was time. "Dad, it *did* happen to me. That's why I left. It's why I stayed away. And now that I'm home—"

"No!" The word came harsh with anger, torn from him.

"What," Regan said, "happened to Mom." No longer question, but demand.

She heard his deep intake of breath—and his capitulation. "She was hit by a car."

It stunned her. "What? A *car?*"

"She went out of her mind once she left our mountain for the facility in Las Cruces. She talked only of returning home, of being broken. The drugs weren't helping— they made things worse. She even agreed to electroshock therapy—but before that could happen, she escaped the facility. She was hit by a car." He paused, gathering his thoughts...and seemed to give up. "It wasn't the driver's fault. She was walking down the middle of the road in the middle of the night."

Regan whispered, "She was coming home." It wasn't a guess.

Frank said, "She was coming home. And so am I. There's no way I'm leaving my little girl there to deal with this alone. I swear, Regan, I never believed this would happen. I was so sure you just needed to come home—to spend some time there, so you could see you belonged. Then it wouldn't matter if you left again for Colorado because I'd know you always *could* come home."

"I know," she said, and they weren't empty words. She did know—she heard it in the misery of his voice, and knew it of the man she called father. He was stubborn, generally taciturn, and to a large extent had let her finish growing up on her own, but he loved her.

And he'd adored her mother.

She shook off the sadness of the moment—the need to hug him and to reassure them both. "You couldn't know," she said. "I never told you, did I? That before I left, I felt the start of it. I didn't think you needed to know. And once I left for the university, I was fine."

She'd left early, in fact, after crunching her high school credits into three years. She'd immersed herself in her painting and she'd never looked back—because she knew she couldn't. She admitted to him now, "It's been so long... I really hoped..."

"Yeah," he said heavily. "So did I."

"How *are* you doing?" she asked. "Is the therapy helping?"

He snorted. "I went miniature golfing last night, believe it or not. Damnedest thing I've ever seen."

A thread of delight found its way through the ramifications of what she'd just learned. "Then it's helping!"

"It's helping."

She took a deep breath. "Then you stay right there, you hear me? I'll work something out. Maybe Kai—"

"You *have* seen him," Frank said, sounding surprised all over again.

"Yes, several times." *More than.* She flushed and struggled to keep it from her voice—her sudden physical awareness of Kai and his effect on her. "He hurt himself, and I patched him up."

"He hurt himself," Frank said flatly, making Regan think she'd picked the wrong thing to say after all. But her father dropped it, and instead picked up the thread of the message she'd left days earlier. "Listen, Rae, you asked about this Arshun…guy." She knew from his tone that he'd wanted to say "asshole" and had kept it clean because he was talking to his little girl. "He came around, all right, and I sent him packing."

"No kidding," she said, using the same flat tone he'd just used with her. "Well, I think he's upped his game a little."

She hadn't had time to think about it—the satisfied sound of his voice on the phone, his complete lack of surprise that she'd been upset.

Not that it made any sense. But her initial distrust of him had turned into something stronger.

"What's that supposed to mean?" Frank demanded. *"Upped his game?"*

"Nothing," Regan said lamely. She tapped her fingers against the phone, considering Arshun. "It means he thought he could take advantage of me."

Frank snorted.

"Exactly. And I don't think he counted on Bob."

"Good old Bob." But he added, "Call Jaime Nez. Fill him in."

The sheriff. "I will," Regan promised. "And I mean it. Stay there. If…if I have to go, I'll head down the hill to

Alamogordo—I won't go far. And not without making
sure things are okay here. Kai—"

Frank snorted again, and Regan hesitated, giving him
room to speak his mind. "Don't you go counting on him,"
Frank said, but where Regan expected warning, she heard
only concern—and she wasn't sure it was for herself.
"Sometimes you see him twice in a week, and not again
for a season. He's his own man, Rae—doesn't need the
rest of us. He's..." The hesitation wasn't characteristic of
her father. "Not like other people."

Regan shrugged. "Apparently, neither am I."

Kai knew, without a doubt, that his life had again changed
forever.

Not because he'd just heard from his da. Not because
the Core had just arrived—and they clearly weren't passing through.

But because of the way Regan had reached him. How
deeply— how naturally, How it happened in spite of their
intent...and how the land embraced her along the way.

He ran on, absorbing the rugged ground, his toes curling around rock—reaching there, leaping here. In human
form now because he was too close to trails and wandering hikers to risk running blindly as lynx. And because
the human could fall into a steady, loping pace that ate the
miles, although Kai was no more meant for extended running than that lynx.

But he could do it. And did. Until Bob barked sharply—
not as distantly as Kai thought he'd be, and his tone held
a warning. Kai took the chance that Bob would recognize him and ran on. He came upon the cabin from above,
glimpsing the strike of sunshine against gold. *Regan.*

Finally, then, he slowed to a trot—loose-limbed and
still contained, but feeling the fatigue of miles across the
mountains. He grew warier, looking for the cause of Re-

gan's fear—whatever had pushed her to reach out across that distance and touch him, when doing so seemed to scare her as much as anything else.

Bob stood at the back of the house, tail waving in slow welcome as Kai stepped down off the mountain and came along the side of the small shedrow barn, finally getting a good look at the paddock where Regan stood beside the horse. A saddle lay in a disorganized heap outside the metal-pipe corral, and a hunter-green blanket hung over the top of one corral panel. The horse stood with his head low and his eyes half-closed, a bucket of oat-scented water in the corner and another bucket by Regan's feet. The horse looked rode hard and put up wet—and so did Regan, her face flushed, her nose reddened and her hair in golden disarray.

"Kai!" she said, and she sounded both surprised and as if she'd expected him all along.

"Regan." He didn't have other words for her—hadn't planned any. He came to a sore-footed stop beside the saddle, his lungs aching for air, his mind and body still reeling from the reverberating cry of the land—from *her.* So when the words came, they were blunt. "What happened?"

She dropped a big round sponge into the bucket and ducked between the corral's rails to come to him—and stopped there, seeing the tremble in him. Her eyes widened, seeing what he already knew—that the greater part of his reaction came from what he'd experienced those miles ago as opposed to the obvious effort of his run. What they'd experienced *together.*

"What *happened?*" It was all he could manage. Now that he'd stopped moving, he felt the heat of his body and the cool air against it, the trickle of sweat down his back. His thighs and shins burned, and a muscle flickered in and out of a cramp along his ribs.

She pressed her lips together; fresh tears shone in her

eyes. "I hardly know," she told him, and then shook her head at his instant anger. "Yes, we have to talk. But…Kai, I don't even know where to start." Pale blue eyes searched his for the briefest moment, then flickered away.

He saw the defeat there and caught her arms when she would have turned from him. "We start *here,*" he said. "We start *now.*"

She shook her head, but this time he saw pain rather than resistance. He released her, but only so he could touch her face, smearing away a tear with his thumb. "Here," he repeated. "Now. Because something is happening to this forest, and it matters."

"Something is happening," she said quite bitterly, "to *me.*"

"And me," Kai told her softly.

He didn't know women. He barely knew people. But he knew instinct better than anything at all, and instinct told him that only honesty would reach her—and only honesty would serve him.

She might have felt the same. She tipped her head and eyed him more thoughtfully. "My father says not to trust you."

The words caused a little twist of hurt; her features softened. "He says," she told him, "that you don't need anyone."

"I haven't," Kai admitted, sticking to that truth.

"That's why Bob didn't know you, isn't it? You've never been here before—even though it doesn't seem as though you live all that far away." It was true, and he knew it showed. She took a step away from him, a token distance. "Mary and Bill know you, but I bet not really. I bet they know *of* you."

"They know me as well as anyone does," Kai told her, not sure what that truly said of him. "And your father."

"Here," she said pointedly. "In this place where peo-

ple do for one another, because that's the way it has to be. We're too remote not to be our own safety system."

But Kai's safety lay in another path, so he said nothing.

"If it wasn't for those men at the dry pool, would I have ever seen you more than the one time? And even then, if the roan hadn't bogged on me?"

He hunted for the truth behind that. He might have co-incided with her in town, but not again in the woods. He'd never have come to her yard, met her father's dog...held her in his arms.

Kissed her or yearned for her.

Except that in recalling the moment they'd met, the spark of the jewel at her briefly glimpsed belly button, the spark in her eye as she'd come up from the ground not shaken from her fall, but furious at his interference, the startling glint of sunlight on the pale gold of her hair...

He didn't truly know the answer to that one at all.

She read his hesitation for the uncertainty it was. "Not all answers are easy, are they?" she asked him, and brushed a strand of hair from her forehead with her wrist. "God, I need a shower. So do you, I gather. Where'd you run from?"

He found unusual solace in the matter-of-fact nature of her words. Unusual relief. So maybe he wasn't quite thinking when he nodded over his shoulder and said, "The peak."

She only looked at him. She looked at his bare feet and at the legs that felt leaden beneath him, and then up the mountain, a most meaningful glance. Then she said, "Let me finish with this horse. We'll take turns in the shower."

And as if it was something he'd ever done before, he said yes.

Regan led the way through the back door, feeling as battered as she ever had—emotionally, physically...conceptually.

There was only one way to live with all that had happened...and that was not to live with it at all. To wall it away.

But here was Kai, reminding her. Not just because he wanted to talk about it, to *face* it...but because he'd been such a deep part of it all in the first place.

His woods. His touch, reaching through the panic and dread to touch her—at first giving her an anchor, and then simply making it all that much harder.

It made her blunter than usual...stripped away the fussy civilities of having him in her home, and of sharing the casual intimacies of physical needs.

Of course, first he had to come inside.

He still stood behind her, lingering at the threshold. No particular wariness or alarm, just...looking. Inside, then out, and then in he came.

"Ice water," she said, and pointed first at the refrigerator, then at the cupboard beside it. "Glasses. Make yourself at home. I'll be out in fifteen minutes." He did not, she realized then, wear a watch. So she pointed at the stove and added, "Clock."

And then, because he just stood there, she asked, "Okay?"

But in truth, she didn't care if it wasn't. Not when she was so grimly trying to deal with the twists in her life.

He seemed to realize it—or he wasn't bothered by it. "Yes, fine," he told her, a calm response that made her squinty-eyed scrutiny of his every action seem damned silly. *He's not like other people,* her father had said.

Right.

The kitchen led to the wide, short hallway and the living room beyond that. The main bedroom sat at the end of that hall—once a private sanctuary for her parents, now full of her father's presence alone. Along the way, opposite the loft stairs, stood the cabin's single compact bathroom.

It had barely enough room for a step-in corner shower, a toilet and a sink set in a rough, handcrafted cabinet.

But it had her mother's tile. Handmade Talavera-style tile, a watercolor wash of color in cool blues and greens and whites with a scattered punctuation of design sets throughout. Her mother's touch, still kept pristine.

Regan shucked her clothes into a heap on that pretty floor, hit the button for the on-demand hot water and stepped into the corner for a quick navy shower. She exited a few moments later still dripping, slathered on body lotion with the faintest hint of peppermint scent and shrugged on a green waffle-weave robe. She dropped a wide-toothed comb in the robe pocket to tame her tousled hair later and gathered her things, detouring to her father's room to dig up a pair of sweatpants and drop them off in the bathroom before climbing to the loft rooms to pull on clean jeans and an oversize T-shirt.

When she returned to the kitchen she found Kai with half a glass of water in hand, looking out the big kitchen window and idly ticking the blinds cord against the glass. The sweat of his run had already dried, and she saw clearly enough where branches had whipped across his upper arms and ribs, the snug wrap of the bandanna still protecting his arm.

For the first time since she'd met him, he didn't brim with energy, ready to bounce into action. The run had worn him down into merely quiet.

She leaned against the door frame and watched. She couldn't believe he hadn't heard her, but he gave no sign of it. She knew exactly what he saw through the window— the mustang in his paddock, the barn behind it, the mountain rising behind that. He studied it with a calm scrutiny bordering on the meditative—and then dropped the cord against the window, letting the wood knob bounce *tick-tickety-tick* on the glass before he reached for it again.

She was just about to clear her throat when he turned to look at her, his clear, hard focus making it obvious that, yes, he'd been perfectly aware of her presence. "This is a nice home," he said as if it surprised him. "Closed where it should be closed, open where it should be open."

"Right," she said, as if that had made any sense at all. "So, hey, the shower's ready for you. I left some of my dad's sweatpants in there, if you'd like to borrow them. Only thing is, we're on well water here, so if you could make it a navy shower—"

His expression made her laugh; he clearly had no idea what she meant. "There's a hand spray," she said. "Get wet, turn off the spray to soap up, then rinse." She cleared her throat, beset by the sudden image of Kai in the shower, water beading the crisp, pale hair of his chest, running across his shoulders and down his torso. She made herself finish, "Don't leave it running the whole time."

He made a little noise of amusement in his throat on the way past. She thought maybe he'd gone punch-tired and added, "Push the button over the sink to preheat the water."

He made that noise again, though he was down the hall and this time she barely heard him mutter, "Hot water."

"There's a towel in there for you!" she called as he closed the door. If he laughed at that, she couldn't hear it.

She shook her head, bemused, and refilled her perpetually lurking plastic travel mug with the filtered ice water, then replenished the pitcher.

Kai came out within moments, scrubbed and gleaming, his hair roughly toweled dry and the sweatpants sagging low—too big at the waist, snug across the butt, too short in the legs. He carried his leggings, belt and freshly rinsed breechclout and headed out to drape them all over the nearest corral panel.

"I don't suppose you wash the leggings," she said as he returned to the back door, briefly lingering at the threshold.

"I scrape them sometimes," he said. He raised his head as though listening to something, and Regan stiffened, wary of what she, too, might hear—and how—but her head stayed silent.

Kai scrubbed both hands over his face, ruffling his damp hair even further. "The gun," he said. "I left the gun here. I wouldn't have done that if I'd realized it was—" He stopped, looking at her as if caught out in something he hadn't meant to say, and finished in a tone that made her think he knew just how lame the words sounded. "It has a bad air about it. It should be in a safer place."

It had a bad air about it. Right.

But because she didn't truly want to know what that meant—not on this morning, of all mornings—she promptly pulled the saddlebags off the back of the kitchen chair and handed them over.

Kai set the gun on the table, a gentle clunk of solid metal against wood. He came up from behind to rest a long-fingered hand on the back of her neck for a silent moment. When that touch fell away, it was only because he'd gathered up her hand as he headed back out the door.

She responded to his gentle tug without question, only belatedly realizing just how much his touch warmed her.

Chapter 11

Kai led Regan past the paddock and the barn and right on up the scrub-covered hill. He didn't take them far; she could feel the weariness in him as much as she felt the lingering kick of fear adrenaline in herself. He wound a path through the elbow-high Gambel oak studding the south-facing slope, and found them a gentle perch within a cluster of tall ponderosa pines, as if he'd always known it was there.

There he sat, and pulled her down to sit in front of him. Still in silence, he wrapped his arms around her shoulders from behind and rested his cheek on her head and...

Simply sat.

"What—"

"Shh," he said. "Thinking. Or not thinking. *Being.* Holding you. That's what I'm doing."

She thought she should protest—or that he should have asked. Or that she should wake up and make her own decisions instead of following blindly along, too shocked by the earlier trauma to do anything else.

But the forest spread out below her, a few sharp ridges jutting out among aggressive folds of land. Her father's little cabin—her *family's* little cabin—nestled comfortably in the snug scoop of ground just before them, with the barn right up against the rise of ground. Beyond it, she could just barely see the top of the mustang's head in his paddock—the flip of his ear as he finally emerged from his exhausted daze, the faint flick of tail off to the side.

She realized she'd relaxed against Kai, feeling the safety in his embrace, his strength supporting her. His thumb stroked the exposed skin of her arm, absently comforting.

"There is nothing to fear in this land," he told her.

She stirred herself to disagree. "Mountain lions," she said. "Bear. And something else I haven't figured out yet. Big tracks down by the seep." Had she seen those only this morning? It felt a week ago. A month. A lifetime, divided in half by sanity and the momentary loss of it.

She thought he'd ask about the tracks. He didn't. He said, "Those are *of* the forest. Not *in* them. Not as you and I are in them."

"I'm *not*—" she said sharply, and then stopped, because she thought maybe she was, even if she didn't want to be.

Her mother had died trying to return to this forest.

He briefly squeezed her shoulders, ducking his head beside hers to kiss the curve where her neck met her shoulders. It was meant, she thought, to be comforting.

She shivered. And scowled. "Do you ever think first?"

He stilled, but didn't respond.

"Before you touch me, I mean. Because as far as I can see, the answer is not so far. Do I even really know you?"

He tucked his head up against hers, breathing deeply; she had the sudden revelation that he took in the scent of her. The movement of warm air across her skin brought up goose bumps—it froze her there, anticipating the next gust of breath, the gentle movement of his thumb over skin she hadn't until this moment considered an erotic zone. She'd nearly lost herself to the subtle sensations by the time he responded.

"Sometimes not," he said. "Sometimes, I just *do*. But not *to* you, Regan. *With* you. Or will you tell me I'm wrong in this?"

She discovered her hand over his on her arm, her fingers twining with his. "No, dammit. And that doesn't seem right, either. I just met you. My head's a mess, and I think I might be going crazy and now is *not* the time—"

He nuzzled her neck, moving a little closer—his feet propped on the hill alongside her thighs, one hand moving splayed across her belly. His weariness had made way for a new tension, one she felt in the brush of his legs, the faint tremor in his arms, his body gone male and hard against her.

"Do you ever *not* think?" he asked

"Mostly not," she admitted in a whisper. "Mostly I never stop. Mostly…I'm beginning to realize just how much it's always there." The fear, she meant. The underlying assumption that she would lose her grasp on reality, the one she'd had since she'd first heard the whispers those years ago.

"I can make it stop," he told her.

She laughed shortly. "Is that reason enough?"

"I don't know," he said, words of vulnerable honesty. "Is it?"

She thought of how right he'd been—that he'd never reached for her when it hadn't been waiting in her, too. She thought of how his presence stunned her, and how she'd already come to look for it. That in some way, he was entirely self-contained.

She had the sudden, blinding insight from that vulnerable honesty, seeing what he risked in reaching out to her. Far, far more than she, who already knew how to have a relationship without truly letting the other person in. More than she, who had lived her life with the assumption of such casual relationships, from friends to employers to lovers.

She twisted within his arms, rising to her knees, threading her fingers through sleek sable hair still damp from the shower. "Kai," she said, and thought it would be answer enough.

His blue eyes had darkened; his hands rested on her hips, and had grown possessive. "Is *wanting* reason enough?" he asked again, forcing her to honesty.

"I don't know," she admitted. "But this is more than that."

He released a breath shakier than she'd expected. "I thought so."

But for the first time, she was the one who kissed him— and for the first time, she felt a tentative nature in his response—as if she was the one who'd made *him* think, and he didn't know what to do with it. She scooted closer, running her hands along his thighs, across the play of muscle in his torso—back down the crisp smatter of chest hair that somehow wasn't black like that on his head, but silver-gray.

And she kissed him hard.

Her reward came in his groan and his shuddering breath—and the way he lay back along the hillside, pulling her with him until she lay sprawled across him, her oversize T-shirt of no impediment at all when it came to keeping his hands away from her skin. She'd donned only a light bra—but that did stop him, his hands suddenly uncertain again.

She straddled him to sit, not at all coincidentally moving against him along the way—stopping to catch her breath at the sharp, unfettered response that flooded heat between them. He thrust up against her with eyes gone wide and then narrowed with pleasure, his lip drawn up in fleeting grimace of startled pleasure.

"I can make it stop for you, too," she told him breathlessly, fumbling between her shoulders for the release on her bra. She should have known he'd take advantage of the moment—her torso stretched, her belly exposed—but she didn't expect him to snatch her at the waist, flip her over and effortlessly control her descent onto hard rocky soil, his mouth closing on her....

Yes, on the tiny diamond glint of her navel piercing.

He tongued it, and she laughed at the tickle and at his warm breath—and then she stopped laughing, for he had no trouble at all when it came to the button of her jeans. He pushed the zipper down, and while she quite suddenly held her breath and waited for his touch, he only rested his hand over her panties—distracted, she thought, by the belly button piercing, by the tangle of shirt and bra, maybe by the tangle of her fingers in his hair.

If he thought she was going to lie here *waiting*—

She kicked off her paddock clogs and then, as he raised his head with his expression gone somewhat dazed, she kicked her jeans off, too—keeping them between her and the tiny sharp-edged rocks scattered among the pine needles beneath them. He might have reached for her then— but she got there first, easily shoving the loose sweats off his hips and over his magnificent butt, and pretty darned certain a man who had arrived in a breechclout wouldn't have come up with underwear after his shower.

Right she was.

He didn't see it coming. He *should* have. He should have known from the look in her eye, from her assertive movement, from her little smile at the sight of him, hard and ready. Most likely he was distracted by her exposed breast, to judge by the whispering, sandpaper brush of his fingers against her sensitive skin, the way he traced the curve of flesh. She arched into him, impatient for a firmer touch, and reached to do her own caressing…such softness, such hard and quivering response.

He made a sound of astonishment and froze, his whole body shivering now, and his lip lifted in that quick snarl of response. He pushed against her hand, losing his breath in a startled huff as she closed her fingers around him.

She laughed in breathless pleasure—and a little of her own surprise. If you were a man who didn't need anyone else, maybe time passed between lovers. Just maybe it had been a while. He probably wasn't truly prepared—

"Oh," she said. "Damn."

He didn't respond with words—just a sharpening of his gaze on hers before he lowered his head to her neck and nuzzled her.

"Protection," she said, tipping her head so his tongue could trace along the soft skin there, hesitating at the little hollow beneath her ear. "I don't suppose you—"

"We are safe," he told her, whispering the words against her ear.

Safe, whispered the voice in her head, for once not inciting panic—not so quiet and lulling, not compared to what she'd felt only hours ago.

She somehow fathomed that they weren't talking about the same thing. "No, I mean—" and sighed happily as his tongue neatly traced the outside edge of her ear, a shiver running through her body to pebble her skin and tighten her nipples, spreading a tingle of warmth in its wake. His hand closed around her breast, gentle but firm—learning the feel of her, she thought. He still moved against her, but more gently—and with a hitch in his thrust and in his breath that told her how hard he worked to keep it that way.

Uncertainty. She realized it through the haze of increasing need—and realized anew what it probably meant.

"No," she said, nonetheless hooking her leg around his to pull them in close, this time expecting his momentary freeze at the new sensation—she wore those thin panties, but nothing else between them. "I mean *protection*. I'm on birth control, but…we need a condom—"

"For what?" he asked, no guile in his voice as he found her nipple with his thumb, circling it.

"Protection!" she said desperately, because she already knew what the answer was.

"You have me for that," he murmured. "You have Bob. You have the land…you have yourself." He followed her collarbone with his breath, his movement gentle and controlled and completely at odds with the tension thrumming under her hands, where her fingers pressed into his flanks—feeling every quiver of muscle, feeling every tremble of thrusts controlled.

"Not *that* protection," she said, and groaned as his breath warmed the upper slope of her breast—couldn't stop herself from tightening her leg around him, from arching into the resulting spear of heat or reveling in his low, involuntary grunt of response. "Safe sex kind of protection! In case one of us isn't as healthy as we obviously think we are!"

At that, he hesitated, pulling back to eye her—his face full of naked vulnerability in his need for her, his response to her. "I have my health," he said, without any obvious understanding. "But I have no—"

"—condom," she supplied for him, disappointment threading through her voice as she tried to slow her response.

Her body was having none of it. She wanted this man—had wanted him the moment she'd seen him. She groaned in frustration.

"Shh," he said, and if he didn't understand, he still accepted—even tense unto breaking, even with a groan in his throat. "There will be tomorrow."

Maybe. And maybe she wouldn't be here. Maybe she'd lose what she had with this man before she even had it.

And if she didn't? He wouldn't follow her to Colorado. She might have laughed at the thought of it if she hadn't been so certain it would turn into a sob—if the morning hadn't rushed across her all over again with all its high emotion. "Tell me again that you're safe," she asked him, running her hand along his arm in a desperate caress. "Tell me again that you're—"

But she stopped, for she'd encountered the bandanna— the one he still wore like a token, covering the deep gouge the bullet had rent in his flesh, freshly applied after the shower. Only now, under her touch, it slipped down from the upper curve of his biceps.

And there was no wound there. There was no deep gouge, no ugly edges, no scabbing or inflammation.

There was only the pink remnant of healing, thin and tender skin that would soon fade without any apparent scar at all.

I'm healthy, he told her. *I'm safe,* he'd said, and the forest had echoed with it in her mind. *I heal fast,* he had assured her when he'd been hurt, not nearly enough days ago to have healed at all. *Not like other people,* her father had warned her, and she thought she'd understood. She'd thought of herself, and his reaction to the things she thought they'd heard together, and she thought she'd seen enough of him to know.

"Not like other people," Regan whispered out loud, and suddenly knew she understood nothing at all.

Chapter 12

Regan left Kai alone on the slope behind the barn. He ached for her touch, alone in a way he'd never felt before—in a way that baffled him and left his body in turbulence and his heart confused.

His body, he could deal with. The Sentinel who'd initiated him had been as blunt about that as in everything, teaching him the ways of her body—and teaching him about his. "Keep yourself satisfied," she'd said. "Learn yourself. When you leave this place and join up with the rest of us, you'll need to know your own needs so you can be a good partner. And you'll need self-control. You'll be stronger than most of us—stronger than anyone just plain human—so you'll need practice, or you're going to hurt someone."

And she'd shown him, bringing him to the brink of release, leaving him unsated—demanding his attention before she would allow him completion.

If he'd been surprised at the intensity of his response

to Regan, he hadn't been surprised at his control. But the twist of emotional pain—the *need*—

That, he'd never felt before.

That, he didn't know how to manage.

So he sat on the hill until he thought he could keep the struggle inside. At least until he figured out those feelings—or until he made it away from this place.

Regan briefly tended the horse and disappeared inside the house.

After a very long while, Kai stood, made his way back to the corral and gave himself the luxury of a long, stress-releasing stretch. Then he donned the damp loincloth—not so damp as all that, after the dry air and sunshine—and pulled on his leggings, and made sure the letter from his father was still wrapped securely around the belt that held it all up. He rewrapped the bandanna around his arm.

Then he went to the door and stood. He had the feeling that she'd come—that she'd kept track of him.

After a few moments, she did. She'd combed her glorious hair and straightened her shirt and fastened her jeans, but high color still sat along her cheeks and sparked in her eyes.

He said, "I don't know how to disarm the gun. It's not safe—I'll find a place for it."

She frowned. "Unload it, you mean?"

He shook his head. "*Disarm* might not be the right word. *Cleanse* it. It's dangerous…it shouldn't be here."

She crossed her arms, and he immediately grew wary— knew he'd overstepped some boundary, but didn't know where it was or what it was called. She said, "I guess I can make that decision for myself."

"I could take it," he said, reluctant and seeing no way around it. Forcing his way inside to take the gun…there was no coming back from that. And whatever the turmoil of being here with her, he wanted to come back.

Even if she otherwise spurned him. And even if she had no idea of the forces that had come to center on this place—or that regardless of what drove her fear, her connection with the land, he could help with that, too.

If not without giving some of himself away.

Her frown grew to a scowl. "And how do you think that would go for you?"

"I think it would be hard, and it would break things between us." He returned her gaze with a steady reluctance. "But it's my fault that it's here, so I'll do what I have to."

She stared at him, then disappeared inside—a few obvious steps to the kitchen table, a few back again—and returned with the gun. "Fine," she said, her face still hard with her anger. "I don't need this particular fight. But I'm really pissed. I don't need you to take care of me."

He accepted the gun with a distaste he hadn't anticipated, finding it heavy and cold in his hand—a metal that didn't warm to his touch. "Maybe if someone *had,*" he said, treading dangerous ground, "you wouldn't be afraid of things now."

Her mouth thinned. "Smart of you to get the gun, before saying something like that. *Bastard.*"

The words didn't sting like they might have—he heard the hurt behind them, and knew it came from that fear, too, from the understanding that he might just be right.

He needed to learn what drove her—how she heard the land, but had no sensation of Core workings; how she had no understanding of that blessing. Why she feared it. But when he opened his mouth to ask, the words wouldn't come. Her fragility in the moment came through clearly enough on her face, in the tension of her shoulders—in the way her arms hugged her slender torso as much as they crossed in defiance. So he only nodded, then turned to go.

She stopped him. "Why have you still got on the bandanna?" When he glanced back, she nodded at his arm. "You obviously don't need it any longer."

He couldn't keep the mild surprise from his voice. "Because it's yours," he told her, and headed off into the woods.

Kai cached the gun in the woods and found himself dissatisfied—knowing it could be found by chance, or that anyone with any faint, subconscious sensitivity to Core workings might find it with something less than chance.

Or that it might draw the Core back to this territory.

But it took him several days of pacing through the forest before he was prepared to leave it to find a safer cache. He patrolled the dry pool; he patrolled the edges of the Adler property. He sat in high places, looking down over the land—listening to it. Hunting signs of the Core, faint clues to their presence and purpose.

When he finally ventured onto the Adler property again, greeted by Bob but unnoticed by Regan, he walked it with a deliberate thoroughness—one that he should have applied much earlier, had he not been—

Avoiding her. Avoiding this land. Too uncertain about the emotions floundering between them, too afraid of hurting her. Too afraid of the strength of missing her, and of his endless impulse to return and pull her into his arms and do the most unthinkable thing of all—to explain to her what he was. To let her understand.

He knew himself for a coward, when what she needed was someone strong enough to help.

And on the Adler property, he found signs of the Core. The faint stench of their passing, of minor workings triggered and already faded. Not of activity so much as *interest*.

He'd have to tell her—to warn her. To explain, as he could, how she should beware.

Beware, Regan, he thought at her as he sat in the scrub of her back hillside with lynx ears flicking. *Take care, Regan.* And then, before he left—before he considered the wisdom of it—he sent her his longing.

Bob the Dog barked sharply, and Kai took to his feet and trotted away over the ridge.

Regan set her paintbrush aside and looked out the dormer window of the loft—the space that had always been hers, and the window beside which she'd always painted, the skylight pouring light across her work and the forest spread out before her.

Beware...

She gritted her teeth, ignoring that echo in her mind— the nudge that had caused her to look up in the first place, even if she wanted to pretend it had been Bob's single and unusual bark.

Just as she had pretended to ignored the startling wash of emotion that followed—the sudden sting of tears behind her lids, the stupid impulse to say, "I miss you, too," even if there was no one here to hear it.

But she set the paintbrush aside and looked out the window—and if she thought she saw a flicker of movement up in the scrubby oak, it was gone before she could be sure.

Chapter 13

Kai dropped the gun into his satchel, pulled on his jeans and shoes, then made his way into town and the general store—too many hours and days of patrolling behind him, too few hours of hunting. And, until Mary silently handed him her own hairbrush from behind the counter, he realized he'd been too distracted to have completely put himself together for town.

After that he borrowed the store's bathroom and mirror and tidied up, but Mary still frowned at him, and she pushed a sandwich at him while Bill agreed there'd been an unusual number of early visitors lingering in the area—scouting for hunting season, they'd told him, and staying for the Apple Blossom Festival. "But they didn't look like hard-core hunters," he added. "Too spiffy."

"Spick-and-span," Mary agreed. "You eat that sandwich, Kai. You heading to Phillip's?"

And since he was, she reached behind the counter and handed over a crinkly grocery bag heavy with material.

"I fixed his uniform," she said. "Tell him we'll settle it out later."

So Kai, the sandwich sitting heavy in his stomach, headed over to the small Tae Kwon Do dojang—and the small and unassuming man who taught discipline and self-defense and who never spoke of his past.

Maybe that was why he'd always respected that Kai never spoke of his present.

Phillip Seamans had a face of experience but indeterminate age, a wiry jockey's body full of wily strength, and a dojang full of young children. Kai hesitated at the door, taking that moment to evaluate the interior. Then he slipped inside, gave his bow toward Phillip, and sat cross-legged against the wall to watch chubby bodies learn to roll and fall and offer proper etiquette, their short limbs all but swallowed by their *dobok* uniforms. Not so many of them in this tiny town, but enough to keep a smile behind Phillip's eyes as their mothers sat along the wall opposite from Kai, emerging to participate as necessary.

Kai watched them with some fascination, as he always did. They were a thing so far from his world, and yet in many ways reflective of it—their blunt honesty and joy and faces screwed up in fierce concentration.

As the class finished, Phillip drew their attention to him and directed them to bow, their solemn little faces bent without precision over randomly placed feet. And then he turned them loose in a pattering stampede. They threw themselves on top of Kai with giggles and shrieks of delight—except for the ones who didn't.

Some children were like Bob—drawn to him, quickly trusting him. And some stood back and watched with large, wary eyes while their mothers puzzled over their unusual shyness.

When the children had been hugged and returned to their mothers to don their shoes and leave, Kai rose to his feet. Had he been a true student, he would have stood as long as Phillip was standing, but here—as everywhere— he was neither one thing nor another, neither master or student. Phillip—like so many in Cloudview—accepted him on his own terms and simply called him Kai.

Kai had been looking for that understanding in the weeks after his family had left. Phillip had accepted his unusual fighting style, a thing of early discipline and instinct; Kai had readily absorbed what Phillip had to teach.

But only Phillip ever sparred with him, then and now. Phillip's rules, to protect Kai from an endless round of challenges and to protect overconfident challengers from Kai's lethal grace.

Kai bowed briefly and held out the bag with its mended *dobok*. "Mary says to settle with her later."

"Something to do with repairs to the boardwalk, if I guess right." But Phillip took the bag with a pleased expression. "I expected to see you sooner than this—I had the impression after that last bout that you were looking for a rematch." He tipped his head, eyeing Kai. "Been under the weather?"

"Obligations," Kai said, a shorthand that Phillip would understand in concept, if not in detail. He didn't say, "I was shot" or "The land is unhappy" or "Regan Adler is here and I want her." He still wore the bandanna—it spoke to him of her—but he didn't expect Phillip to ask about that, either.

He tugged his satchel around from where it had rested on his back. "I have a favor to ask. Something to keep safe."

Phillip offered a wry expression. "Since when can I hold something more safely than you?"

Kai was supposed to shrug amusement, he knew that. To respond in kind. But he found himself too caught up in the events of the past days. "This can't be with me," he said. "It can't be in the forest." He hesitated, torn between the need to keep secrets and the need for Phillip to understand. "It needs a neutral place, behind concrete and metal."

Phillip's brow raised. He might not understand the things gone unspoken, but he understood that they were there. Still, when Kai reached into the satchel and brought out the gun, Phillip made a sound of surprise.

But he took the gun—holding it as Kai had, as an object and not a weapon.

"It's not safe," Kai warned him.

"Kai," Phillip said, true humor warming his voice, "it's a *gun*."

"It's more than that," Kai said, coming down hard on those words—a hint of his nature coming through in the ferocity, the protective imperative.

Phillip regarded him as a man who'd heard those things—as a man with a long habit of thoughtful response. "Where did you get it?"

"From the one who tried to kill me with it," Kai said and shook his head. "The important thing is to keep it neutral…and that, I can't truly explain. I just need it believed."

"The sheriff—"

Kai interrupted him, a rarity of broken etiquette here in Phillip's dojang. "Would he believe?"

Phillip's wry grimace came with understanding. "He'd ask a lot more questions than I am. No doubt that's because he's a smarter man than I." He slipped the gun inside the bag with the *dobok,* but his expression said he had his own questions, and that he hovered on asking them.

He just might have, had Kai not caught a hint of distress from the land and lifted his head to it, eyes narrowed.

Phillip had never seen him go on the hunt…but he recognized it well enough. By the time the two men appeared in the open doorway—big, muscled, clad in dark shirts, loose, light pants and silver studs at their ears—Phillip had turned to meet them.

Aeli and Hantz. And still well adorned with fading bruises from their previous encounter with Kai.

"Sentinel," Aeli said, the sneer of a single word. Kai lifted a lip at him—a warning that Phillip was an outsider, and not to be drawn into the truth of their worlds. But the lynx pushed hard against him from within, recognizing the danger—the enmity. *The men who had threatened Regan.*

Hantz gave his partner a meaningful glare, and Phillip intervened with polite courtesy.

"How can I help you?" he asked, as congenial as ever—but he stood balanced and ready, and the Core minions were fools if they saw Phillip as he seemed, a small innocuous man with a bag in hand.

Hantz said, "Just looking for a good place to work out while we're here." But his attention wasn't quite all there, and his thumb rubbed over a unique metal coin—the active amulet Kai had felt. *A seeking amulet.*

Maybe hunting Kai and what taint remained from the bullet. Maybe hunting the gun itself. Though it didn't quite make sense that it mattered so much. Surely the Core had other guns, other bullets?

Unless they were trying something new.

Unless they'd lost something truly important—or something they really didn't want him to have.

Or even to know about.

A bad move, then, to have shot him with it and failed to kill him.

"You're looking for a place to work out," Phillip said, eyeing them. "I'm sorry to say I doubt this small establishment can meet your needs. You might try Alamogordo."

"Alamogordo," Aeli repeated, staring flatly at Kai.

"Down the hill," Phillip said helpfully, and pointed.

"If we wanted—" Aeli started.

Hantz interrupted, pocketing his coin-size amulet. "Thank you," he said. "We'll look into the options." He eyed Kai, an expression of dark promise—an acknowledgment that they couldn't pursue this in Phillip's presence in spite of undiminished intent. Then he caught Aeli's gaze and jerked his head at the open door. "Then maybe we'll be back."

Phillip watched them go and—most tellingly—he closed the door behind them. He turned back to Kai and raised a brow, casting an obvious scrutiny for bruises and injury. "You left your mark on those two, I see." He frowned then, a faint thing of true and rare censure. "Stand down, Kai. Or you can follow them out."

Kai took a startled breath, feeling the lynx so close to the surface—closer than he'd realized. Feeling in himself the ferocity of protectiveness toward Regan, toward the land. He took another breath, deliberately pushing the lynx away. Another, and felt again the weariness that had dogged him through the most recent days.

He was only man, trying to fulfill an inborn imperative. A single Sentinel in the middle of a Core incursion, and not truly a Sentinel at all.

Phillip nodded at the door. "Better. You still look like crap, though, which is a blunter way to say what I politely implied when you arrived. Now, you going to tell me about them?"

Kai hesitated. "When I figure out how. Will you still keep the gun safe?"

"From them," Phillip said, and it wasn't a guess. "They following you?"

He could answer that one readily enough. "I'm not sure. Maybe."

Phillip hefted the bag. "I'll keep it safe," he said. "Under the condition that you don't lie to me—not ever, but spe-

cifically not about this. *Not answering,* that's one thing.
But don't give me crap."

"I haven't," Kai said. "I won't."

"Okay, then." Phillip gave him a companionable clout
on the arm. Kai's lynx snarled up inside, overreactive...
still wanting to strike out. And Phillip nodded, as if that's
what he'd been waiting to see.

But he didn't judge it. He simply noted it. "I'll put this
away and go check in with Mary. I think you'd best do
forms today on your own."

This, Kai realized, was no more than truth—although
it chagrined him. He couldn't recall when he'd been unable to tame the lynx...and he couldn't recall when Phillip had ever looked at him this way.

Or when, in spite of all his understanding, he'd ever
turned back to use just this tone in his voice when he said,
"I can keep *this* safe, Kai. You'd better think about what
will do the same for you."

Regan parked in Cloudview's upper lot and pulled the
keys from the ignition, musing on her day so far.

No matter how far out in the woods the cabin, no matter how close it was to being completely off the grid and
self-contained...it wasn't quite there yet. And real life still
happened. The septic still needed to be pumped, the well
water tested, the plumbing fixed.

And in desert country, if the kitchen sink started to
drip it didn't matter if the land was poking away at your
mind or if your body wouldn't stop thinking about the man
who frightened you on one level and inexorably drew you
to him on another. Down the winding narrow road you
went, five thousand feet below to Alamogordo and the
nearest significant hardware store. Because if Regan left
this place—*when* she left this place—she would leave the
cabin in good shape.

She'd found the faucet cartridge and then done the grocery shopping—because the other thing one didn't do was waste a trip down the mountain. Or leave home without a big cooler in the back of the car.

It was easier to hit the Cloudview post office than the one down below, so once Regan had wound her way through the switchbacks to the top again, she headed up to park here at the boardwalk.

When she emerged from the car, she held a bundled accumulation of her father's mail. It was a quick jog to the post office just below, and a quick jog back to the car—where she looked to the main street below and considered the virtues of ice cream versus a nice, sinful doughnut.

Because unless something had changed, today was doughnut day at the general store.

In that moment, she got a glimpse of herself—preteen, laughing as she crossed the road with her mother, each trying to top the other's description of the world's most indulgent doughnut. A stupid little thing—

But if it brought the sudden sting of tears to her eyes, it also brought a little smile to the corner of her mouth. She left the car and headed downhill—past the garage, past the gas station—

Matt Arshun stood gassing up his fancy car.

His presence punctured Regan's bubble of connection to her past. Suddenly, she was more aware of her strides, of the impact of asphalt against the soles of her lightweight hikers. Suddenly, she was aware of the chilling breeze against her bare arms and the way it cut through her thin shirt—the way it tightened her skin.

Arshun glanced at her breasts, and she knew she should have pulled her jacket on before leaving the car. But her stride faltered at the additional two men who emerged from the store, coffees in hand. One each, and…an extra.

Aeli. Hantz. The men from the woods, if not the man

who had commanded them—although that extra coffee suggested he might be close.

If only Arshun hadn't glanced aside in response to Regan's reaction, and moved his head in the merest fraction of a negative—and if the men hadn't eased to a stop because of it, trying to look casual as they sipped their coffee and made their small talk, that one leftover coffee speaking volumes.

If only they hadn't had such similar styles. It didn't matter that Arshun was in a suit and the men in their snappy but more casual outfits, or that Arshun had a sleek club of gathered hair while the men sported tighter styles. They had the same cast of skin, cast of feature…the same dark eyes and dark hair. The same spark of silver in their rings and watches and tiny stub earrings.

"Regan," Arshun said, pulling the nozzle from his gas tank and hooking it back into place on the dispenser, as if she wasn't smart enough to realize he was now with two of the men who had attacked Kai that week earlier with Marat. "I'd like to talk with you about that land."

"Please don't waste your time," she said stiffly. And then, in case that wasn't clear, she added, "Or mine."

He only smiled.

She made it across the street without being hit only because the road was characteristically empty, and only when the general store bell jingled the door closed behind her and everyone turned to look did she realize she'd come inside with a rush. "Doughnuts!" she said brightly, and headed for the bakery display.

"Regan Adler," Mary said. "What wind got up your butt?"

Regan stood in front of the bakery glass and tried to think about sprinkles versus chocolate, but could only see the knowing look on Arshun's face—one that wouldn't have spooked her nearly as much if she hadn't seen those men in the woods, armed and coming for her, or if she hadn't seen Kai's blood, or if she hadn't so recently taken flight up a mountain road on a bolting mustang.

"Regan?" Bill's voice was quieter and came from waist level; his wheelchair hummed to a stop beside her.

"Chocolate," she said, determination in her voice, and Mary moved from behind one counter to the other to pluck up a pastry paper and acquire the selected doughnut.

"Regan," she said. "No one looks that shade of pale from a doughnut craving."

She felt a sudden flash of irritation, remembering this, too, about living here—the difficulty of keeping secrets, of even keeping one's thoughts to oneself. It was a wonder her mother's ailment hadn't been known to all before Kathleen's indiscretion.

With a jolt of realization, she tore her gaze from the pastries to find Mary's rounded face—to understand that the concern there came from more than today's fluster.

To realize for the first time that others *had* known all along. That they'd cared. Her mother's secrets…never really secret at all.

It choked her for a moment, making swallowing impossible. And then, because it was suddenly important that Mary know this *wasn't* about her mother, she said, "A couple of men startled me, that's all."

She frowned, and looked out the storefront window. "They *bother* you?"

Because this, too, was the kind of town this was. Regan relaxed, if only a little. "No, no…I was thinking deep thoughts, that's all. You know, whether I'm going to mess up the faucet when I replace the parts I just bought. Didn't see them, so they startled me."

"Big men," said one of the other customers, inviting himself into the conversation. Regan found him with a hammer in hand, a short and wiry man of middle age who looked as though he could have ridden a horse to the wire in the derby—except something in his movement reminded her of Kai, and something in his eyes told her not to make assumptions. "Dressed dark."

"Yes," she agreed.

The man exchanged a look with Mary and Bill. "The men who seem to know Kai."

"At your place just now?" Mary asked, though she anticipated the answer with a slight nod.

"They didn't bother you?" the man asked, prodding, his attention back on Regan.

"No," she said, and thought it truth enough. They'd very much bothered her...but not, as it happened, just now. And talking about *them* would have meant talking about Kai, and the woods, and things that didn't feel completely like hers to tell.

Besides, she didn't know this man—and she let that show, too.

He responded with immediate chagrin. "Manners," he said. "My name is Phillip Seamans. I own the Tae Kwon Do dojang. I've been here since before you left, but I don't expect you remember me...or it."

She heard what he meant her to hear. He knew of her; he knew of her family's loss. "Regan Adler," she said anyway. And then, reluctant words she couldn't keep herself from saying, "You know Kai, then?"

"Since I got here," Phillip said. "Although I only saw him once in those early years. His father, now...there was a man with things on his mind."

"Kai grew up here?" Regan tried to fathom it—tried to imagine Kai as a boy, living so nearby...and she'd known nothing of it.

Then again, she'd been preoccupied at that point. Too busy watching Gwen Adler fall apart.

"Kai's got plenty on his mind from the looks of it,"

Mary said, meaning in her voice—and in the glance she aimed at Regan. "Did you see how worn down he looked today?"

"Excuse me?" Regan said, rising to that occasion. "You think I've been gone so long I don't remember those *looks?* I haven't seen him for days. And from what I've seen, he can take care of himself just fine."

But she hadn't meant to blurt out such revealing words, and she shut her mouth on any more of them.

Mary stuffed the doughnut into a tiny white bag and rolled the crinkly top down with brusque movements, handing it over the counter. "I did tell you, Regan—don't mess with that boy."

"Boy!" she said, and gave Mary an incredulous look. Had Mary seen Kai lately?

Or maybe just not in those leggings.

Bill gave her an affectionate look. "Mary's been keeping an eye out for too many years, maybe. Truth is, he probably doesn't need that help anymore."

"He's a wild thing," Mary grumbled. "And like most wild things, civilization is the thing that will end up hurting him."

Phillip cleared his throat. "He wasn't himself today, I'll say that much. But I think we can safely look to those men for the real reason. I might just have a word with Jaime Nez."

"It's hard to imagine what the sheriff can do," Regan murmured, thinking again of the strangeness of it all—and only afterward realizing that her words made little sense without that context. She managed to add lamely, "After all, they're only hanging around. Along with that Realtor who won't get off my back."

Phillip shifted his grip on the hammer. "You've seen them before?"

The doughnut bag crinkled in Regan's grip; she pushed

cash over the register counter and figured change couldn't come fast enough. This man was far too astute…and Regan was far too distracted.

This, she realized, was a conversation to be having with Kai. Whom she'd effectively chased off, and hadn't seen since. But who, in the end, was the only one she could truly tell about seeing the dry-pool musclemen with Matt Arshun—and the only one who would truly understand what it meant.

The only one who already seemed to understand the things she didn't want to talk about at all.

Chapter 14

Kai did the forms Phillip had taught him, focusing on the details—the exact level of his clenched fist, the smooth, accurate motion of arms and legs, the balance of his body. He moved on to his own forms, the spin and tuck and roll that came so naturally.

Phillip had helped him integrate the two, giving him discipline without destroying flexibility—understanding, even at the start, that Kai would fade back into the woods to follow his own instincts before ever suborning them to things entirely human.

Even if he'd never understood why.

Alone in the studio, he focused on the slap of the mat, the sharp exhalations of his own breath, the sensation of muscles at work.

He no longer felt the influence of the gun and its bullets, secured as they were in Phillip's floor safe. He no longer felt the lingering, muted whisperings of Core activity in the woods—a thing so subtle that he hadn't recognized its presence until he'd encountered its absence.

Of the Core, Kai knew little more than what his parents had taught him—that their workings drew upon the earth, sapping energies and spitting back the twisted remnants of those same energies. *Poison.* Poison to the earth, to the unwitting humans who shared it, and to the Sentinels. Most of all to Kai, who not only had the ability to perceive the merest whisper of such workings—the miasma of the Core's very presence—but who found them so hard to bear.

Temporary freedom from the subliminal taint of Core activity made its renewed presence all the more evident to Kai when he emerged from Phillip's dojang—a faint taste at the back of his throat, a light pressure against his skin. All things he'd felt prior to interrupting the amulet dump at the dry pool, but simply not recognized.

I will find you, he thought at the Core, hesitating outside the dojang to lift his face to those invisible currents, sensing the direction and strength of them. *You will not touch this land.*

Or Regan.

He caught a ride back toward the wild lands that held his home, disembarking—as he always did—nowhere near the game trails of that place.

This time, he headed straight for Frank Adler's land.

Already the air here felt cleaner than before he had removed the gun, clearer—absolving itself of the taint. Kai pulled the satchel off his shoulder, shedding his clothing and packing it away to tuck behind a clutter of rocks—his trappings of civilization, none of which would take the change with him. He stood naked and unfettered in the trees, stretching into a grand yawn…shaking off the feel of asphalt from beneath his feet.

When he bounded forward, it was as lynx—the brilliance of the energies from the change still coruscating in his wake. In this form, he moved swift and silent, running the boundaries of the property—noting Regan's new tree tags, stretching up on his hind legs to leave marks of his own, the late-afternoon shadows falling long around him where the sun sliced through the trees.

Because the Core had been here. Not active, but…here. Here more than anywhere else, making themselves familiar with the several hundred acres of the Adler property… and pushing in close to the house.

Regan might hear the land, but evidently she didn't have any particular sense of the Core. Kai found their scent, their footprints…and up on an outcrop with a perfect view of the cabin, he found the lens cap for a camera.

He hesitated there, looking down at the cabin. He knew it for what it was—a remarkably independent dwelling, here where no maps truly traced the roads. Solar panels lined the roof, soaking up the sun even in winter; the woodstove warmed the house without help from the gathered electricity. The well pumped into a vast cistern buried into the hill, and the horse drank from the same rainwater collection that watered the garden beneath greenhouse panels.

From here he could see the barn, see the horse, see the spot on the hill where he and Regan had very nearly coupled.

He tried to tell himself that the depth of his response to her came simply because he found her beautiful, the bright gold swirl of her hair and the strong active nature of her body, the perfect curve of her breast in his hand and the wink of the jewel at her navel.

But he'd found other women beautiful—the hikers he'd guided in the off-season, the women in the hunting parties and the tourists traipsing through the general store. Some of those women had features more beautiful than Regan, bodies more lush—and they had offered of themselves to him, obviously enough so there was no mistaking their invitation.

No. It was simply Regan. He didn't know why, and he didn't know if that was because he knew so little of the outside world—of *women*—in general, or if men simply never knew such things.

He yawned hugely under the weight of the thoughts, eyes squeezed shut and ears flattened. He resettled his tongue in his mouth, working his jaws...lips resting over long canines and sharp, carnassial teeth. *Lynx*.

She would never know. *Could* never know.

But he could still protect her. Whether she knew it... whether she wanted it.

Sentinel and lynx, both.

The morning after her drive downhill and her encounters in town, Regan found her mystery footprints right at the edge of the yard.

"Suddenly this place is Grand Central Station?" she asked Bob, who had left his porch vigil to lean against her leg with a low and solemn wag. Even the old cat was out today, sunning himself in the driveway—although neither animal appeared particularly concerned about the tracks Regan was so very certain had to be lynx.

She found herself not particularly concerned, either. If there was truly a lynx in this area, however it had gotten here, it needed all the help it could get. She found her mind's eye wandering, putting together images of a mountain forest painted in shadows and sunlight, a lynx just barely emerging to be picked out in those edges of light.

She also found the second set of tracks. As fresh as the lynx tracks if not fresher, the imprints of those massive hiking boots were still drying into hardness along the damp edge of the woods where the dew lingered.

She tried to imagine Kai in shoes, and recalled with

crystal clarity the library, where he'd looked—almost—like anyone she might meet in town. His feet had borne hiking boots, all right—but they'd been lightweight and low profile.

She suspected he'd ditched them as soon as he'd thought no one would remark upon it. How crazy was that, to go barefoot in these woods? *Barefoot down from the peak.* As if the average hiker made it to the top of this range at all, never mind in bare feet—never mind to come running down the whole way at the signs of her distress that he shouldn't have been able to perceive at all.

It was all part of the big picture of her decision to go. Men who shouldn't be on this land...that was one thing. But the land itself, invading her mind...*Kai,* and his preternatural ability to use the land to reach her...

Concepts to which she couldn't even put words, and to which she really didn't want to.

"I'm leaving," she told Bob, who merely wagged his tail another few beats, still leaning his great shoulder against her. She'd meant to say something about her departure to Mary and Bill—to look for someone who might watch this place.

Maybe it was too hard to admit it out loud—that she would leave this place when her father needed her here. Especially with someone prowling around so invasively.

As if she didn't know exactly who. Whatever his reason, Arshun wanted this place. He and those men.

Kai...

"I don't need your help!" she snapped at that insidious whisper, and then muttered an apology when Bob's ears flattened in concern. She ran a hand over his big head. "You're one of the reasons I'm leaving."

Although she couldn't blame the whispers for expressing what she'd already managed to think of on her own.

If anyone could make her feel safe here, it would be Kai.

Then again, if anyone could make her feel *unsafe*...it was the man who heard what she did, and apparently embraced it. The man who spent his time in the woods like some modern-day Grizzly Adams, guiding hunters and hikers on some irregular and highly sought-after basis. The man who had healed from a bullet wound in an impossibly complete and swift fashion.

The man to whom she responded in such a swift and primal way that she hardly knew herself. And that was hardly what she needed, when what she knew of herself was unraveling all on its own.

No doubt that's why she had come back from Alamogordo with those extra steaks and with a packet of condoms.

Kai...

"Let's go inside, cat," she told the lounging feline. "I have to call Dad—maybe he knows someone who can stay here."

The cat rolled to his other side, stretching hugely—his whiskers rippling and claws spread into extrusion, his whole body full of satisfaction.

"Nothing stretches like a cat," she told him, and led the way back to the cabin.

But the whispers wouldn't leave her alone. Not in the loft, working at the rough-edged painting of the woods and surprised to find it finished, to see that the rough edges were part of it. Not in the kitchen, where the new faucet cartridge installed just as it was supposed to. Not over a solitary dinner, or the phone call she didn't quite make.

Leave. Stay.

And the whispers curling around in her mind.... *Kai... safe...beware...* A confusing contradiction of thoughts and feelings, all imbued with a kind of longing.

She sat curled in the overstuffed chair of her loft, bathed

in the natural light of the specialized fixtures she'd been given in the early days of her art, when her mother was still there to nurture such things. Sketching out drafts of a new painting between random, quick impressions of the tracks she'd seen…pulling out her old reference books to make quick studies of a lynx in motion and surprised to find how much of those images drew not on learning, but from something inside herself.

Something trying to find freedom through her art.

Because the work wasn't for someone else's project—illustrating someone else's words, or making clear someone else's treatise—she let herself go. She submerged herself, sketching from one page onto another, shifting from quick detail to sweeping strokes, and when the purr surrounded her, she didn't even at first realize it. It seemed an extension of her own pleasure, this sensation of just being what she'd always been meant to be. Only when she stopped to switch to a softer pencil did she realize the sensation came from without as much as within.

That the whispers could purr.

It jarred her from the serenity of what she was doing, and turned her back into a woman at the end of the day, surrounded by books and paper, her tackle box of an art kit gaping open beside the chair and night fully fallen around her.

"I wasn't done yet," she said to the darkness outside the window, knowing that she'd have to get the woodstove going if she didn't want to shiver half the night, that Bob hadn't been fed and the mustang should be checked before she went to bed even if a full slow feeder would keep him supplied for days.

With reluctance she put the pencil down, but she couldn't stop from flipping through the pages of what she'd done. "What is *that* supposed to be?" she muttered at the sight of a languid line that stroked across the paper, and snorted at herself—until she suddenly remembered doing it, seeing suddenly the line of Kai's side, his torso flowing into hip and along the join of his leg where muscle shifted, so casually beautiful. And here…a tassled ear above the eye of a lynx, smeared with the natural kohl of its coloration…looking wise. Looking right into her soul.

She touched it with her finger, tracing around the outside of it…feeling a kind of reverence for the mood that had gripped her and what had emerged. Allowing herself to quit fearing and to relax into vulnerability.

But the whispers ground down into a moan, a taste of ugliness and merest hint of a word.

Beware…

And the lynx eye transformed before her, whirling down into a tight pinprick and exploding back out into dripping ugliness, skin sagging from flesh and bone peeking through. Thorny vines wound around an exposed eye socket and reached out from the page to circle her fingers. "No," Regan moaned. "No, no, no…."

But when she jerked her hand back, the vines came, too. And when she flung the sketch pad away, it skimmed across the room to land faceup, and the vines had unspooled between them—tightening around her hand and arm, pricking her…flowing up and around to bind her torso and crawl into her hair and poke at her lips and tickle into her nose.

She clamped her mouth shut on her terror and clawed at herself, ripping her shirt and her skin, shrieking deep in her throat and knowing she couldn't let it out—tripping and stumbling and sending the cat streaking away down the stairs. *Kai!* she cried inside, and didn't even know why—except that as she fell to her knees, it seemed the only safe retreat, there inside the insanity of her own mind. *Kai!* She crumpled into a ball and tucked herself tight, feeling the vines braid and weave around her…capturing her.

Kai...

The whispers were right there with her. But instead of warning, they brought the sudden memory of flesh against flesh on a hillside, of rocketing pleasure and gasping response. Of Kai's touch, strong fingers gone gentle...of his *presence*.

Abruptly, she found herself alone in the loft, curled into a tight ball on the floor. Her pencils lay scattered, the tackle box overturned...the sketchbook in the corner, the pages gently fluttering. When she pushed herself upright, she discovered her hands whole, unpierced by thorns. The damage to her shirt was only that which she'd caused; the damage to her skin only that from her flailing.

A new panic arose, stronger than any outside fear. Her mother had never been like this. *Never.* Never violent, never so completely lost to hallucination.

I have to go. Now.

But first she had to find Kai.

He owed her answers...and she owed him a warning.

Chapter 15

Regan found herself outside the cabin with her breath puffing cold into the frigid spring night. Her day pack hung over one shoulder simply because this high-woods girl didn't walk out unprepared into the darkness.

That the pack hung ready by the back door had helped. Because she'd hardly been in a position to start from scratch, with her mind so fully wrapped and tangled around what she was about to do.

Terrified.

She hadn't meant to send that thought out into the night, but maybe she had. Because the night answered.

Safe...

"Oh, you must be kidding!" she snapped at it. "Did you not see what just happened? You are breaking my *brain.*"

Or the whispers weren't the problem at all. Maybe it was just her brain.

There was only one way to find out.

And only one way to find *him.*

Unless she was truly crazy after all, and not just being driven there.

"Kai?" she said, the word hesitant and uncertain against the backdrop of silence.

And only the silence came in response. She faltered then, understanding what it would take—that rather than running from the whispers, she would have to speak to them. That if she was to warn Kai at all—about Arshun's involvement with those at the dry pool, and about their presence in town, and about the new poisons swirling through the land—she would have to stop running from being her mother...

She would have to become her mother. And she didn't know if she would ever come back.

The light from her red LED flashlight careened eerily through the trees before her. At first she followed the southward game path, heading in the general direction of the area where she'd first seen Kai. "I'm coming," she muttered, knowing only the night would hear. But she had to gather her nerve for that final, necessary step: reaching back out to the voice that had spoken to her. And through it, hunting for echoes of Kai.

Kai?

Safe, purred the land.

"Yeah," she muttered, her heart pounding ridiculously hard, "we've had that discussion." But nothing had reared up to slap her, and the forest remained stable around her. She took a deep breath and tried again...less tentatively this time. Trying not to think about what it would mean if this actually worked—about her, about her mother, about the nature of the world she seemed to live in but no one else saw. *Kai. I need to talk to you.*

After a moment of utter silence, she snorted quietly to herself. As if she'd truly thought to get a response of some sort. She might as well just bellow into the peaceful night.

?...

The flashlight spurted through her suddenly clenched grip, falling to the ground and turning itself off. She made no attempt to retrieve it, standing frozen in the darkness.

She could pretend that had been her imagination, that sleepy, wordless query. She could pretend it had been wishful thinking. She could pretend—

But she knew. Deep inside, where she didn't have to justify it to anyone else, where she didn't have to explain...

She *knew*.

Kai?

And the land spoke to her.

Kai slept wrapped in fleece and comfort and bare skin, nested in his low bed with only Regan's bandanna around his fully healed arm. He'd fallen into dreams of darkness laced with exhaustion, shifting against the gentle confines of the blankets—until the dreams themselves shifted, and became Regan. Became the scent of her, all warmth and gentle fragrance. Became the flashing gold of soft hair, tumbling free after a shower. Became the touch of her inner self that she didn't even know she offered—and became the touch of her hand.

Kai?

Even in sleep, he reached back to her, open to her presence. His breath quickened; his fingers twitched.

Kai?

He welcomed her, responded to her, groaned in the happiness at the feel of her—

And woke with startled surprise to the still quiet of the night—tangled in blankets, soaking in the aroused state of his body and the understanding that he'd not just wakened to his dreams, but he had *been* awakened.

Kai?

The tentative whisper came like an afterthought in his

own mind, recognizable only by the dint of his years alone with the land—with its echoes and its connections.

Never had anyone deliberately reached him this way. *Regan.* Not an unknowing ripple of need or a flailing, fearful shout, but an uncertain and brave query into a world that had done nothing but frighten her until now.

For of course it was Regan. Her touch, filtering into his dreams. Her essence, flavoring his sleeping thoughts.

Still half-asleep and reveling in the intersection of their worlds, he reached back to her. Nothing so bold as a greeting…merely the soft sigh of a welcome.

It wouldn't do to scare her now.

She searched for him, he understood that much. And he understood the strength it must have taken for her so much as try. How frightened she'd been by what she'd experienced here, and how he himself had frightened her simply because of who and what he was.

He'd stayed away from her for a reason.

But now she searched for him, and if he didn't quite understand why, or what had driven her to overcome her fears, he didn't quite care at the moment.

Kai?

Yes, he thought back at her, a little more strongly than before. *Here.* He rose from the mattress, two of the blankets wrapped sloppily around his shoulders. He slipped through the slash of an entry and out into the night, where the chill air bit at his ankles and seeped into his feet.

He didn't go far. Just far enough to protect his home, even from Regan.

For she was close now, the red flash of her light slashing against the trees, her progress steady after crossing the many acres between her home and his. Whatever her purpose, she'd given herself to it.

He held himself still, waiting—absorbing her through

her subtle, inexpert connection to the land and breathing in of her essence…offering his own back to her.

She might not recognize it, subtle as it was. Or she might—

"Kai!" As intensely as she spoke his name, she kept her voice low—in deference to the night. Her light flashed briefly over his chest, rose to his face—never went as far as his eyes before shifting away. "Oh, God, Kai, I must be crazy—"

He had no words to take away the breathless distress in her voice, this woman trying to bridge two worlds. He merely opened his arms, and when she dropped her pack and stepped into them, he closed the blankets around them both.

Her hands were cold against his ribs and her cheek was cold against his shoulder; she carried the subtle taint of the Core. He gave her warmth and waited.

"I have to leave," she told him, holding him yet a little tighter. "But I had to come here first. How backward is that?"

He made a noise in his chest. It was the best he could do—the only words in his mouth would have asked her to stay, and he thought if he did that she would push away from him and run. Or if he had reached to her through the land instead of merely inviting the essence of it around them, a wash of cleaner energies to brush away the remnants of the Core.

They stood until she stopped shaking and he grew more and more aware of the soft press of her breasts, the fine grace of her spine, the tuck of her waist and the curve of her hips. He tried desperately to think of other things, to remember the control he'd been taught and practiced, but as she relaxed, her fingers no longer quite clutching along his ribs, he collected tension.

She said, something of surprise in her voice, "You're *naked*."

"I was sleeping," he said.

She lifted her head to regard him, a gesture he could see clearly through a darkness that was hardly dark for him at all. Not with Sentinel eyes.

"Of course you were sleeping," she said, and loosened her hold on him. "You must be freezing."

He made another noise in his chest, something of desperation and humor combined. If she hadn't been wrapped in her coat, she would have known better. "Not really."

She closed her eyes, and something shifted in her expression—an awareness of him…and maybe of herself. She smiled ever so faintly and stepped back within the circle of his arms—just far enough to unzip her coat and shrug it off her shoulders, revealing the tear in her shirt. The soft skin above one breast showed through; the ripped neckline folded over the other.

"Regan," he said, and heard in his voice not just concern, but warning. "The cold—"

"I'm pretty sure you'll keep me warm." She shifted aside an errant fold of blanket, brushing her hand across his hip, then down into a bold caress. He jerked against her touch, and then he was the one who trembled. "Yeah," she said. "Pretty sure I've got that right."

"Regan," he said, somewhat desperately—remembering the hillside behind the Adler cabin, remembering how he'd frightened her—his healing arm, his reach for her through the land. His ferocity and strength, just as he'd been warned. "I'm still who I was. Before. On the hill."

"That's okay," she told him. "I'm *not*." She looked up at him, searching his features in the darkness and no doubt able to see very little in the absence of her flashlight. No doubt assuming the same of him. Her mouth opened… closed again. Not saying something.

She pressed her cheek against his chest and held him suddenly very close. "Before I go," she said, not quite making sense. "It won't be enough, but I can't *not* want you as much as I do."

His breath gusted out over her hair; he wanted to stroke it, to feel the sensation of gold. He wanted to run his hands over her soft skin and clamp them over her hips and feel her movement around him. He *wanted,* in a way he never had—in the way he knew he should beware. He knew he should reach for control, or warn her or tear himself away and put distance between them.

He knew just as certainly that he'd do none of that, just as he could say nothing of reassurance or desire. But he didn't have enough practice with words and he'd already gone beyond them.

Regan didn't seem to need them or want them. She tugged at him, pulling him not closer—as if that was possible—but downward, so they went to their knees together.

"Okay?" she asked him, her lips against his neck and sending hot chills down his spine, his skin both furnace-hot and goose bumping in the cold air slicing through a gap in the blankets. He shivered and sucked air into his lungs and forgot to respond. She took his face between her hands, her mouth brushing his. "Okay?"

The question felt more profound than it seemed but he couldn't think beyond it. *Okay,* he managed—and only when she stiffened slightly did he realize he'd done it silently, letting assent filter through the land. He managed to find his voice. "I am what I am," he reminded her, words and tone fraught with warning she wouldn't and couldn't understand.

"Yes," she breathed. "Right. You are. *I* am." She kissed him—a light brush of her lips.

"No," he said, more desperately yet. "I mean—" *What I am. The lynx. The Sentinel.*

"Kai," she said on a breathless huff of frustrated laughter, not understanding at all—but holding back, her lashes brushing his cheek. Waiting, with the question of it hovering between them like a live and vibrating thing. *Ready?*

"No," he said, because he wasn't and couldn't possibly be ready for this. But then, desperate again, "Yes!"

She laughed and brought her mouth down on his. They rolled within the blankets, mouths demanding and closer to biting than caressing, kissing deeply one moment, scraping teeth against skin the next. Kai made no careful seduction, had no plan from one instant to the next. He bared his teeth and gave way to white-hot sensations, driven by her eager hands and gasping response. Her damaged shirt tore away under his hands; the bra somehow gave way before him.

He found the strength then to hesitate—*barely*—buffeted between desire and pounce and the sharp, gripping need to keep her safe from what he could be. She tugged him forward with a suggestion he couldn't resist. With a growl in his throat, he bent to lick at tender skin and pebbled nipple.

Regan arched into him with a cry of welcome and just as quickly rolled them over to sit atop his thighs. Both of them fumbled with her jeans, finally shucking them away and her panties with them.

When she settled on his thighs again, already fondling him, it was all he could do to keep from grabbing her, putting her hips just where he wanted them and thrusting deeply into her. He went so far as to reach for her, feeling the snarl of intent on his own face—

The feel of it stopped him short, slapping at him with his own loss of control and his own greed for sensation, the heat coiling around to overtake his mind.

"Shh," she said to him, her hands on his chest, then

his stomach—stroking his tension, stroking the tremble. "Shh, Kai...it's *okay*."

But he couldn't think, and he had no idea what she meant—only that he'd gone wild inside in a way he'd never experienced and didn't know how to handle. He thought she'd be far from okay if she could see his face in the darkness the way he could see hers—if she could see how close he was to taking her in a way it couldn't possibly be okay to take a woman. *Control,* the Sentinel had said. *Restraint. Please her, don't take her.*

And so he froze, his fingers clamping into her skin and his shoulders slipping back off the blanket, grinding into the pine needles and stones as he arched beneath her, his body betraying him by just that much.

"Kai," she said, and it felt like a caress; it *was* a caress, soothing over his soul and his trembling body. She stretched over him, reaching, and he didn't understand until she'd rummaged briefly in her small pack and pulled out something crinkly.

"Ready for you this time," she said, leaving him no more wise, no less desperate. She tore the thing open and reached for him, shattering what he'd regained of his control—rather than clamp his fingers too harshly at her hips, he slapped his hands to the ground and dug in there, feeling the tight prickle of lynx claws within his fingertips and with it a sudden rush of fear.

He'd been warned. In no uncertain terms, he'd been warned. *Stay gentle. Stay in control.* But Regan...

Being with Regan...

The fear of it struck deep—that with his body in such extremes, the lynx would take him, just as he habitually took the lynx. With his mind in such turmoil, he'd turn—if not into fur and claw and tooth, into the wild thing that ran so close to his human nature. But with her hands on him, caressing him, enclosing him—

"What—?" he managed, a strangled travesty of a word.

"Shh," she said again. "Condom. Almost… There. Okay?"

"Regan," he said, because he couldn't find anything else and because *what if—*

"You're thinking too much," she told him, with no idea how little he was thinking at all. She moved above him, positioned them together…slid over him with a warm and enclosing welcome, tipping her head back on a blissful sigh.

"I knew it," she murmured. "Oh, I just knew it." She tightened around him, a flutter of internal muscle, and Kai bowed up against her, creaking with the strain.

"Kai," she said, creating a gentle rhythm that belied the breathlessness in her voice, "it's *okay.* This is what we are. Just let it *go.*"

His control slipped, a dangerous thing—one hard thrust before he found himself again, the sensations rocketing through him.

Her breath warmed his chest; her tongue lapped around a nipple. "Kai," she said. "Let it go."

Kai flipped her over, a growl in his throat, a pounce in his movement, *wild pounding strength….* He kept to his knees and yanked her up at an angle, pounding into her with a fierce abandon, a creature of sensation seeking the hot gathering coil of pleasure and only vaguely aware of her rising cries, her hands clutching at him. He curled down over her, fingers tangled in her hair and propped on his forearms to seek her mouth with his, to drag his teeth down her neck and over her shoulder—to twist his head aside to avoid biting her.

Her cries escalated into a soundless scream, and she went wild against him, and when he snarled it turned *wild pounding hot,* nothing but sensation and reaching and clawing for that completion. It was a rush that crept up far too slowly and then at the end took him utterly by

surprise, twisting him in a snarl of rigidly exquisite perfection that meant nothing would ever be the same again.
Nothing.

Chapter 16

Regan throbbed in a haze of sensation, Kai's most wondrous, final gasp of astonishment echoing in her ears, in her mind…in her heart. Still propped on his elbows, his forehead dropped to her shoulder, his breath warming her skin—panting hard, in a way that running across a mountain had not wrung from him.

Another gasp and his body released from its climax to collapse—but not quite on her. Somehow he rolled aside, and then there she was again, straddling him—this time with the cold biting at her skin.

She let herself fall over his chest, groping for the blankets. He offered an unsteady hand in assistance. The whole of him was unsteady, as far as she could tell. Where she lay over him in cuddled bliss, he seemed less certain, fingers moving through her hair to guide the strands of it away from her face—and then continuing to stroke just for the feel of it.

Just as he drew breath to speak, she understood. "Hey," she said. "I'm all right, you know."

He drew another breath, let it out slowly, and said, "I was not gentle."

She laughed, a single huff of air. "You were just what I asked you to be."

In his following silence, she raised herself off his chest enough to look at him—or as much as she could, in this darkness, and she realized out loud, "You're really worried." As if she hadn't been the one to start things, or as if she'd ever so much as hesitated at the fervor that had gripped them both. Surely he'd—

Or maybe not. Slowly, she said, "You don't get into town much, do you?"

After all, he was gorgeous. He was brimming with vitality. And he was a man. *Surely*—

Kai stroked her back beneath the blankets. It felt as though he was memorizing her, a slow path down her spine, a hesitation as his hand encompassed the curve of her bottom. It felt as though she was being...

Worshipped.

It felt wonderful.

And then he startled her by skipping the entire cautious conversation to respond to the gist of her question. "I was with someone, once... I was young. She said I should take care. That I could too easily hurt someone without—" He hesitated. "To hurt a lover."

Someone. Singular. She couldn't imagine what that woman had said to him to leave such concern over lovemaking that had been vigorous, but not rough. Responsive and unfettered and completely, resoundingly perfect.

Not to mention so touchingly vulnerable that it had reached her in ways she hadn't expected...wasn't sure she even truly understood, just as she understood so little about Kai or the forest or this entire situation.

But she didn't want to think of Kai with anyone else, not even long-ago Kai. Instead, she said, "Well, I'm fine. No, you weren't gentle—and neither was I. Reach for my pack over here, and I'll show you *gentle*."

He'd been quiescent inside her; at those words he stirred. "Uh-huh," she said, and grinned into the darkness. "But not without a fresh condom."

"Birth control," he said. "But I can—" He stopped himself and left it at that.

A man with secrets.

But he didn't yet stretch out to snag the pack, a dark lump just out of her reach and just within his. Instead, he scraped his fingers gently through her hair—petting her. "I want you again. I've wanted you since I met you, and I think I'll always want you."

Always? It nearly distracted her from the rest of what he said, that single word.

It hadn't distracted him. "But this isn't why you came here."

"Maybe it is," she said, putting a little edge in her words. "Maybe it's an important part of why I came here." Even if she hadn't thought it to be true at the time. But she'd tucked those condoms into the day pack, hadn't she? Earlier in the day, to be sure, but she'd known of them when she'd grabbed the pack and headed out into the woods.

"It's an important part of what happened here," he agreed, following her hair out to its unruly length and continuing the caress down her back, just enough of fingernail against skin to make her squirm in tingling response, and just enough squirm so his hand closed more firmly across her bottom, fingers pressing skin as he shifted against her. He floundered and found his words again. "But it's not why you called to me or found me. You said...you have to leave."

The events of the evening washed back over her in an

overwhelming swamp. She rested her cheek against his shoulder and let herself feel buffered by darkness. "Yes," she said. "I do. I can't deal with…" *Whispers. Shouts. Thoughts that aren't my own. Living my mother's life… and dying because of it.*

He stiffened as though he'd heard her. "You are what you are," he said. "Embrace it. Find balance in it."

Or lose yourself to it. Regan opened her mouth in protest as that thought pressed against her—one that didn't feel like her own. She shook her head, rejecting it. "I don't want to have that conversation," she told him. "But I couldn't just leave. I needed you to know—"

"This?" he asked, sounding unconvinced as he pressed them closer together yet, his hand spread over the small of her back.

"Maybe in part." She breathed in the scent of him, absorbing everything she could of him and letting that buffering darkness magnify the sensations—the crisp feel of his chest hair against her breasts, the planes of his body; the strength beneath her and the strength within her. "But more. Because I was in town today, and I saw those men from the dry pool. The two muscle-bound ones."

He grunted, his chest moving against her. "So did I." His voice darkened, offering more danger in those three words than in anything she'd heard him say yet. His hold on her tightened.

But not uncomfortably. *Protectively.* Or so she told herself.

Not that she wasn't seeing glimpses of him that reminded her of lessons long learned in childhood—things wild and untamed were never truly safe, no matter how it seemed. No matter if they were trained and nurtured and meant to be pets. Eventually they bit down hard in one way or another.

They were what their natures made them.

Don't you go counting on him, her father had said.

But here she was…and she had no choice. Not anymore. "They were with Matt Arshun when I saw them," she said. "They tried to pretend they weren't, but they're not very subtle people."

She heard the frown in his voice. "Matt Arshun."

"The Realtor. Or actually, the man who's pretending to be a Realtor. If he actually is one, I haven't found any sign of it." She tried to remember if she'd mentioned it to him, couldn't recall. "He's been at us to sell the property—first my dad, then me. He's damned pushy."

He made a sound in his chest; she realized with a start that he'd growled. He seemed to realize it, too, for the sound cut abruptly short. "You're not safe there."

"It doesn't matter. I'm leaving, remember?"

From the way he briefly stopped breathing altogether, he'd lost that detail to their lovemaking. "Regan," he said, and kissed the top of her head, his arms wrapping around her in gentle possessiveness. "What happened?"

Right. As if it was possible to explain her family, here in the middle of the night in what should have been the afterglow of passion. As if it was possible to explain her mother, *ever.*

As if it was possible to explain Regan Adler.

"I need to go," she said, the only words she could find. "I was hoping…you might… The horse. The dog and cat. I need to find someone to feed them."

He didn't respond—at least, not directly. "What happened?" he asked. "Not just now. But *then?*"

She tried to roll away from him; he didn't let her. Not when she pushed against his chest, and not when she tried to throw off the blanket and outright bolt. For the first time, she felt his strength when she didn't want to. Instant panic flashed over her, tinged with anger—and then subsided.

Either you trust him or you don't.

With her body…with her mind.

"Damn you," Regan muttered, not sure she was talking to Kai at all. She didn't expect to be kissed in return. Not to be pulled down with strong gentleness and into something tender and caring, soothing against lips bruised by recent passion.

She sighed, not so much beguiled by the gesture as immersed in it, and subsided to again press her cheek against his shoulder.

"It matters," he said. "Maybe more than you know."

"Trust me," she told him, and couldn't keep the edge from her voice. "Not more than I know." And then, since he hadn't done it yet, she rose just far enough to grope for the pack, dragging it close to find familiar pockets by feel, briskly unzipping what she needed. He never quite relinquished her—his hand on her arm, resting against her leg, her hip…his fingers running through the trailing ends of her hair. She tucked the condom in one of the tiny plastic bags she kept for trash and used a wet wipe to clean them both up before jamming her legs back down into her jeans.

By then she was thoroughly chilled and glad to snuggle up close again—beside him this time, her head on the pack and her hand roaming across his chest—finding the sharp definition of muscle, running her fingers down the center of a six-pack that twitched beneath her touch. Before he could ask again, she said, "When I was twelve, my mother admitted to hearing voices. She said she'd heard them since she'd come here and that they'd never bothered her…but she thought that since I was getting older, I should know. In case maybe it wasn't just her."

"Voices," Kai said. Not with curiosity, or judgment… but with a certain care.

"Not *voices*," Regan admitted. "That's just…well, shorthand. Whispers, maybe. Intentions. She said it was as if the woods were speaking to her. She used to spend hours hiking on her own, and Dad couldn't get her to stop—he could barely get her to leave a note saying where she'd gone. She said she felt safe."

Safe...

"That doesn't sound like a bad thing."

"It wasn't." Regan looked out into the darkness and saw her mother instead—saw the serenity in her, the smile on her face—her gentle distraction as she plied her craft, hand spinning and weaving fine alpaca wool scarves and hats and art pieces. A sharp breath brought her back to the here and now, the press of a rock through the fleecy blanket that carried Kai's scent, the awareness that her jeans barely rode her hips and hadn't yet been fastened.

"It sounds like a good thing," Kai suggested, if carefully.

"Maybe it was," Regan said, and made herself say the next words. "Until the rest of the world heard about it from a teen who couldn't keep her mouth shut, and decided she needed to be cured." *I'm so sorry, Mom. I wouldn't have said anything to her if I'd known....*

"Cured," Kai said flatly. "Is that a thing from which one can be cured? Living fully in the world?"

Regan's throat tightened up on her, and her words came out strained and raspy. "Apparently not." She took a deep breath—or tried, because it suddenly seemed that she'd forgotten how. "There were drugs...they only made things worse. And worse. And my mother stopped being happy, and she stopped walking in the woods, and she stopped weaving and she started hurting herself. And then they took her away, and I..."

She stopped, gulping against the words as they lodged right there in her throat, and this time when Kai tightened his arm around her, she welcomed it. She barely managed to say, "I always thought maybe she'd killed herself because no one would tell me. Dad just said there'd been an accident. I only just—" Another deep breath, or what passed for one. "She was trying to come home, and she was hit on the road. She was *walking* home, Kai—back to the voices! There was nothing left of her, only those damned voices!" Her voice broke on the sob she'd never meant to allow, and then on another, and he held her— murmuring to her, humming some tuneless thing with a rasping undertone.

She didn't let herself cry long—she didn't dare tap that deep well of grief. She wiped her face on her torn shirt and said thickly, "So I have to go. I can't let that happen to me."

His voice sounded a little too careful. "Why would it?"

She made a derisive noise. "Don't pretend you don't know. I hear things, too, Kai. *Voices.*"

"I do know." His voice held an intractable note she hadn't expected…maybe even a touch of impatience.

She flung it back at him. "Then you know that's why I left this place? I went to Colorado and I had *peace* in my head. Right up until I came back here." She would have pushed away from him if the night hadn't been so cold. "No, that's not even really true. Right up until I first saw *you.*"

He rolled up on his elbow, his leg resting over hers, his hand at her waist and tugging her closer. She couldn't see his expression clearly, but everything about him—the renewed tension in his shoulders, the harsh note injected into the normally gentle rasp of his voice, even the pressure of his fingers against her skin—spoke of an intensity. A kind of desperation. "And was that truly bad? To have some sense of me?"

Sudden caution struck her hard—and not just because of the power in him, the unbidden flash of memory encompassing how he moved in a fight, how easily he overcame not one but three armed men.

She could hurt him now with her words—that was the

power in her, and the gift he'd just given her. It loomed between them, a fluttery and breathless thing.

She measured her words carefully. "If that was all this was…maybe not. But this isn't like what my mother experienced. This is…" She couldn't help a shudder at the cold brush of those moments in the loft. "It's horrible," she said, forcing the words out. "It's horrible and frightening and it takes over my mind."

"Workings," he said, but not as if they were words meant to be spoken out loud. "You came with the taste of workings."

Still, she asked, "The what?"

He shook his head, just visible in the darkness. When he lowered his mouth, she thought he would kiss her—but instead he brushed against the side of her face. "Listen," he breathed.

By the time she understood, it was too late. She felt the wash of green and blue and brown, not so much color as a cool thrum of energy. She wanted to roll in the green, let the blue brush against her skin, and sink into the brown. A faint warble of high notes teased her ears above the distant warning yowl of something wild, and she sucked in a breath so deep, so fresh, it sparked waves of tickling energy along nerve and bone.

Just when it started to become too much, when she would have panicked, the sensations eased. She became aware of a more stable presence—warmth and spice and an undertone of raspy purr…a work-rough touch on the bare skin beneath her shirt, a solid, unwavering presence with hints of all those previous sensations woven throughout.

"Kai?" she whispered.

He responded with a wordless affirmation, adding texture to sensation. Only then did she realize that her hands roamed his body, and that he'd grown hard against her—that she already lifted her hips to him, gripped with a

mindless yearning for more. More of what she'd just experienced, more of *Kai*. That she held a quiet emptiness
more than just the physical, and that the need to fill it suddenly consumed her.

She found his face with her hands, turned it…kissed
him deeply. Not as fiercely as before, but in a more encompassing way, a more personal way. She slanted her mouth
against his and explored him, feeling his body change
against her and feeling the lick of fire around a new in-
trusion of reds and golds, her being awash with rich color
and reverberating with his deep groan.

She played him, her hands wandering his sides, caressing his flanks, tightening around his buttocks—tugging
him within reach to explore firm muscle, to cup him and
fondle and realize that with his gasps came a change in
pitch and color. The golds spun from the burn of an ember
to the deep glow of fire, the reds crept to orange, and the
cool blue breezes turned sultry. He'd shoved his way past
her pants to find the heat of her—touching and explor-
ing. White heat shot through her nerves and through her
mind, and even as she realized that part of the song came
from her, Kai made a startled sound in response, his body
encompassing hers.

She lost track of who was what. Kai's presence mingled with her response, mingled with the song of color
and sound and feeling that twined around them. When
he entered her, they both cried out in joy. When she met
his gentle thrusts, they sighed together in pleasure. When
her fingers clamped down around his arms, gold threads
wrapped them in a tightening spiral, and when he trembled, his pleasure wrenching from him with each startled
breath, the fire slapped against her in a series of waves that
built into a twisting spire of suddenly fearsome potential.

She would have moved faster against and around him,
clutching wildly, her ankles hooked as if she could some-

how pull him beyond *close* to make them physically one. But he didn't let her—and the colors and sounds and vibrations didn't let her, controlling the pace so the feelings swelled. The intensity of potential swelled, spilling between them and wrapping them up, and still Kai moved with deliberation, with a control she hadn't expected. He paced them, building them, leaving Regan sobbing with need until she flung her head back and cried out loud with it.

The sound turned to sharp energy, shredding through sensation with shards of spiking pleasure and shredding right through Kai's restraint. He snarled, a sound that struck both memory and primal response, and Regan cried out again, a plea beyond words—but he didn't increase the pace so much as he simply slammed into her, hard and steady and just...

One...

More...

Time.

The golds turned to fire and the reds to lava and Regan spun helplessly in the center of it all with Kai twining around her and through her, his body jerking with release and his snarls gone harsh in her ear.

When sensation faded, leaving her awash in paler color and the faintest larklike melody, conscious thought started to trickle back in. Kai's breath panted across her skin; the cold night air cut through a gap in tangled blankets. She'd lost her pants again, her feet were cold...and Kai still pulsed quietly inside her, flesh within flesh and no barrier between them.

Safe...

She sighed across his shoulder without the energy to disbelieve. "What did you do?" she asked him, something of wonder in her voice. Not to mention the faintest edge of accusation. He didn't answer—at least, not with anything more than a nuzzle he probably didn't even realize he'd given her. "Kai, *what*—"

"Nothing," he said, but with an unfinished sound that kept her temper from spiking back into place. That and the languid waves of fading gold still lapping through her body. Finally, he amended, "Nothing more than I ever do."

She knew he wasn't talking about the love he'd just made to her—she knew well enough it was no familiar thing to him, as naturally as they'd come together the second time. As *completely* as they'd come together.

"I listened," he said. "And I shared it. I wanted you to know...how it really is." He rubbed his nose against her shoulder, a thoughtful gesture. "I wasn't expecting it to take us like that. That was a..." He hunted words and finally offered, "Surprise." But his voice held the dry awareness that he would never find a word adequate to describe what had happened between them.

Regan knew, because neither would she.

And she knew, too, that buried within all that sensation and response and ecstasy, what they'd done had gone far beyond the physical and straight through to the very human connection of emotion and mutual vulnerability and silent commitment.

She might not truly know this man. She might never truly understand him. She might not see him again after this night.

But she loved him.

And it didn't change a thing.

Chapter 17

Kai stayed awake into the night with his body more alive than it had ever been, the land whispering contentment across his skin...absorbing the memories of what had happened here.

And at the same time finding himself far too aware that Regan had arrived coated with the taint of the Core, and that what she'd described—her fear, her horror, the changing voices—had not come from the land.

Not directly.

He didn't fully understand what had happened to Regan's mother, only that it had not gone badly until civilization had interfered, damaging what lay between the woman and the land. He knew it to have been unnecessary...to have been tragedy.

He held the living scars of that tragedy in his arms, warm and sated and—for the moment—trusting. And between the land and this woman, he had never felt the imperative more strongly—the need to protect them both.

To stop the Core.

If only he knew the first thing about them. He needed more than just his innate ability to sense them; more than what Aeron Faulkes had been able to imply in his letter. More than what he could learn in his patrols and in a few short encounters.

But this Core presence wasn't about wiping a few amulets clean; it wasn't about lingering to reclaim a gun with special properties, one they couldn't afford to have fall into either Sentinel or mundane hands.

No, they'd turned invasive and they'd launched harsh workings. And they had a distinct interest in Frank Adler's land.

He'd have to get help.

Going to the Sentinels meant painting a target on himself for both Core and Sentinel interests. It meant the end of his way of life, even if he somehow managed to evade both factions in the end—for it meant the rest of his life would be spent doing just that. Not here, with the home he'd always known and the land he'd always protected, but higher, deeper…further away from the world.

Do what you have to, his father had written him.

And Kai would.

Regan opened her eyes at dawn to discover Kai already awake, and to discover her body rueful both from such vigorous lovemaking and from a night on the ground.

He had no such problem from what she could tell. As she sat, he stretched hugely beneath the luxury of the blankets, his nakedness a reminder of his haste to meet her the night before, when she'd radiated such distress.

And the evidence of his ability to hear her, and of her own to reach out through the voices she didn't even want to acknowledge in the first place.

She looked sharply at Kai, but he seemed totally caught

up in waking—yawning to stretch again, revealing the play of muscle to the early light, the shift of stretch and beauty. His eyes were sleepy within the faint lining smudges of color, their blue dark and clear beneath strong brows, hair black in the diffuse light and mussed to a high degree.

Her fingers had a pretty good idea how it had gotten that way.

But as he rolled out of his stretch to sit, the blankets falling away from the unnecessary bandanna to reveal the entirety of his torso, she frowned—reaching out to touch the silvery hair on his chest, to touch a face with clean lines and faint hollows beneath his cheeks and the long dimples that showed at the faintest hint of a smile.

A face without stubble, or even the hint of a shadow.

He held for her touch with such stillness that she understood the effort she asked of him—*wild thing, fighting all his ingrained responses to her*—and withdrew. A nearly invisible tension flowed away, and she thought it wasn't her imagination at all.

She thought she'd felt it as much as seen it.

"I still have to go," she said, quite simply and without truly planning it.

He looked sharply at her, eyes darkening...silent. Understanding that *go* meant not just back to the cabin, but away from this place altogether.

She shifted, stiff and aching in unaccustomed ways. Aching *inside,* which she hadn't expected.

"Last night..." she said. "It changed everything." She closed her eyes so she wouldn't have to see his expression, already far too aware of the pain she would cause him. "Last night changed everything," she repeated. "But...it changed nothing." Now she did look at him, finding his steady and silent regard, his body so still he might have been carved. Utter attention. "There's something wrong with this place. It drove my mother crazy—it *killed* her.

But, Kai—" she took the deepest of breaths, meeting his gaze in what suddenly felt like a shared misery *"—it can't have me."*

He leaned over, curling a hand around the back of her neck with such smooth intent it took her entirely by surprise when he drew her in for a kiss. Not fierce, not primal…but gently caressing. When he released her, she had the startling sensation that he was stepping back in all ways.

The thought brought a stab of unexpected grief, and she almost didn't hear his low words. "Regan, I *am* the mountain."

But she did hear him, and she took a deep breath. "I know," she said, and she did.

She didn't try to make sense of it, or to defy it. There wasn't any point, not after what she'd felt the night before. She felt the tears come to prickle at her eyes, but she didn't look away from his face, not even when it blurred or when she had to blink so hard or when her voice cracked, coming out barely more than a whisper. "I *know.*"

They hadn't spoken much after that. They hadn't needed to, in their shared and somber state. Kai had gone, promising a quick return—standing naked and unabashed to shake the blankets free of pine needles and head off into the woods.

By the time Regan had pulled on her clothes, brushed away a number of inexplicable buff and silver hairs, finger combed and braided her hair and had a rough toilet, he approached again, clad in tunic over breechclout and leggings, and damned well taking her breath away.

She made herself pretend not to notice and finished policing the spot as he arrived, greeting him with mundane words. "All clean," she said and added, in case he hadn't followed, "Leave no trace."

He shook his head with the faintest of wry smiles. "Not quite," he told her, and she flushed at it, looking away. She didn't have to see his fist hover over his heart to know what he meant.

And she still had to go.

So it was Regan who shouldered her pack and led the way, her stomach growling about food and her body somehow now hypersensitive to the brush of jeans and shirt and jacket against her skin…and her own heart aching.

But he hadn't tried to talk her out of going. He'd said, briefly, that he would spend time at the cabin, making sure animals were fed and the place stayed warm enough to avoid frozen pipes in what remained of the late-spring nights. And now he came along so she could show him the details of such mundane things.

She smeared a tear off her cheek and tackled a particularly steep part of the trail with more vigor than strictly necessary.

But Kai, when he came to the top of that slope behind her, hesitated. Regan turned back to him—and her question faded in her throat.

Kai, and not. Kai, and more. He stood with such simmering potential, such imminence of action, his expression and entire body so utterly focused—

She sucked in air and stumbled a step back, her heart suddenly driving into overtime—the most primitive of reactions, deeper than instinct and beyond all thought.

His gaze flicked toward her, and everything changed.

Wild.

Truly and entirely wild, and capable of…

Anything.

She stood stiff and still as he closed the distance between them, frozen in the stark wonderment that she'd made love to this man, *touched* him and been touched… had been so arrogant as to think she knew him.

If he had any inkling of her reaction, it didn't show. His voice emerged a low growl. "It isn't safe here."

She managed to say, "You're not talking about the voices."

His gaze went out over the woods. "Something else— something that changes how the voices speak to you." When he shook his head again, this time it was with frustration. "I can't explain. But you're right. You should go. I'll—" He took a deep breath, fraught with tension that didn't quite make sense with the words to follow. "I'll get help."

She touched his arm, sensing his struggle—not understanding and not able to help…and frightened by it. "I wish I knew what you were talking about."

He didn't even pretend to answer, but he caught her gaze and held it, as direct as ever. "If I make it safe again, will you come back?"

She froze again, slapped not only by the fear of it, but by the yearning. She managed to whisper, "It will never be safe for me here. You know that."

"Be with me," he said, "and I can show you how."

Tears spilled over and took her by surprise again, and this time sparked her temper. "Dammit," she said, wiping one cheek and turning away from him, surprisingly close to stomping her foot. "I never cry like this!"

He put his arms around her from behind and rested his cheek on top of her head. "Neither do I," he said, and it startled her to realize his voice held more than its usual hint of rasp.

So they stood for a moment, and at some point Regan took a deep and shaky breath, and Kai kissed her hair, and she managed to say, "I can't promise. But…I want to."

"Then I'll promise," he said. "And I'll be here."

Rather than cry again, she struck off along the game path, no finesse in her steps. The lay of the land looked familiar again—the stark lines of a dead tree against that south slope, the jumble of limestone tumbling off the side of the ridge to the north.

Kai moved with increasing caution, straying off the game path to parallel her—ghosting in and out of sight and only coming in close again as they approached the cabin clearing.

Then he came close enough to stop her—not with his touch, but by coming in to crowd her, his expression troubled, searching hard, one hand reaching as though he might just tug her to the ground.

Beware!

She startled, her gaze darting through the trees. "What?"

BEWARE!

Kai caught her glance, and she knew suddenly that he'd heard it first, that he'd never stopped listening at all. "Kai…" she said, not sure if she was warning him or pleading with him—taking a step back from the rising of the wild in his eyes, and from the sudden impression he was on the verge of turning on her, driving her back down the hill—

He jerked, astonishment on his face. Regan stood startled and stupid as he stumbled back to lose his balance, falling against the rough rusty bark of a massive ponderosa. His gaze caught hers for an instant of what looked like inexplicable *pleading*.

Then the booming report of a large caliber rifle echoed between the ridges, and the blood bloomed up high on his chest, and Regan understood.

She might have stood stupidly for another instant—but as Kai's eyes rolled up and his knees gave way, she lurched to catch him. His weight took them both down, surprising her with his solidity—with the instant memory of how he'd held himself so lightly over her the night before, loving her with every fiber of his being.

Run...hide...beware...

She didn't waste time looking wildly for the shooter. She hooked her hands under Kai's arms and dug her heels in, straining to get him behind the tree.

Because the one thing she did know was where the shot had come from, and he still lay right out in the open.

All the same, she got nowhere. Not until Kai groaned and rolled away from her, first to his hands and knees and then rising with a snarl, surging away in blind intent.

She snagged him as best she could. "Kai! Over here!"

He escaped her grip, staggering, and she leaped up in sudden inspiration, plastering herself behind the tree where she wanted him. "Kai, I need help! Please!"

And then she knew.

For *her,* he could do it, even through stunned confusion. He made it back only as far as the tree before falling again, but it was far enough.

For now.

"Let me see," she demanded, first nudging and then shoving him, drawing frantically at her artist's familiarity with anatomy—the arteries, the ribs, the lung housed up high under the collarbone. But he was remarkably uncooperative, bent over himself to clutch at the wound and then so suddenly turning on her—that snarl on his beautiful face, that wild look in his eye.

Regan shrieked, scrambling back against the tree in a purely visceral reaction. "It's *me,*" she said, and—more desperately than she'd ever imagined—reached out to the place the voices lived inside her.

Somehow she'd come to take them for granted. Somehow she'd gotten used to them, learned to *use* them. Learned, so deeply, that connection with Kai.

When she encountered the solidity of his silence, it hurt. Her own voice bounced back at her in a distorted echo, evoking from her a breathy gasp; her whole body recoiled from that blow.

And she knew, looking at that wounded, wild eye, that he hadn't done it deliberately. *I am the mountain,* he'd told her.

Except now, somehow, he wasn't.

"Hey," she said, making her voice no-nonsense—the same one she would use on the spooked mustang…or, when she was twelve, on her mother during a bad moment. "It's me. And whoever did this is still out there." Her mind flashed to the men she'd seen at the dry pool and with Arshun in town.

Men who liked guns. Who *didn't* like Kai. And who wanted this land.

Kai pressed the heel of his hand against his brow, panting like the untamed thing he'd become. "Regan," he said, the rasp pronounced in his voice.

"Get over here!" she said, filling her voice with authority she didn't feel. "We've got to get into the house and call for help."

"Core," he told her, not moving—just swaying there. Every word came from a distant place, as if he had to fight his way through something other than pain. "The phone won't work."

"It's voice-over internet," she said, baffled. "Satellite provider. It should work just fine."

"It *won't*," he said, grinding the words out. "They wouldn't let it—"

"Okay, okay—" She couldn't let him waste energy on the point. Either the phone did or it didn't, and he *still* hadn't truly taken cover, even if no one had taken a second shot. She darted out into the open to wrap a light arm around his waist, guiding him to the tree. When they got there, he put his back to it, and only the rough bark kept him from sliding down. "Look, before the satellite connection, we only had CB radio. I bet it's still stuffed in Dad's closet. Either way, the house is still the best bet."

He gave her a blank look. "I don't know *CB radio*—" and then lifted his lip in that snarl, folding over to clutch at his shoulder. When he looked up, the wild was back in his eye, the rasp back in his voice. "Core poison," he said. "Workings. I can't—"

"Let me see," she said, using her firm voice. "I have no idea what you're talking about, but that's going to take a lot more than a bandanna."

"Won't heal," he said vaguely, fingers curled over the blood of his tunic as if he might rip the bullet out by force, or at least by force of will. "Take it *out*—"

She pulled his hand away, taking liberties—getting her first good look at the wound's location and cursing with it. He wasn't having trouble breathing yet...but he would. Breathing...and *living*. "The house," she said. "We've got to reach the house—"

"Why?" Kai lifted his head to look at her straight on, and she didn't understand at first, because wasn't it just obvious? The house was shelter, the house was their only chance to call for help, the house held her shotgun and the .22 and maybe her father still had his .30-06 tucked away somewhere—

"Why," Kai asked, closing his bloodied hand around hers, grabbing her attention with the intensity of his grip, "do they want this land?"

"Finally. Someone asks the right question." Arshun's voice took them both by surprise, along with his presence at the edge of the clearing.

Regan shot Kai a look of concern, startled that anything, anywhere, could take this man by surprise...but especially in this forest. Even wounded, she'd somehow expected his untamed nature to warn them.

"Core," Kai said, and offered that little snarl of lip.

"Sentinel," Arshun said, and his returning smile seemed more genuine that it should. "Bless my heart. A little lost sheep of a Sentinel, with no idea what he's gotten into. I'm even sort of sorry about killing you."

"Not," Kai said, "dead yet."

Arshun said equitably, "Give it time." And then, to Regan, "You really should have talked your father into selling this place. His particular injury was one of our more subtle achievements, but there's a limit to our patience."

Regan took a wary step back from him—and only then realized he wasn't alone. Hantz and Aeli from the gas station were there, and Marat from the dry pool who'd been managing them and the disposal of the strange dull metal disks.

Core. Sentinel. She suddenly realized how very little she knew about any of this—how very stupid she must look, indeed. She took a step back from Kai—from the others. "My *father?*" She couldn't stop her horror from showing. *"What have you done?"*

"Much less than we could have," Arshun said briskly, giving Kai an annoyed look. "Fortunately for you, we truly don't want to draw attention. If it wasn't for your little stray Sentinel, none of this absurd drama would have been necessary at all." He scowled at the man who'd managed the metal disks they'd called amulets back at the dry pool. "It still shouldn't have been. For God's sake, Marat, it's a stinking little log cabin in the middle of nowhere."

Marat didn't seem discomfited by Arshun's annoyance. "And unlike the other homes in this area, it's almost entirely self-sustaining and off the grid, surrounded by land that remains a completely untapped resource—and in an area the Sentinels have left entirely to its own devices." He smiled darkly. "There aren't enough people in this area for them to hide themselves, and aside from our *little stray Sentinel,* they wisely know it—but it was their mistake to think they could effectively monitor the area from a distance, wasn't it? So we'll do well here, once we acquire the place. Her father is being taken care of as we speak, and by the time we're done today—"

"No!" Regan said, panic creeping into her voice. Panic, the way any sane person would panic under these circumstances.

Was she still—?

Yes. Completely and totally sane. The voice of the land whispered in her mind no more than it had ever done— and maybe the only thing in this moment that was truly familiar at all. And so she took another step away from Kai, and he lifted his head to look at her not with the wild in his eyes, but his pain—a wounded expression, pleading for understanding.

But she didn't understand. Not at all.

My father. "You leave him alone!" she snapped at Arshun, and she didn't mean Kai. "You leave *us* alone."

Arshun shook his head—more relaxed, more matter-of-fact, than when he'd been playing the role of Realtor. "That's not going to happen. But don't concern yourself. You won't remember any of this—not this encounter, not what you think you've learned about the land...or about yourself. No more hallucinations, no more nightmares. No more Kai Faulkes."

"Not," Kai said, though his voice lacked force, "Dead. Yet."

But his pulse beat rapidly at his neck, and the blood spread down his tunic, and Arshun merely looked at him and said, "Soon."

Hantz made a sound of satisfaction through his broken nose and glanced at Arshun, who nodded permission. *Permission for—?* And Regan realized only far too belatedly, as Hantz reached for her. Presuming, assuming, overconfident—

Kai pounced.

The wild in him broke loose, splashing through the land to slap up against Regan—to stun her for that instant in which Kai reached the man, her mind filled with images of flashing canines and a narrowed feline eye, whiskers lifted in snarl, claws slashing—

When she blinked out of it, the broken-nosed man was going down and Kai rotated over him, around him, freed from gravity and the constraints of civilization but his hands still caught in the jerking twist of motion that had wrenched the man's neck into snapping.

"Get her out of here!" Arshun snapped at Marat.

Regan skipped back, slipping out of the day pack and wielding it at Marat just as Aeli slammed his rifle at Kai, using it like a club—missing and jerking it back to use in a two-handed defensive position when Kai turned on him.

Marat ducked against Regan's flailing pack and snatched her arm; Regan shrieked fury and kicked out at him, always skipping backward, not quite able to take her eyes from Kai—

Kai, leaping at his enemy and grabbing the rifle with both hands not to jerk it away but to twist around it like a gymnast around a bar, raising himself up, *up* and over, slamming his knees into the man's back, his elbows on either side of the man's head—and then riding the man down to the ground, grabbing the rifle and flinging it far into the woods.

Marat swore, losing his grip on Regan, hesitating—leaving her to help with Aeli.

"No!" Regan cried, and threw herself on him—wrapping over his back to cling and beat at his head and face.

"Control her!" Arshun snapped at Marat, stepping into the fray as Kai rolled away from Aeli, briefly crouching in a gathering leap for Arshun—

But Arshun got there first. As Marat rammed Regan back against a tree, jarring her loose, Arshun stepped in to land a simple, brutal kick to Kai's ribs, right below the spreading stain of blood.

Kai rolled away from the force of it, came back to a crouch—and stopped short, astonishment on a face gone utterly pale, the veins distended at his neck. He coughed hugely, spattering blood across his lips, and gasped air in quick, heaving effort.

Arshun stepped back in satisfaction as Kai lifted his face to Regan, a dazed look. *"Run,"* Kai said, though there was no sound behind it. Only pain and the awareness of her rejection, the desperation of the situation.

Run...RUN...

Regan caught her breath on a sudden sob and turned away, losing the pack to sprint into the woods.

RUN!

Marat's heavy weight came down across her legs, a tackle driving her into the ground, grinding her face into the needles and trapping one hand beneath her body while she shrieked in anger and protest and fear.

And behind her, a gunshot rang through the trees.

Chapter 18

Kai fought in a wild rage of desperation, the lynx struggling to break free—the sensation of claws pushing at his fingertips, ears flattened, tail lashing. He fought with Sentinel strength, agility impossible to even the most deadly of humans. He left one man dead and another man dying and he did it with a poisonous Core working lodged in his body.

But his blood streamed down his side and tasted sharp in the back of his throat, and even a Sentinel needed blood. And air. And to be able to see when the world started to go gray around him.

Run, Regan. RUN!

But he heard her shriek of fury, gone muffled in struggle, and knew she hadn't made it. And when he turned to Matt Arshun, one last man to kill after a life dedicated to preservation, he saw the gun.

But it was just a gun. No workings, no poisons.

And Kai, too, knew how to run.

For now.

* * *

Regan fought them every step of the way. Marat hauled her up and clamped a cruel hand above each elbow, shoving her in front as they headed toward the cabin—but she didn't make it easy.

Her face had taken the brunt of her fall, and blood trickled from a split lip and the sting of myriad little cuts along one cheek; her knee throbbed where she'd hit a rock. And then she thought of Kai, fighting for his life—for *her* life— and felt none of it, twisting and fighting until Marat released one arm and cuffed her so severely that her ears rang and her vision jumbled.

And in her mind she heard nothing but that final report of sound, the shot in the woods behind her.

And the silence that followed.

When she could see straight again, tears blurred the cabin before her—and the giant dark form of the dog on the porch, his tail stiff and his head low, his warning unmistakable even through tears.

"Don't you hurt him!" she cried as Marat stopped, spitting a curse in her ear. "He's just an old dog!"

"He's got teeth," Marat said, which was a point. Bob had teeth and knew how to use them. "You don't want him dead, you do something about it."

Regan drew a shaky breath. "Bob," she said, trying to sound reasonable. "Get off the porch. Go on. Go check out the woods." She made a restricted half gesture at the trees, jerking against Marat's grip in annoyance. He gave her a little more latitude to do it again. "Go on. Go check out the woods!"

Come…safe…

Maybe Bob, too, had some sense of the voices. He stalked down the steps, never looking away from Marat, a deep grumble at the curl of his lip—not trusting, but obeying.

Regan barely had time for relief. Arshun came striding out of the woods, and his face looked like hers felt—one side of his mouth puffy, his brow split, his cheek scraped. Bits of bark stuck to his face, and she realized with sudden hope that Kai had flung him against a tree. *And escaped?*

That hope must have shown on her face. Arshun appropriated her arm on the way past, never slowing—dragging her when she stumbled. She didn't catch her balance until they'd topped the stairs to the porch, and he didn't stop moving until he'd yanked her through the screen door that Marat hastily jerked open before they reached it. Arshun hauled her right into the house and flung her at the couch, where she bounced once and came to her feet.

He was ready for her—he shoved her back down. Then he took several quick strides to the little hall nook to scoop up the phone with one hand and hold the handset up with the other, pointing it at her so she could hear the stutter of the dial tone at the earpiece—the indication of a voice mail.

Even as she absorbed his familiarity with the cabin, he replaced the phone with a little jangle and returned to stand in front of her. "That message is from your father. It seems that his injury is worse than suspected. The doctors don't know how they missed it, but he's going to need surgery to fuse some cracked vertebrae." He gave her a meaningful look. "It's a surgery that usually goes quite well. But sometimes not."

The blood drained from her face in a prickling rush as his voice faded. After a moment she realized she sat with her head shoved between her knees and an impatient hand at the back of her neck, steadying her. Her mind whirled, her body ached…her heart ached. "Get your hand off me," she said as distinctly as she could.

The pressure disappeared. She sat upright, pushing

loose hair from her face. Marat stood uneasily by the door
as if to block her escape...or warn of approaching trouble.
Kai? In spite of it all? Arshun stood before her with legs
braced, pulling a handkerchief from his pocket to dab at
his split brow. Now she could see that his suit was torn,
his knuckles bruised...his face truly battered.

Good.

"Kai got away," she said, finding the words a comfort.
A faint susurrus whispered across her mind, a sense of
satisfaction. Kai's name, curling around her mind.

Arshun sent her a sour look. "He won't survive."

She sent him a stubborn look. She didn't understand
their enmity, but she understood that it somehow went
deeper than one encounter over boxes of waste metal. And
she didn't understand Arshun's purpose here, his need for
this land, but she knew the threat he represented—to her,
to her family, to the land itself.

She knew if Kai lived, he would be back to stop them.
If he lived.

Arshun gave her a perceptive look. "We shot him twice,"
he said bluntly.

"And still," she said, looking at his face, "he did that
to you."

His expression went sour.

"He heals quickly," Regan offered, and knew that to be
true, too—beyond all fathoming, his skin already whole
and unblemished beneath the bandanna he now wore simply because he wanted to.

Because of her.

"Generally," Arshun conceded. "But not this time."

And she remembered, too, Kai's reaction to the gun—
calling it poison, and how he'd so emphatically taken
it, hidden it. She remembered his expression from the
woods—more than just a man shot, but a man struggling
against that poison's effects.

"Kai Faulkes is no longer of concern to us," Arshun said.

"Liar," Regan muttered, and knew from his expression that she'd scored a hit.

He didn't acknowledge the interruption. "You need to think of yourself right now. Of your father. We don't want to hurt either of you. It would draw too much attention to your home, and to this pending sale, and we prefer...*subtlety.*" He looked at her, reading her expression—letting his words slide home. "So he still has the chance to survive this surgery with no impairment.... He can return here and use our generous settlement on this property to purchase a modest home closer to town, more appropriate for his situation." He dabbed again at his trickling brow, sending her a meaningful look. "Or the surgery could go very badly indeed, and he'll never return to these mountains again."

She didn't faint this time. She'd seen it coming. She fisted her hands where they rested against her thighs and forced her voice into some semblance of normalcy, drawing on the confusion of memories from the woods. "I don't understand why you're telling me any of this. You said I wouldn't remember this."

"And so you won't." Arshun nodded at Marat, who dug into his pocket and withdrew, of all things, one of those chunky metal medallions, this one on a long thong of tightly braided leather. It shone with the same oily gleam as those at the dry pool, looking both ancient and heavily handled.

"It's silent," Marat assured Arshun.

"Kai knew," Regan said, realizing it—not understanding any of it. Except suddenly she did—knowing how Kai heard this land. "That's the problem, isn't it? You didn't think anyone would know you were here—what you were up to. And he did. He *does.*"

"Not any longer," Arshun said. He tucked the handkerchief away and accepted the amulet. "And the reason we've had this conversation is that although you won't remember, some part of you will still *know*." He stepped closer—close enough to brush up against her knee and take her chin in an unpleasant grip between smooth fingers. "Some deep part of you will still understand that unless you welcome us, your father dies. Your heart will know that your lover *is* dead, and that you are, in fact, utterly alone here."

No. Kai wasn't dead…he *wouldn't* be. She would have heard it through the land if it was true. And she wouldn't be alone, not truly—not as long as the voices whispered into her mind, reminding her of what had happened here, warning her…beckoning her to places of safety.

Arshun must have read something in her eyes—her defiance, her determination. He smiled tightly. *Cruelly.* "Yes," he said, taking her fisted hand to pry the fingers open and push the medallion into her hand—a thing of biting and startling cold. "You won't even have your secret little connection to count on. You are," he said, patting her hand closed around the metal, *"alone."*

Regan opened her eyes to find herself on the couch, the cat sitting directly in her line of sight with his implacable stare fastened to hers. She sat, startled at the stiffness and bruises…and only vaguely remembered taking a tumble in the woods.

She looked down at herself to discover clean clothes, a couple of colorfully whimsical Band-Aids sprinkled across her hand…a quilt wrapped around her shoulders, and a sprinkling of unfamiliar silver-and-buff hairs across the couch. "Wow," she said to the cat. "I must have taken a good one." Just to be sure, she felt around her head… found no soreness, just the fat numb feeling of her puffy lower lip. "Huh."

But beneath her puzzlement, she felt a disquiet…an uneasiness. The feeling of something missing.

Something important.

Chapter 19

Kai made it as far as the nearest shelter, a copse of Gambel oak obscuring an undercut of land. Rough, inadequate…and a welcomed relief. His calf burned, a wound made by Arshun's untainted bullet—no longer bleeding, already healing with the preternatural speed of a Sentinel body under extreme duress.

He'd pay for that healing with days of intense hunger and cramping—if he lived through it.

If he could pull himself together long enough to *think* and survive at all.

His chest throbbed, full of heat and Core poisons, the stink of it filling him from the inside out. It tore at his thoughts, his strength…his sanity.

He reached for the lynx without much thinking, hunting relief—hunting the strength of his other. The form he'd been taking since childhood, as natural to him as this broken human body.

He reached, and found nothing. Only the pain and the poison.

Kai pressed up against the cool earth of the shadowed shelter, tipping his head back against the uneven crumble of it. Wanting to curl up on his side, knowing his impossible, ragged breathing would only get worse, and so instead sitting upright, arms wrapped around his torso to hold the pain in.

He was Sentinel. He could do this.

But could Regan?

Kai realized he'd passed out only as he jerked awake, broken rib grating up high under his collarbone.

Not alone.

He sank his fingers into short black fur, dropped his head against a strong shoulder. Bigger than his lynx, sturdier...

Smelling distinctly of dog.

Bob gave an undertone whine, barely breaking into sound.

Kai found himself unable to muster words. But he offered a brief and raspy hum, the hint of his lynx's rich purr. Bob took his for the companionable welcome it was, and slumped more firmly against Kai—sharing their warmth and grief. And if Kai still couldn't think past the pain and the poison, for the moment he didn't truly have to.

His father had tried to warn him. *Do what you have to do.* Agony shuddered through his chest, a spurt of warmth and wrongness. He'd seen this coming. He just hadn't understood it.

Kai clamped his hand around his arm, digging fingers in deep to keep his thoughts straight. He'd never learned the *adveho*—he'd known only that it was a Sentinel-wide cry for help, a Mayday of piercing effect. No Sentinel would ignore it; most Sentinels could hear it.

He had no idea how to send such a thing.

"There's no point," his father had told him. "The help it might bring would end up killing you in the long run— Southwest Brevis would learn of you, and no field Sentinel with your strength is allowed to run outside brevis. They wouldn't mean to cause you harm, but they won't understand. Not in time. And the Core…"

The Core had already found him—likely thought they'd killed him in spite of all strictures against what they were doing here. Workings against the mundane population, manipulation of unwitting families—a sniper's shot through the woods and the slap of impact.

The Sentinels could do no worse than that, should he reach them.

And they could save Regan.

Kai didn't know the *adveho*. But he knew the land. He knew how to talk to it…and talk *through* it.

He threaded an arm around Bob's shoulders, shivering, and thought he imagined a hint of warmth from the ground at his back—made no sense of it, and couldn't spare it the effort. Not when he had to pour himself into the land, pushing out a shout of despair and demand. *Help us!*

He was Sentinel. Surely he could do this.

Hang on, Regan.

"Yes," Regan said into the phone to the Realtor named Matt Arshun. "Of course. I'll check with my father, but I'm sure he'll be interested."

Not that he didn't still love this place. But it didn't seem likely he'd be returning to it—even if the surgery went as well as it possibly could. He'd enjoyed El Paso, it seemed.

"I'll let you know. Thanks for your call, Mr. Arshun," she said, and settled the handset slowly back into the cradle.

Not that she, too, wouldn't miss this place. But her home was in Colorado now, and had been for a decade.

She bent to give the cat an absent scratch and winced, trying once more to remember just how she'd bruised herself. Sure they weren't still coming up from her fall off the spooked mustang. That was over and done with—or should have been.

It was too easy to lose track of the days in these woods.

But a fall from the horse didn't explain the exquisitely sensitive tenderness between her legs. She climbed the loft stairs slowly, hyperaware of that sensitivity—of how alive her body felt, and how oddly…sated. Had she dreamed…?

The mirror showed her a split lip, a cheek with a few tiny cuts, a bruise beside her eye. It showed her a faint red mark on her neck, nipples that looked as tender as they felt and a puzzled look staring back out at her.

Some of what she felt might be explained by the imminence of a particularly strong period. *If* she was due.

What day was it again?

She hunted up her favorite old T-shirt, couldn't find it—unexpected, given that she was only working with a suitcase of clothes, not a full wardrobe—and pulled on the red bandanna print instead. In the bathroom, she looked more closely at the cuts on her face—tiny as they were, they seemed fresh—and then forgot to care until she ran across a blotch of blood in the soft crease of her elbow.

Not her blood, as near as she could tell. And there had been a considerable splash of it, mostly rubbed away but not entirely.

But once she finished washing it off, it didn't seem important. She brushed out her hair, pulled it back in a bouncy ponytail and returned to the loft to stare in surprise at the unfinished painting there.

Not only that she didn't recall starting it, but…

The way it called to her. The glimmer of the lynx's eye, the sensation of wild freedom and green life and reaching connection.

"Dammit, Dad," she muttered. "Did you lace those cookies with pot?" It wasn't as if he'd never done it before, when the memories of her mother grew strong.

Regan found herself surprised at the dim nature of her own memories. Could it be—*could it?*—that she was finally starting to heal from her mother's casual abandonment?

Her sketch pad sat askew on top of her toolbox; she picked it up, flipping through pages of wild things, mere lines of suggestion and eyes peering from darkness and then, abruptly, the unmistakable impression of a man's side, from muscle-strapped shoulder and torso to the intimate line of hip and flank, strong obliques and the long stroke of a strong thigh.

She found her fingers running over the page…stopping there as if she could perceive the flesh beneath flat paper, her body responding.

"Wow," she breathed, and resolutely put the sketch pad aside. "Girl, you need a date. Or *some*thing."

Or something.

Fine. A trip into town would help. She'd check out an audio book from the library, see if Mary had any more jerky, grab a treat for Bob…wherever he was.

She'd get herself out of this place. It was time to let go.

Chapter 20

The woman at the post office greeted Regan with a distracted smile; the guy behind the counter at the gas station convenience store fumbled her change and scooped it up with a distant smile.

Maybe it's not just me.

It seemed as if the entire town of Cloudview walked through the day listening for some forgotten music.

At the general store, Mary looked at her with some surprise. "What happened to your face?"

Regan waved a dismissive hand. "It looks worse than it is." And then, before Mary could narrow her eyes and ask for details, she said, "Anyway, I just wanted to see if Bill had any of that great elk jerky hidden away in the freezer."

"You walked out of here with a big sack of jerky just the other day. Don't tell me you've gone through that already!"

"I did?" Regan looked down at herself as if she'd find answers there, raising her voice slightly to speak over the sound of Phillip Seamans and his drill on the boardwalk, still finessing his repairs. "I feel like an idiot. I guess I've got too much on my mind." Even if she couldn't quite think of what it was.

Mary sent an understanding look her way. "How's Frank?"

Regan felt the puzzlement of it all over again. "He needs surgery, they say. I offered to go be with him, but Uncle Cal is handling things just fine. And then…I guess he's going to stay there."

"What?" Bill exclaimed from the nearby aisle in which he'd been pricing items. He wheeled out to give Regan a disbelieving stare. "That doesn't sound like Frank Adler!"

No, it didn't.… Did it?

But Regan shrugged. "I'm going to wrap things up here and head down to Texas, I guess—my uncle's going to be in over his head with the surgery. I'll just have to start on the next contract while I'm there." She'd renegotiated the deadline, so she still had time. But sooner or later she'd have to get back to her studio.…

"What do you mean, 'wrap things up here'?" Mary said, alarm in her voice. Phillip eased over and lurked in the doorway. Odd.

Regan shrugged. "We've had an offer on the place. I guess Dad wants to sell."

"The hell you say!" Bill blurted out, wheeling up to her. "Just like that?"

Just like that.

Mary looked equally aghast—even a little pale. "What about his dog? The horse?"

Regan frowned. "Bob's old.… I don't know. I'm sure we can find a good place for the horse. Maybe with one of the hunting lodges. I had thought to ask…"

Ask who?

Phillip crossed his arms. "Surely you weren't thinking of asking Kai to deal with them."

"No," Regan said, startled. "Kai?"

Phillip's eyes narrowed and, although he didn't move, he suddenly seemed less casual than he'd been. "Have you *seen*—" he started, but Mary's mutter stopped him.

"Oh, Lordy," she said. "Just what this day needs." But then she put a smile on her round face and moved toward the cash register. "Hey, Kathleen—got everything you need?"

Kathleen. Regan couldn't fathom the curious jolt she felt at the sight of the woman—a childhood friend not seen for years, her features matured, her childhood plumpness grown to generous adult curves, her expression...

Wary?

"Kathleen," she said. "It's been a long time."

Kathleen looked startled as she set her produce and milk on the counter, almost as if she felt she was interrupting something. "Yes," she said, a strange bit of hope in her expression. "A very long time."

Mary spoke with what seemed like determined cheer as she rang up the purchases; it matched the expression on her face. "And how are those boys of yours, Kathleen? Enjoying Phillip's classes, I hope?"

Kathleen's face lit up. "Oh, Phillip—I'm glad you're here. I wanted to tell you how much the boys enjoyed it when Kai stopped by the other day. You know, if there's any way you two could be talked into putting on another demo—"

Phillip glanced Regan's way, shifting as though he suddenly wished he hadn't lingered at the door. "Such things aren't for entertainment."

"No, of course not." Kathleen flicked a glance at Regan as she handed Mary a twenty, not one Regan could interpret. "But it certainly is inspiring. They started asking for extra practice after the last time."

Phillip smiled faintly. "I'll see how Kai feels about it."

Kathleen scooped up the cloth bag of groceries. "That would be so great." She glanced at Regan again, hesitating only briefly on her way out. "It was good to see you again, Regan. Maybe I'll run into you at the festival this weekend."

Regan murmured something she hoped was appropriate, waiting to hear Kathleen's steps on the access ramp before she said, "Huh. Not in a talking mood, I guess."

Mary snorted. "Don't know what else you expected, the way you've given her the cold shoulder since you two were girls." When Regan sent her a startled glance, Mary put up a placating hand. "Not that anyone blames you, of course, given what happened with your mother. But you must know she never would have told your secrets if she'd known what would happen—"

Regan shook her head. "I feel like I should go back to bed and start this day all over again. Nothing quite makes sense. My mother left—that was no secret, was it?"

Bill made something of a choking noise, and Mary's mouth fell open. Finally, she drew herself up and said, "No. No, I guess it wasn't."

Regan drew an exasperated breath. "This is a strangest day."

"There's something in the air," Phillip agreed, watching her more closely than she expected.

"Go home, do the chores and go to bed," Mary said by way of her own agreement. She snorted again. "And if you ever figure out what this day was all about, let me know."

Regan left without the jerky she apparently already had, and was headed down the stairs when the door opened and closed behind her. She glanced back to find that Phillip had followed her, already reaching to gather his tools. But something about his expression stopped her.

"I'm worried about Kai," he said. "I don't suppose you've seen him?"

"Kai," Regan repeated, trying to make the word mean something. It didn't, but she couldn't quite bring herself to care. "No, I haven't," she said, instead of asking, and then raised an arm to wave as Matt Arshun drove his classy little sedan down the street, slowing for the wide, marked pedestrian crossing. Matt waved back, expression unreadable from inside the tinted windows.

"That looked like—" Phillip cut himself short, looking over at her. "Are you all right, Regan?"

Once more in this day, she found herself vaguely surprised. "Of course," she said. "Why wouldn't I be?"

"No reason," Phillip murmured, but he watched her with a gaze that suddenly seemed too knowing, and maybe even a little invasive. "If you do see Kai, let him know I'm looking, will you?"

"Sure," Regan said, heading for her vehicle.

And then promptly forgot about all of it.

Who are you?

The voice pierced Kai's thoughts with startling clarity, jerking him into awareness and back into pain. Bob lay pressed against his side, ears pulled forward in worry. Outside this crude little overhang, daylight faded and the cold sank down on them.

Or should have. Kai had the vaguest awareness that he lay against warm earth, a little hollow of deliberate welcome.

Who are you? Where are you?

And Kai thought stupidly that he was here, and that he lay poisoned by the Core working trapped in his body—and when he tried to push his thoughts back out in response, they grew sticky and entrapped by that poison. The tarry nature of it infiltrated his body, taking with it heat and sickness. Keeping him from healing, while his own nature wouldn't quite let him die.

Trapped, he thought at the voice in his head. *Here and trapped.*

And they were barely human thoughts at all, because the poison wrapped itself through his mind as well as his body.

My name is Annorah, said the voice—distinctly feminine in tone, and it couldn't seem to decide if it was annoyed or concerned. *I'm at Southwest Brevis. I heard your call—but we don't know you and we can't find you.*

Kai twitched as water dropped against his cheek, barely needing human thought to know the wrongness of it. No water ran down the rock close over his head—not on this dry spring evening with no clouds overhead. No water *could.*

Yet there it was again. It was the merest effort to shift his head to the side, to open his mouth…to take the first drop and realize just how intense his thirst had become. Blood lost, fluids lost…the high dry air, pulling water from his body.

Getting nothing, said Annorah's voice in his head, as if she hadn't bothered to disconnect before turning aside to address someone else. *Everyone else is on silence protocol…. I'd hear it if anyone answered….*

Keep looking. That voice came to him as a curious echo through Annorah, a male timbre and definite bite of command. *You're sure it was Sentinel?*

Sentinel, said Annorah. *But not like anything I've heard before.*

Another drop of water fell into his mouth, imbued with the taste of soil and sap, and then the next—falling a little more quickly this time.

Keep looking, said the man again. *We don't leave our own out there to die.*

Might be too late. Her words came as a dull surprise, knowing she was probably right. That if the earth hadn't come forth to warm him, if the water hadn't even now come forth to renew him…

That even so, it might be too late.

Regan, he thought—and found strength in that thought, the piercing quality of fear and need.

He'd killed two of the men from the Core. But he hadn't killed them all. And that meant Regan was alone with them.

Wait! Annorah said, and fell so silent that he almost held his breath with her.

Almost. If he'd had breath to hold. If the taste of blood didn't live in his throat, the fire of poison didn't coat his veins, the breath didn't rasp in his own ears.

No, never mind. I thought I heard… A pause, a mental sigh. *I'll keep looking.* And then, more clearly, *My name is Annorah. I'm at Southwest Brevis. I heard your call—but we don't know you and we can't find you. If you can, send us a location call…,..*

Kai sank into the dark earth, his mouth just barely open to catch a few drops of water, and he thought only, *Regan….*

Regan faced the evening with a trepidation she didn't quite understand. She paced through the house, running her fingers along the smooth log walls, dusting the stone mantel surrounding the woodstove pipe, fussing with the fire itself. She admired the bathroom her mother had tiled, spent long moments with her head tipped up to the pot shelf that held what was left of her mother's life—her pottery, pieces all charmingly hand shaped and splashed with bright glaze.

Of course she ended up in the loft, the area that had once been shared with her mother and had then simply been entirely hers.

She decided to recognize her mood as a completely reasonable nostalgia at the impending sale of this place, and ended up in front of her easel—personal photos and references scattered around her, a gesso-prepped canvas before her, and the warm, familiar scent of linseed oil with the sharp note of brush cleaner cutting through.

She found herself sketching in broad strokes of a dark forest, sunlight slashing off to the side...

The lynx peering through.

When she finally crawled off to bed, she'd flushed her head of nostalgia and regret and barely left the meditative daze of her painting at all. She pulled off the oversize men's shirt that served as her painting smock and tugged her jeans off and otherwise slept in the shirt of the day, tumbling into...

The brush of fur, the twitch of whisker...the solemn gaze of a Sentinel in the green depths of the woods...

She tumbled into dreams. There, those solemn feline eyes insisted on looking back at her, deep blue instead of the pale green of a true lynx. There, she saw shuttered lashes—and felt the brush not of fur, but a man's touch. She instantly yearned for it, stretching into it; she welcomed warm breath against her skin, and the press of lips and hint of teeth. She arched to meet silky skin and crisp hair, and opened her legs to invite hard, thick sensation—feeling herself stretched and reveling in it, whimpering in the request for more, for the fulfillment of hard thrusting and strong hands holding her just where she needed to be.

So quickly, pleasure tightened close within her, building between them, so sweet that she cried it out loud, imploring him for release—so strong that he gasped with each thrust, a helplessly guttural sound building to explosiveness right along with her. Together they tangled and clawed and ached and cried out; together they strained. Together they reached completion, going rigid against each other to tremble and pulse in the white lightning of pleasure.

But he had barely gasped out his climax, his hands still tight at her hips and fingers pressing into soft flesh, when he jerked his head up and rolled away. And though she could *feel* him—knowing the familiar solidity of a torso hard with muscle, thighs long and strong, shoulders broad—she couldn't *see* him. Only glimpses—the clarity of his eyes, the strong line of a cheek, the straight line of nose and flare of a well-defined nostril—but never the whole.

When she cried out for him, she had no name on her lips. And when he responded, it was with a rasping snarl of warning—his touch trailing across her belly, his leg briefly entwined with hers.

And then he was gone.

Regan scrambled after him—

And woke on her knees in the bed, reaching out, fingers stretched for what she'd lost.

Slowly, she sank back onto the bed, her body still throbbing with its very real climax and very real pleasure. In the darkness, she looked over toward the easel—the faintest gleam of wet paint in the moonlight, the vision that had captured her evening, and somehow captured a part of her.

And she had no idea why.

Chapter 21

Kai jerked from pleasure straight into agony, snarling up out of the earth to pant in confusion, hands already reaching for claws—all reaction, no thought, and what was left of his humanity still lingering with Regan.

He didn't wonder for an instant if it had been real. He knew it. More than a dream, more than wishful yearning. He didn't need the fast fading throb of his climax to know it.

Regan. Still there, in spite of the Core. Still reaching out to him—if only in her sleep.

He pushed out through the land, hunting her—hunting for any sign of her. But beyond this little nurturing shelter—the dog still warming him, the Core still closed dark around him—the clarity of his thought quickly made way for threads of cloying poison.

He snarled back at it. *Regan, I won't lose you!*

But he did. And as he fell back, surrendering thought to the grip of twisting pain, he lost not just Regan.

He lost another piece of himself.

Another voice intruded—the woman who called herself Annorah. She sounded tired, but still determined—renewed, as if she'd caught some hint of him. *Who are you? Where are you? We want to help!*

Who are you...? Where are you...?

In a sudden panic, he realized he had no answers. He just *was*. He was agony and grief and hunger, no grasp on the past, no grasp on the future.

Who, she said, an echo into his darkness. *Who. ARE. YOU?*

Something snapped, from lynx to human to darkness to the final clarity of a sharply snarled response—one with claws behind it, and a slash of anger. *I DON'T KNOW!*

And he didn't.

He searched for himself in a poisoned darkness, gathering a final thrust of energy to reach for the thing that had never failed him. *Lynx.*

The dark bulk of an aging canine shape scooted away with a yelp as Kai unfurled fingers into claws. He lifted his head to open angry feline eyes and flattened tasseled feline ears, snarling his way into the other half of himself.

And when he stood as unsteady lynx, the night unfurled before him, sharply delineated in the faint blue tint of a Sentinel's preternatural night vision—a hint of moonlight carried within his eyes.

The big black merle dog stood nearby, offering an uncertain wag of his tail. The lynx twitched a stubby tail, flicking ears forward...took a staggering step to bump his head against the dog's shoulder and offer the briefest purr, a deep and scraping sound.

And then he limped off to find himself something to eat. Alone.

Chapter 22

Regan greeted the morning with horse chores, but she was surprised when she discovered her father's old dog standing at the corner of the house, his tail wagging with a grave uncertainty she'd not seen in him before.

"Bob!" she said. And then, in discovery, *"Bob!"* Dried blood crusted his fur—his shoulder, his side, down his front leg. Dread hit her stomach, and she quickly knelt beside him, searching beneath the fur and watching for any sign of a flinch.

He gave her arm a solemn lick and his tail wagged gravely onward—and soon enough she realized that the blood lay entirely *over* his hair, failing to penetrate his soft, dense undercoat.

But the dread didn't diminish. "Where have you been?" she asked him, as if he might even answer. And, without thinking, added, "Who have you been with?"

Snarling cries, a grunt of pain, a glimpse of wild eyes and swift, twisting action—

Regan pressed fingers against her forehead and her world wobbled briefly around her, a cry of earth and sky and rending pain. She sucked in a breath, feeling as though she'd forgotten something important…and then feeling the distinct sensation of memory skitter away.

She climbed to her feet without any particular grace, grasping for a practical next move. And because she didn't have one, she did what her father would have done. She went into the house and grabbed up the little .22 rifle, heading out into the land.

Whatever Bob had found might still be alive. It might be in pain.

The lynx hunted. Doubly wounded, unsteady, knowing only instinct and need, it padded down toward easier prey. Domestic daytime prey.

A chicken wandered the edges of a garden plot of covered spring greens, too early to find much in the way of insects, but nonetheless pleased with itself, clucking softly and ruffling russet feathers in the sunshine.

One weak leap, one squawk, one wild flap of wing… hot sweet blood pulsed into the lynx's mouth.

A human shout followed it back into the woods.

Driven by irritable restlessness and persistent, jarring pieces of memory, Regan took again to the woods— searching for she didn't know what. She left behind her painting, voice mail to her father and the faint guilt of her failure to return the most recent calls from that nice Matt Arshun.

On the first day of walking the land, she found an area of trampled undergrowth and patches of dried blood— on the ground, smeared down a granddaddy ponderosa, splashed on low leaves. She found drag marks, too, and spent no little amount of time hunkered down with the rifle over her knees, trying to understand how an event of this obvious magnitude had occurred so close to the cabin without drawing her notice.

On the second day, she found further signs of trespass on their land—a careless cigarette butt, instantly raising her ire—it was the most inexcusable carelessness, here on a land that caught fire so readily.

On the third day, a week after she'd woken on her couch with dim memories of a fall in the woods and the bruises to prove it, she stayed home—and the hunters found *her*.

With her father in prep for surgery and her hand never far from the phone, she'd tucked her feet up on the couch to balance a sketch pad on her knees and doodle idle, pointless notes for her *Bats Are All That!* contract work.

Not that her father wasn't doing well—in fact, better than expected after the doctors had made their inexplicably delayed discovery of the damage to his neck. And not that she didn't have enough to do, between the delivery date on the sketches and what seemed like an inevitably pending sale on the cabin.

She just couldn't seem to keep her thoughts together. The half-finished painting in the loft again called to her, fueled by her hiking. She stubbornly resisted it, telling herself she had other obligations and pretending not to know that she'd spooked herself with the intensity of the grip it had on her.

The land itself still drew her, full of secrets and unexplained drama. And the town drew her, too—tugging at her with the ongoing impulse to go talk to Mary. If Mary didn't know what was going on in this area, no one did.

But that didn't explain her equal impulse to go talk to Phillip Seamans, a man she had just met and wasn't even sure she liked.

The cat stretched at her side, extending his front legs

stiff and straight, claws pricking at air. *Nothing stretches like a cat.*

Except for Kai.

What the—? Where had that thought even come from?

Bob's barking interrupted her efforts to pluck apart her tangled thoughts; he drifted back to the porch along the way. She glanced out the window to see three men hesitating at the curve of the driveway, each of them toting a hunting rifle—one of which had the pistol grip and a high-capacity magazine of an assault weapon.

Charming.

She put the sketchbook aside and joined Bob on the porch. Sometime during recent days, she'd gained the privilege to rest a hand on his head. When she did, he leaned against her leg.

She wasn't quite sure when all that had happened, either.

The men moved forward when they saw her, but she didn't let them come too close. "I'm sorry," she said. "I need you to stay back there. Is there something I can do for you?"

"Sure," said one of the men. He was a sturdy man, looking decently fit and prepared to hike around the high woods in his tan shirt and woodlands camo pants. His hair curled around his ears beneath a gimme cap, while the other two either had their hair scraped high and tight beneath similar caps, or were lacking it altogether. "We just came to get permission to hike around this area."

Right. With their rifles.

Regan tipped her head toward the woods. "Seems to me you've already been doing that." She gave one man a meaningful look—along with the cigarette pack in his front shirt pocket. At their blank expressions, she added, "Cigarette butt."

To judge from the chagrin on the one man's face, she'd guessed right, indeed. But the man with the pistol grip rifle didn't care. "You can't expect us to know when we cross property lines if they're not marked."

Regan smiled a little to herself, thinking of a ride on the mustang, an encounter in the woods—

No, wait. *What?*

She shook off the moment and told the man, "The lines are marked, if you're looking. And I do expect you to know that nothing's in season right now."

"Lady," said the man with the least available hair, his nose a bulbous thing and his lips too thin beneath it, "we've got a right to protect ourselves."

She laughed. "If you're that concerned, get out of the woods."

"Haven't you heard?" The man with hair shifted his cap back on his forehead. "Something's gone rogue out there. Staying out of the woods is no guarantee—it's coming out to hunt. The tracks look like a big cat, but the sightings look like—"

Lynx. She knew it without knowing how. *Of course, Lynx.*

"Bigfoot?" she suggested, since he hadn't finished his sentence. Not that she blamed him. Canadian lynx in the Sacramento Mountains... Bigfoot would have been a better bet.

The man with the nose scowled at her. "It's no joking matter. This thing is taking chickens—"

"Oh," she said, more drily than the desert spring air. *"Chickens."*

"We've got a right to protect our property."

But his tone put a growl in Bob's throat. Regan struggled to keep her reaction appropriate, her voice appropriate—and to understand the strength of her reaction in the first place. For it wasn't just ire at poachers on the prowl; it was a fury that went beyond. It was *personal.*

She managed to say, "I very much doubt you're from

around here at all, but even if you are... *No, you don't*. If you have a problem with Bigfoot, then call the Forest Service. But you absolutely don't have the right to hunt off your land, or permission to be on mine. And you can bet the rangers will be looking for you now."

The man with the nose shifted the grip on his rifle, looking as if he'd prefer to be shifting his grip on Regan. "I get it," he said. "You're one of *those*. A righteous, tree-hugging *bitch*."

She stood straighter. "You want to go there? Then yes. I *am*. And this is my land, and *that*—" she waved a hand to indicate the sprawl of rugged earth around them "—belongs to the creature that you hunt." Struck by thought, she held up one finger. "Hold on a moment—"

That took them by surprise, and though she half expected them to stomp away while she ducked back into the house and grabbed up her cell phone, they still stood there, uncertain, when she returned. She held the phone up just long enough to snap a quick photo.

The rudest of them cursed and turned away from the house, jerking his head at the others in an indication they should follow. The man who'd first spoken, the one who must be playing the good-poacher role, looked back at her. "Listen, lady—"

"Regan," she said. "Regan Adler. In case you want to resent me by name."

"Listen," he said. "You might want to rethink this. We know it's here on this slope. We've tracked it here."

"Good," she said—though her heart pounded at his words, striking fear not at the presence of the lynx, but for its safety. "If it's here, then it's safe."

But she didn't waste any time after the men left. She transferred the photos to her laptop, plugged into the satellite internet access and uploaded the images to a photo site. Just as quickly, she called both the sheriff and the local ranger station, identifying the men as active hunters on both private and national forestland. Someone in town would know who they were and where they were staying. They'd find themselves facing trouble sooner than they expected.

If maybe not soon enough.

What if they're not the only ones?

If the word had spread about a lynx siting in this area, they wouldn't be.

Find it. Find it first.

How absurd was that?

But she found herself changing clothes, grabbing her day pack…leaving her work behind and planning to be back before any reasonable expectation of word of her father's surgery.

Out on the porch, Bob sat at stiff attention, his gaze riveted to the driveway. As Regan caught a brief glimpse of a newly familiar sedan through the pines, Bob escalated into a growl, already more riled by the approaching car than he had been by the three hunters.

Arshun. Coming to discuss the offer on the property.

Irritation flickered through her, coming as a surprise. Arshun had been understanding of her father's situation… gently persistent in his pursuit of the property, offering what seemed more than a fair price. She had no reason for the resentment suddenly sitting hard in her stomach.

But she trusted Bob. And she had nothing to tell Arshun, not with her father in surgery—and after that, recovery.

She hesitated, locked the front door for the first time in what was likely a decade and slipped around the side of the house as the car curved up the driveway, getting the back door on the way by. Bob left the porch to stalk along at her side—another surprise—but drifted away to sit by the paddock as Regan climbed on up into the woods, not truly caring if Arshun spotted her. The irritation flared again, surprising in its strength.

She chose her path without thinking, first walking the game trail along the side of the mountain and then breaking away to climb upward, looking for and readily finding the high point her mother had called her favorite—a slab of towering, fractured limestone studded with amazingly persistent little oaks and clear enough at the top to sit, dig into her pack for water and ponder the land before her.

Welcome...

"Hello," she said out loud, without truly noticing that her impulsive acknowledgment came in response to the infinitely quiet sensation of greeting. "How strange to think that I'll miss you, after all this time of being away. I should have come back sooner."

Welcome...

"I just needed some time away," she told the woods. "To come to grips with losing Mom to you." She frowned, not certain why she'd even said that. "I mean, with losing her at all." For what did an accident down in Las Cruces have to do with these woods?

Those hunters had rattled her more than she'd thought.

Find him...

They'd rattled the hell out of her if she even thought she could track down a lynx in this forest. She was no hunter, no tracker.

Help you...

She made a face, fingers pushing against her brow... full of impulses and certainty and not understanding any of them. No longer truly able to resist them. She stuffed the water back into the pack, impatient with herself

Her fingers brushed thin, crinkly foil.

She pulled the condom wrapper from the pack with nothing less than astonishment. An *open* wrapper. A little more frantic digging revealed a baggie with a used condom, some used tissues.

"I must be losing my mind," she said, too stunned to do anything but stare at the things in her hands—understanding immediately what they meant.

She'd not only been with someone, but she'd been with him in the woods. *Leave no trace.* She'd cleaned up after them, come home...and completely, immediately forgotten it. Forgotten *him.*

But her body remembered. Even now it tingled, flooding with warmth in some places, with tight anticipation in others. And her body had certainly remembered those two days earlier, when she'd woken pleasantly sore and still half aroused, remembering when she'd dreamed of—

Kai...

Honest, deep blue eyes and gentle hands and wild strength, the line of torso and hip—not on paper, but hard muscle beneath her touch, surging passion beneath her body—

She sucked in a breath, dropping the baggie as if it could sting her—and maybe it could. Maybe it *had.*

Find him...

For the first time she realized that the stinging impulse came from outside of her, imposed upon her instead of generated by her. She lifted her head, casting a wild glance over the woods—the intensity of big bright sky, impossibly blue; the majestic nature of pines spearing into it, carpeting the abrupt and sometimes jagged land and making way only for the thrust of limestone and bare cliff.

Find him...

It was distinct now, recognizable, and so profoundly insane that she shouted back at it.

"Stop it! *Stop it!* Get out of my *head!*"

Her words rang out over the land and faded into silence—long silence, until finally a scrub jay ventured to scold her, and a small flock of pine siskins resumed their chaotically breathy twitter.

And then, quiet but insistent, the sensation in her mind. The *knowing* in her soul…. *Find him…*

She'd come out into these woods to find a lynx. A wounded lynx.

Or…

Maybe to find a feral man named Kai who had touched her, loved her, made her body sing…and then somehow been forgotten.

"If I'm going to find anyone," she told the sky, "maybe it ought to be *me.*"

The sky gave her no argument.

Regan jammed the telltale trash back into her pack, slipped it on over her light jacket and headed down the hill to pick up the game trail, circling back around to the dry pool.

She gave up on thinking. She just walked the woods, as her mother had always walked the woods as they had sometimes done together.

Her mother had always known just when to stop, to pull behind the cover of a big corrugated ponderosa trunk and point quietly at browsing elk or a passing mule deer. More than once, a bear…more than once, a mountain lion. And once, just once, a pair of mountain lion cubs, playing with clumsy fervor outside their den.

"How do you always *know?*" Regan had asked, her childhood self just barely able to manage the terrain.

"The land tells me," her mother had said, quite simply. Quite happily. With no idea of what was to come of it—

No. Wait. Her mother had died in a car accident, far from home. Nothing to do with—

Her friend Kathleen, crying—braces glinting, youthful teen face distorted with emotion. I'm sorry! I'm sorry! I never would have said anything if I'd thought this would happen!

Her father, full of conflicting grief and guilt. She was trying to come home...back to the land....

Dark blue eyes and heady presence, a voice with a lurking rasp, body with a primal strength and unexpected grace. Cherish what you can hear.

She stood stiff and still, battered within...memories fluttering to the surface and sinking away again. Her body relived its own memories—the throes of a struggle, of fighting and losing the battle to escape as cruel hands dragged her away. She heard again a final, sharp gunshot—

Felt again the land cry out in dismay—

Heard the echoing cry of a wounded animal.

Kai.

Yes...

"I don't understand," she said out loud, and her voice sounded broken.

Trust...

Right. As if she could trust anything right now.

But her body told her the truth of it all. It had been well loved...and it had been bruised and manhandled. It had warm, sensual memories, and it had bruises she couldn't explain. Just as she couldn't make sense of the blood in the woods or Bob's growling resentment of a man who hadn't been anything but solicitous—but to whom Regan, too, had quite suddenly developed an aversion.

She laughed out loud, a short and bitter sound. "What," she said, to no one at all, "have I got to lose?"

Things went easier after that. She quit thinking so hard—she quit thinking at all. She strode out along the whisper-thin game trail, watching her feet, listening to the faint crunch of needles, the rustle of wind up high in the trees...and to the small, murmuring voice in her head.

That voice, those impulses…they took her further than she'd been before, and left her with the uncertainty of how and when she'd return. Fortunately, the horse had days of hay and water and Bob was well-fed. When her own stomach growled, she ignored it.

For the land suddenly dumped her out at the mouth of a cave, a thing so well hidden she couldn't believe she'd found it at all.

She slipped in past the aspen stand of an old burn, and behind the screen of brush and vine. There she faced a narrow slot in a rock, finding deeply within it a completely incongruous wooden door—not a square door, but one cut in rough angles that matched the rock…and one left completely ajar in its mortar-sealed frame. She pushed past the open door to slide sideways through an unevenly narrow passage and came through into…*a home.*

The cave had a low wooden floor and simple, sturdy furnishings, a wardrobe incongruous against one slanting wall, a pantry cupboard nearby, a minimalist camp stove set off in one corner and a basin and pitcher sitting on an old-fashioned washstand beside it. Diffuse light scattered through the space, startlingly effective but still dim to her eyes, its source not immediately obvious.

It took a few moments before she saw the bed tucked against the wall—only a low mattress, sitting on a set of storage drawers. Blankets lay over it, a generously rumpled mess.

From the middle of that nest, a lynx regarded her with unblinking eyes.

It knew the moment she saw it, growling a deep threat that curled up into a brief yowl and lift of lip and whiskers, ears slanted back in anger but not fear.

"Oh," she said weakly. "Hey, there. Sorry I bothered you."

Her mind caught on the reality of it, logic and sanity

warring with what lay before her. With the worn nature of the floor, the established nature of the furnishings, and the slap of truth—this hillside home had been here across the years, and she'd known nothing of it. Her mother had known nothing of it. And she'd found it now only because she'd—

Because she'd been led here.

The lynx shifted—big for its kind and glorious, its mottled buff-and-silver fur still thick with winter, dried blood gone black high on chest and leg. It growled again, a lingering sound that came as a definite threat.

Regan took a step back, feeling for the exit. "Okay, then," she said, her voice as quietly steady as she could manage. "You hang out here in your Batcave. I'll just… I'll leave, shall I?"

She'd done what she'd come for, and more than she ever expected to. She'd found the lynx. And now she could report this location to the rangers who would set live traps—they'd care for the creature and return it to an area where its mere inexplicable existence wouldn't turn it into a target.

After all, someone had already shot it.

The lynx shifted to face her more squarely as she backed away, its eyes flashing blue.

Blue.

Blue as in her dream, blue as on her canvas, blue instead of pale, wise green.

"Kai?" she said, and instantly felt infinitely stupid, connecting this animal to a man she couldn't even remember knowing, except—

A bite of cold night air slipping through blankets, the warmth of a man's arms, the wild strength of him—

She looked at the nest of blankets and felt the blood rush from her face and her knees stuttered out from beneath her, leaving her leaning against uneven rock and even then just barely on her feet.

She would never forget those blankets. Not as she'd seen them in the light of rising dawn, luxuriously soft and patterned in a wash of earth tones and what she'd noticed then and simply never understood—a scattering of silvery hairs.

She still didn't understand. But the lynx looked at her with an inscrutable interest as she slid a halting path down the wall to sit there looking at it.

"Kai?" she said again.

When had her world changed so it made more sense to call this animal by a man's name than to assume any of the other wildly improbable possibilities? That a man named Kai lived in this woodlands bunker, or that he lived here with a lynx that didn't belong anywhere near this area but still had never before been spotted, that the lynx had been wounded at the same time the man had gone missing, his friends worried and asking...

That she would call the lynx by the man's name.

"Kai," she said more firmly.

The lynx responded with a feline sound she couldn't quite interpret. It might have been threat or warning.... It might have been confusion. Either way, its eyes had gone narrow. It made an aborted movement, thought better of it, sinking back against pain with ears flicked back and whiskers bristling.

At the foot of the bed sat a satchel. Regan closed her eyes with a strangled sound, seeing in her mind's eye that same satchel—on the ground beside a man at the library. A man standing relaxed and yet not, a face of masculine beauty and a flashing glance with the same heat she'd felt in her dreams.

Trust...

The concept pressed in around her as a warm sensation—surrounding her as the cave surrounded her. And it spoke not only to her.

The lynx's ears flipped forward, then back again. When it snarled into a quick hiss, she thought it reacted not to her at all…but to what they'd both heard.

She got to her knees…inched closer to the bed. Knew her insanity and did it anyway. Watched the lynx…watched the lynx watching back. Slow but steady, no longer truly fearing…

Until her fingers sank into a fur more luxurious than any shared blanket.

She looked at the lynx, astonished at herself. The lynx looked back, as if just as surprised. No longer *it* in her mind, but *him*—recognizing the masculinity in beautiful feline features, in the large and rugged build of the animal.

In the acknowledgment that filtered back to her on the whisper through the land.

"Kai," she whispered without really knowing what she was saying at all.

Chapter 23

The lynx poised, stunned in his own confusion.

Kai had wanted to strike out at her; he didn't. He'd wanted to growl and hiss at her; he didn't.

He just watched her approach, and then he watched her touch him.

"Kai," she said, her human voice and human words meaningless in his world. *"Kai,"* she said again, touching him somewhere inside his mind, a place so recently gone dark and smothered and confused.

He flicked an ear, absorbing the invitation without responding to it—except that there was a purr rising in his throat, deep and raspy. He squeezed his eyes closed on it, floating in the mix of pain and pleasure—the hot throb of his wound, radiating darkness; the gentle knead of her fingers in his fur.

He might just have floated away on it if the memories hadn't risen between them, twining with the clear, cool green taste of the land.

Touching her, her human skin beneath his human hand, all silky smooth curves, all softness, all heat and responsive warmth.

A startled sound escaped her, her fingers stilling along his neck just as his purr cut off into silence.

Her hands eager down his human back, grasping at his buttocks, stroking his shoulders and tunneling through his hair. Her warmth surrounding him in all ways. Their pleasure, their gasps, their wild shouts—

"Kai!" she cried, and this time with recognition—with meaning.

The woods around them, the fiery impact of a bullet, the world of pain and confusion and fighting back, the lynx pushing hard at him and Core poison spreading fast and deep...

The Core. Enemy, invader...destroyer. Even from that wound, he should have healed. For he was—

"Sentinel," she said out loud, a certainty without true comprehension.

Fighting back—fighting hard. Killing men, when he had never wanted to take such life. Her cries against his ears, the sound of her struggle—her sudden silence. Another gunshot, laced with pain but not poison—

He blinked, found his claws extruded and puncturing the mattress...found her bent over him, crying against his neck.

"I forgot you," she said, choking on the words. "How could I? How could I just go on with my tiny little world!"

His impulse to soothe her came through in a brief and ragged noise that couldn't be called a purr. Impatience gripped him, twisting something within him, and he reached for his voice, suddenly remembering that he had one. That the *human* had one.

He closed his eyes against flashing blue-and-silver energies, coruscating light and flickering shards of intensity. His lynx's yowl turned to a shout. Regan cried out and flung herself away, her forearm up to block her eyes.

Kai found himself tangled in blankets, folded over with white-laced fire coursing through his wounds, his chest, his arm. Darkness still pressed in on him, and all around him lay...*silence*. He gasped against it, shivering.

"I can't believe..." Regan's voice reached him in a whisper as she rose as far as her knees beside the raised mattress.

He didn't need her to fill in those words. *I can't believe what I just saw. I can't believe what's happening. I can't believe what you ARE—*

But she said, "I can't believe I could ever forget you."

She moved slowly, gently, giving him the benefit of being the wild thing he was—but not hesitating as she touched his cheek, wiped the edge of his damp lashes and bent to kiss him. Firm, sweet connection.

She knew him now, whatever the Core had done to her. She knew him, she'd come for him and she'd found him.

Kai hadn't meant to let a groan slip out with his relief or to shiver against her.

"Shh," she said, easing back. "We'll figure this out. Together. It's okay if it doesn't make sense right now."

"I can't hear anymore," he said, little more than a whisper, and then realized he'd made little sense.

Except she understood anyway. "I can," she said, and rested her hand on his. "Listen through me."

He forgot to breathe in the relief of it, the wash of the woods through his mind, the taste of green and growing, the heavy weight of rock and earth. She stayed with him there for a long moment, waiting for him to relax, to slump against the comforting familiarity.

When she finally spoke, she kept her voice low. "There's so much I don't understand," she said. "So much I think... maybe I never will. But I know this." She took a deep breath. "I'm not crazy. My mother wasn't crazy. What happened to her—"

Kai grabbed her hand, stopping her—filling in his own words for hers. "Is what will happen to me, now. *Alone.*"

She shook her head in quick denial. "No. Not you. You…you're so much more than she was. Than *I* am."

He squeezed her fingers. "To *me.* This Core working…" He closed his eyes in the desperation of it and tried again, seeing her utter lack of comprehension. "This injury. The people who did it, and who want your land. Call them the Core. The injury holds a working—"

"It's okay," she interrupted him. "If there's one thing I get, it's that I have no idea what's going on—not in the details. You're hurt, and I have to help you. I *need* to help you." She bent to touch his forehead with hers. "I need you."

"Regan," he said, and found he'd been in the darkness too long, still the grip of the lynx over his mind and his words. In the end he simply pushed gently back against her forehead with his, a soft head bump with a faint rasp in his throat.

She laughed. "Finally," she said. "*Finally,* I know what that sound reminds me of. That's your man-purr, isn't it?"

The look he gave her shifted into skepticism. "Man-purr."

"Oh, yes," she said. "And Kai Faulkes, I have a mind to find out just how many ways I can make you purr."

She kissed him again, quick and assertive, and then sat back on her heels to regard him, leaving him her hand—and his connection to the land. "But first, you need help. This tunic has to come off." She eyed the blood-soaked material with disgust. "And we need to get back to my place—"

A new, stunned look crossed her face. "Oh, my God.

While it still *is* my place. My *father's* place. What have those people done to him?"

Kai frowned. Hard enough to think through cloying Core workings, through pain…but what—?

She shook her head, a decisive motion. "Arshun," she said, "took me back to the house after you got away, made noises and threats…. I'm not supposed to remember the details, just how much it matters. He'll kill us if we don't give him that land, that's what it amounts to. Starting with my father—starting by *crippling* him. In his surgery—" She looked at him, despair in her eyes. "It's happening today. *Now.*"

"No," he said, firmly enough to belie the new shivers of pain that swept through him; she gave him a startled look. "Your father is fine. Arshun thinks things are in hand."

She nodded slowly. "They *were,*" she said. "My father gave him verbal acceptance of the offer yesterday. They must have done something to him, like they did to me…" She looked at him, understanding shining in her eyes. "What they did, it wasn't strong enough. It wasn't stronger than what we already had—"

"Shh," he said, because it was the only thing he had to say. He gave her hand the slightest of tugs, and she came to him; he eased over onto his back to welcome her, wrapping one arm around to hold tight while she lay over his chest and clung to him, her face buried against his neck but her weight carefully shifted away from his wound. "Shh," he said, and clung to her in return, knowing that neither of them quite understood what had happened to their lives, but that there was only one way to make it through.

Together.

Regan pulled back and wiped her eyes and tried to regain her balance. "Where," she said as matter-of-factly as she could, "is your knife?"

He looked at her without understanding, his eyes shadowed in the darkness and shadowed by pain, and she thought they probably had a very limited time to accomplish what had to be done.

And then it would be too late, with Kai lost to whatever had been done to him.

So she marched on with what had to be done, hoping the rest of it would eventually make better sense. "Your knife, to cut that shirt away," she told him. "It's ruined anyway, and I don't think you'll be very happy if we tug it off."

Understanding flickered over features gone hollow. He nodded at the stout little chest of drawers, and she reluctantly disentangled her fingers from his, seeing instantly how his expression turned bleaker without the connection her touch seemed to offer.

My mother wasn't crazy, and neither am I.

Well-meaning people had killed her mother. She knew better than to ever let it happen to her.

Or to ever let her father know what he'd so unwittingly helped to do.

She readily found the knife, and—helping herself to the dresser and its scant contents—also found another shirt. Emboldened, she rummaged in the pantry area and discovered a salve redolent of juniper and sage; then she found a clean, full bucket of water and helped herself to it.

Beware...

She placed the bucket beside the bed, scowling at the land. She supposed it was a bit much to expect detailed messages or profundities, but a *hint*....

Kai made an inquiring noise; she picked up the knife in one hand and placed her other over his forearm just long enough for him to understand.

And Kai, who knew the land better than she, said, "Someone's coming." And at her raised brow, added, "Not necessarily friendly."

Panic flushed through her chest. "I didn't hide my tracks—I didn't even think of it. I don't even know *how*."

"Hurry," he said, though he looked unutterably weary. "We must be out there. Making *new* tracks."

"Stomping all over the old." Regan put the knife under the tunic and sliced upward, away from his skin and careful of the point. Glad, in a way, for the need to work swiftly, because otherwise she would have hesitated and fumbled and made it harder for both of them. "Tell them I came here to meet up with you and hike out. I'm making reference sketches, and you had some places to show me."

Kai twitched at the slide of cool metal along his torso. "Do you have sketching things?"

She laughed shortly, cutting through to the tunic neck and then along the sleeves, peeling the material away so he lay on top of it—and without pausing, worked the sharp blade through the cleanest section at the bottom to make herself a rag. "I *always* have sketching things." She dipped the rag into water and offered him an apologetic look. "This is going to be cold."

He growled under his breath as the wet cloth hit skin, a sound she'd heard before and that now suddenly made so much more sense. His skin pebbled as she washed the dried blood streaking his chest and side, staining the light pattern of coarse, silvered hair; his breath hitched as she washed around the wound itself, a simple but ugly hole, as if someone had taken a slightly misshapen paper punch to smooth skin.

I heal quickly, he'd told her once.

Not this time. No doubt only his preternaturally fast healing had kept him alive at all.

He took a ragged breath, coming out of his self-imposed trance to follow her gaze. "It won't truly heal until the bullet comes out."

And she realized with a sudden shock that he would

never allow her to take him to Alamogordo to the hospital. With just as much surprise she realized, too, that she understood perfectly. For if the medical system had so badly failed her mother, who lived outside the norm in only that one, distinctive way, what would it do to Kai? Discover and exploit him? Or simply kill him with misguided kindness because he wasn't what they expected?

"First things first," she heard herself say, reaching for the pungent salve and spreading it gently around the wound—and using more of the torn tunic as a patch, letting the salve serve as an adhesive. It had to stay only until they could reach her father's cabin—there, she'd have extensive first-aid supplies and food. And the people who had done this to him—to *them*—would have no idea that she'd remembered herself...or that she'd found Kai, and he still lived. They had no reason to think things weren't going exactly as planned.

Just as quickly, she tended the wound in his calf—almost healed, that one, living up to all his previous allusions to his own unbelievable nature. "Let's head off whoever's skulking around out there. Can you sit?"

With help, he did, allowing her to ease the clean shirt over his arm, taking over to manage the rest of it himself in quick, rough motions. He took the knife and shoved it into the sheath hanging from his belt, and by then Regan had planted herself slightly to the side, bracing herself—offering her bent arm as a solid support in case he needed it to rise.

He did, giving her cause to startle all over again at the solid weight of him—realizing again the deceptive nature of his movement, his gravity-defying twists and grace when in confrontation with Arshun and his men.

But now when he stood he wavered, and she quickly moved up beside him, steadying him.

Beware...

He felt the warning come through her and nodded at her pack. "Your things."

She grabbed the pack on the way out, settling it over her shoulders as they emerged and hesitating there while Kai reached up one-handed and tugged a swath of camouflage netting down over the door. A few steps into the woods she looked back and did a double take. "If I didn't know it was there…"

He gave her a short, grim smile with satisfaction in it— and confidence. Of course. He'd been living this way for a long, long time. The smile fell away as he noticed her face—a little scabby, full of faded bruises…the lingering signs of a violent assault she still barely remembered those days earlier. He reached over to touch her and didn't quite, fingers hovering over the healing insults. His jaw hardened as he turned away.

He led her from the entry and limped up to the aged remnants of a fallen tree. There he sat, buckskins and breechclout and tunic over bare feet, looking much as he had when she'd first seen him—an integral part of these woods.

But wounded. Hurting. Defying all probability to be sitting there in the first place. Surely, whoever came would see it in him.

He nodded out at the area just below them. "Walk circles," he said. "Over your incoming tracks. Roll on the ground."

"Roll—?" But she did as he asked, first walking ever-bigger circles and figure eights, then dropping to the ground. As she climbed to her feet, brushing away crisp brown oak leaves and pine needles, the sound of their approaching intruders reached her ears—a mutter of male voices in conversation, the faint crackle of a broken twig.

She climbed back up to reach Kai—startled when he took her arm and tugged her down, but going with it. Even more startled when he hooked his hand around her neck and drew her in for a kiss, but going with that, too—so easily sinking into the moment of it, his lips warm and firm on hers, moving with an assurance they'd not quite had when they'd first done this.

By the time he drew back, he'd brought color back to his pale face and a flush to hers, and while his breathing hitched in a way it shouldn't, her own chest rose and fell with betraying rapidity—and when she looked up into the woods, she found the three poachers watching from only fifty yards away.

Watching…and smirking.

She shot Kai a look; he lifted one shoulder without apology. "There is much I don't truly know about the world," he murmured. "But I know what gets a man's attention. They won't think too hard about your sketchbook now."

"I might just hit you," she told him. "At some better time."

But she knew she wouldn't, and so did he. And it wasn't hard to jump to her feet in an embarrassed way and go instantly on the offensive.

The poacher with the most attitude beat her to it. "Now we know why you wanted these woods to yourself."

"This is national forestland," she told him, pretending he hadn't been watching her enthusiastic embrace, then spoiling the effect by brushing futilely at the needles on her light jacket. "You don't belong here with those guns. I warned you—"

"Yeah, yeah," said the man, propping the butt of his rifle against his thigh. "And you took a picture."

"I already sent it to Jaime Nez." She took a step back, bumping up against Kai. He rested a hand at her lower back.

"Who has nothing better to do than to rush out here and

search the woods for us?" The man snorted. "It's a sleepy little town, I know—but these are big woods."

Kai stood, and then the hand at her waist served as subtle support. "But it has only so many places to pull off the road," he said. "And the rangers here know them all."

The poacher in the back resettled his hat, impatience on his features. "We haven't tracked anything but the girl since we started looking."

Quiet land...quiet creatures...

Regan understood, with a flash of surprise, that the land had listened to the events of the day—had listened through Regan. Had soothed and quieted its own creatures, sheltering them from the dangers wrought by Core interference.

Trying to...

"We saw those tracks down by the seep," said the smallest of them, protest in his voice.

Kai's weight wobbled against her, stabilized; he suppressed a faint grunt of pain.

"And nothing since, and he's goddammed right about the rangers. If they start looking, it won't take them long to find the truck. Doesn't matter how far we went up that crummy little access road."

Kai put his hand on the back of her neck—skin on skin. It felt cooler than it should have, weighing heavily upon her, even while seeming a casual touch, and it made her intensely aware of his struggle to hide his pain. She leaned into him, not quite understanding his purpose—not until she felt the push of sensation. Uneasiness and anxiety, the ominous impression of darkness and shifting branches, lurking dangers.

Kai said, "You don't belong here." But he was looking at Regan, and suddenly she understood. *This, too, is something I can do.*

She could be a conduit in the other direction. From Kai to the land—instructing it, guiding it. A subtle *no trespassing* sign that these men would never hear clearly enough to question consciously, but to which they would nonetheless respond.

She caught the thread of it, reaching out to the land as she had done not so long before while sitting high on her favorite outcrop. She added her own concern, her anxieties, and steeled herself for the vulnerability of being so open—the sense of grief that came from nowhere, the awareness that her mother had deserved to understand this connection, too.

That they were not victims, but were in fact shepherds of this unique and lingering patch of true wilderness.

Even if it didn't come without cost.

That emotion, too, went out across the land, combining into a slow ripple of *leave this place* that had its effect.

The smallest poacher swiped a hand over his face, looking out around them. A visible decision crossed the features of the youngest poacher, the one who'd already been the most aware of the lines they all crossed. The most aggressive of them frowned, took a step back…and looked up to find the high sun through the pines.

"Eh," he said. "Whatever this thing is, it's holed up by now. Besides, it's been eating chickens, and I don't see any of those here. We'll see if the Delgado orchard wants us to stake their place out. It's been there twice already… it'll be back."

Note to us: avoid the Delgado place.

Not that the guy was done—he gave the disturbed ground cover a significant look, and another to Regan's disheveled hair, her dirty jacket. "Though you might want to keep your eyes out, you and nature boy," he said. "It wouldn't pay to get too distracted out here." He eyed Kai. "You're the one they were all talking about, in town. They seem to think a lot of you. Just one more freak in the woods, if you ask me."

Kai's growl vibrated against Regan's side, not quite audible...not quite truly human. Definitely not steady.

She pressed herself against him, making of herself a soothing presence. After a hesitation, he squeezed his hand at the back of her neck, subsiding. "Maybe," he told the poachers. "But I'm a freak who's welcome here."

It couldn't have made any sense to them. But then, neither could the unease that inexplicably assailed them, seeping into their minds, through their bones, through the soul of them, sending them shying away in spite of their intent on capturing—on *killing*—the unique, wounded creature they'd come after.

Regan held her ground as they left, absorbing more and more of Kai's weight—until they'd gone far enough and she'd taken all she could, and Kai slid down beside her to land with a jarring *thump* on the uneven ground, releasing an involuntary grunt.

She knelt beside him, letting him tip forward to rest his head on her shoulder, stroking along his back...giving him time.

And knowing they didn't have much of it.

Chapter 24

Kai lost his way long before they reached Regan's home, losing himself in pieces to give way to the lynx...to the darkness. Claws scraping, teeth bared, ears flat...the energies of the change roiled against his soul.

Her hand slipped into his, her lips whispering against his ear—words he could no longer understand, but the meaning clear regardless. Encouragement. Understanding. Support he could no longer do without.

She guided him, inexorably drawing him onward, using touch to impress her own strength into him—her determination, her new belief in herself...in him. *I'm here,* she whispered to him through the land.

She had learned so fast. But he still felt himself giving way to the growl within.

"Kai," she said firmly, no longer whispering. "Kai. Whatever they've done, you've got to fight it harder than this."

Spongy darkness seeping into his soul—stripping away humanity, turning the lynx wild and just a little bit stupid.

Capable fingers gripped his jaw. "Don't you dare," she snapped at him, though there might have been a hint of a sob at the back of her throat. "You pull yourself together!"

He lifted a lip, pushing back in ire more feral than human.

"Think again, buster," she snapped right back at him, still with that edge of a sob. When her cheek brushed his, it was wet—and the prelude to warm lips on his, kissing him hard. He groaned in protest as it brought him back to a greater awareness of the battle—of what he had to lose, and what he had to win.

"Good," she said fiercely. "And I'm *sorry*—"

Which made no sense until she jammed a thumb against his shoulder near the injury. He roared up in the sudden deliberate agony of it, feeling not darkness but jagged, hot lightning.

"I'm sorry!" she cried. "I'm *sorry!*" And then did it again.

He twisted away from her, came up spitting mad and crouched on all fours, ready to strike back and to do it hard—and then blinked, vision clearing, to find himself looking at Regan's tearstained face. Tearstained and pale and exhausted, her pink day pack sitting off to the side, the porch boards beneath his toes and hands, and Bob sitting back against the rail to regard them both with dignified uncertainty.

She must have seen the sanity return to his eyes; she threw herself at him with a single stifled sob, held him tightly and then released him. "Quick," she said. "I need to understand how to help."

"Get it *out,*" he said instantly, his voice so ragged the words barely came together. And then, as she struggled to hide her horror at the thought, he recognized how much he was asking, and said, "Call Phillip," instead. Wearily, he rolled back to sit on one hip. "Call Phillip."

That, she scrambled to do—fumbling at the lock, slamming the screen door behind her and leaving the interior door open so he could hear her flipping through the phone book, hear her dial the old phone—hear her frantic message to Phillip's voice mail. Then she barely hung up before she lifted the handset to dial again.

"Mary!" she said. "Thank goodness. Is Phillip there? Do you know where he is? I *really* need to—" She cut off for a moment, and then said faintly, "What? My God— is he okay?" More silence, and then, with subdued relief, "Thank goodness. Did they catch…?" And finally, slowly, "No…no, never mind. Obviously, it can wait. Thanks…. No…no, I'm fine. I'll see you soon, I'm sure."

He wasn't expecting to hear the phone dial one more time—or to hear her greet her uncle, murmuring words that came with relief. "Give Dad my love," she added. "And please, this is so important—don't let him talk to the Realtor, that Arshun fellow? I can't go into details, not now… but the guy is running something on us. I know Dad trusts him, but…please, just don't let it happen. Tell Arshun that Dad's sleeping, or that he's out in physical therapy, or *whatever*." And finally, "I know, I know. Blame it on me when the time comes. Okay? Thanks…. Love you, too!"

And finally, the handset hit the cradle, and Regan emerged from the house—no less pale or bedraggled, a glass of water in each hand. She crouched gracefully beside him and thrust one at him, even as she tipped the other to her mouth.

He needed no urging. He downed the entire thing with water spilling over the sides and down his neck and leaned against the porch rails as he returned it to her.

She said briefly, "Someone broke into Phillip's place and he caught them at it. He'll be okay—he's coming home from the hospital tomorrow. And he did them some damage—all the blood there wasn't his—but there were two of them."

"Arshun's people," he said shortly. "New reinforcements."

She nodded. "That's what I thought, though I can't imagine why they would bother Phillip. Of all the people in that little town, they went to the one who knows how to defend himself?"

"He has the gun," Kai said simply, struck with the sudden understanding of it.

She looked at him blankly a moment, and then her gaze shifted to his shoulder and back again. "With the poisoned bullets."

"The ones that carry workings," he said, by way of agreement. "Do you know if they got it?"

"They never made it past the gym area," she said. "If it was somewhere else, then…no. Not yet."

Not yet.

Because the Core would keep trying.

And so would they.

He caught her gaze more strongly, found her pale blue eyes rimmed faintly with red, bruised with fatigue. "I'm sorry," he said.

"I know," she told him—understanding in her face, as well as renewed determination. "And I'll do my best."

Needle-nose pliers. Shish-kebab skewer. The sharpest of cuticle scissors. Turkey baster. Alcohol and boiling water.

She'd done her best.

And so had he, lying across the old kitchen table with his feet propped on a chair, his hand curled around the edge of the table and gripping hard.

"What if it's close to a nerve?" she'd asked, stepping back to rinse her hands and recharge the cloth she used to damp the sweat off his face, even in this cool kitchen. "Or a blood vessel?" After all, she'd taken anatomy for her life drawing work, even if she'd gone on to focus on things that stung—or leaped or crawled. She knew well enough how much structure was crammed into that area. "What if I break a clot loose and it goes to your lung?"

And he looked up at her and laughed, though it had come with bleak eyes and between rapid and strained breathing. "If it stays," he said, "it kills me, and then the Core destroys the soul of this place. It destroys you. If you take me to a hospital, they will kill me. But if you take it out, it will hurt me and then I heal."

"Because you're Sentinel," she whispered, not quite able to say, "Because you're also a lynx and you do impossible things."

He nodded, but she'd seen the hesitation in his eyes and bought him time by trailing the cloth down the side of his face and neck. By then he'd settled his hand around the solid curve of her hip bone, a touch both comforting and intimate. "If it happens," he said, not taking his gaze from hers, "if there is bleeding or if the poison is too deep already, then it will not be a thing you have done. It will be a thing we could not stop."

And so she used her makeshift probe and her clumsy faux forceps, and she found the damned bullet buried just deep enough to cause its havoc, and she gripped its blunt, misshapen metal and tugged it past broken, grating rib and she wished to hell and back that he would just pass out like a classic Western hero.

But he didn't. He kept his gaze riveted to her face and his hand slipped down for a bruising grip on her thigh, losing himself in her as best he could while his eyes widened and teared, and the mouth that kissed her so well lifted lips in defiance and showed her the distinct nature of his canines, just ever so slightly defined beyond the norm. And finally, when she'd pulled the ugly thing out and dropped it beside him, *finally* his lids fluttered and his eyes rolled back.

She wanted to let her knees go and plop down into the remaining chair, put her head against his shoulder and cry big hearty stress tears. She thought she probably should.

On the other hand, she also thought she should get moving while he wasn't really there to feel it, so instead of that big hearty cry, she gently wiped down his face, kissed him right on his beautiful mouth and pulled out the cuticle scissors to trim and neaten the edges of the skin before she filled the turkey baster with the saline eye rinse from the barn and irrigated the wound.

That got him stirring, as she thought it might. She moved quickly now, cleaning things up, liberally smearing on the triple antibiotic from the barn, taping down a thin sanitary napkin in lieu of bandaging. By the time he groaned and muttered a rare, weary curse, she'd taken to sponging down his chest and arms. "Let me," she said when he pushed vaguely at her. "You'll feel better, and it's calming me."

So he subsided, and she continued her work, running the damp cloth over the amazing structure of his torso, muscles defined and wrapped around broad shoulders down to lean hips, layered over the gentle rise and fall of his chest. She removed the last traces of blood, wiping down the hard curve of deltoid into biceps and then down his forearm to each finger.

When she set the cloth aside, he sighed deeply and opened fully cognizant eyes, bright behind their faint natural-kohl lining. "Thank you."

"Just being selfish," she told him.

"Loving," he said, correcting her. "Being loving."

It startled her, hearing that word out loud.

Then again, what else had driven her to find him, to

batter through the web Arshun had put over her thoughts? To stand up on a rock along the mountainside and throw herself to her instinct instead of running from it?

To face, finally, that from which she'd run all her life? "Maybe," she told him. "Maybe so."

Kai leaned on Regan not on his way out to the couch, but up the stairs to her loft, with the thick scent of linseed in the air and canvas and easel set up at the congruence of skylight and window, shelves of books and art supplies lining the walls with a dusty hint of permanence in diffuse evening light.

Only one corner spoke purely of bedroom, such as Kai understood it from his mildly curious study of the world beyond his own. A sturdy chest of drawers painted bright yellow with pine-green accents, a bed of wrought iron and piled-on covers, and a closet plunked in against the wall with yet more shelves built up the side of it—these containing a score of carefully placed pottery pieces, all glazed in earth tones with a lacy agate effect.

He had little time to notice anything else, with the heat and darkness still pounding through his shoulder and the renewed taste of blood in his throat where she had, indeed, disturbed fragile tissues.

But beneath that—beneath his certain knowledge that he needed to take to that bed before he simply fell on it—there rose a stinging warmth of a different kind, one he welcomed: his Sentinel nature, finally coming to the fore, and finally channeling his considerable connection to the earth's energies. Finally, it would overcome the wound that had tried so hard to kill him…and it would do so with a speed that would likely alarm Regan all over again.

She helped him sit rather than fall, flipped a quilt out to cover him, and then quite casually tugged off her own dirty jeans, giving him a glimpse of the tiny glinting jewel at her belly button and more than a glimpse of skimpy, high-cut underwear in bright jade-green.

She laughed ever so faintly at his expression—a little bit surprised, a whole lot yearning. "We have a lot to talk about," she said. "Like who these Core people are and what they're really about, and how they did what they did to me, and how to protect my father from them, *and* how we're going to get them out of here. And, like, why your eyelids are marked and the hair on your chest is…well, like your…"

"Fur," he murmured.

"Fur," she said as firmly as he thought she probably could. "But then why your eyes are blue and your hair is black."

He laughed shortly, barely with the energy to put sound behind it. It hurt anyway, his hand going involuntarily to his shoulder as she settled carefully into the bed beside him, tucking her legs up and under the quilt. She made a dismayed sound in her throat, something not quite a tsk of disapproval, and leaned on her elbow to stroke her fingers through his hair, a blatantly crooning sort of gesture. Comfort.

And it was. The touch, the intent, the intimacy behind it. He turned his face into her hand, kissing the palm. "Because my family roots go back to Northern Ireland, and my father had the look, and so do I. Because how the *other* expresses itself varies."

She narrowed her eyes. "That sounds far too sensible for a man who—who—"

"Takes the lynx," he offered, saying it for her.

She opened her mouth…and settled, not quite able to say that much out loud. But her fingers never stilled, stroking his hair and tracing his ear and the line of cheek and jaw and nose until he couldn't help but rasp out a sigh that edged on his lynx's purr.

At that, she said, her voice low, "But…because of this *other*…now you'll be okay? The bullet and its stupid poison is gone, and you can heal?"

"I am," he murmured sleepily, "a very fast healer."

"Uh-huh," she said. "So you've said. Me, I'm all normal and everything, and I need a serious nap now. After that…we'll talk."

"We'll talk," he promised her, even if not sure exactly what he would tell her. What he *could* tell her. Or whether it was simply too late to protect her from all the things she shouldn't know.

Kai stirred from healing sleep, somebody else's voice in his head—reaching through with a power and focus he'd never had, even without the interference of the clinging darkness.

My name is Annorah, I don't know if you can still hear me. But we're looking for you…and we'll keep looking. We're coming for you.

He eased his breath out on a long sigh.

He'd called them because he'd had to. Because without him here, there was no one to protect this place from the Core's newly persistent invasion. Because he hadn't believed he would be here to find at all.

So yes, they were coming. *The Sentinels.*

But he didn't know if their search felt like a threat, or a promise—or maybe just another enemy to face.

When Kai woke again, he found himself restless. He slipped from the bed and limped down into the kitchen, where he drank deeply from the cool pitcher and then headed for the porch, scratching under the chin of the marmalade cat on the way.

He stood for a long time, leaning on the railing…testing

his legs, assessing the faint lingering ache in his calf—barely a wound now.

The high chest wound, he still guarded. That one would take time, even once the traces of the Core working had faded away. He tucked his thumb into his belt to keep himself from testing it, stretching it.

Instead, he looked out over the forest dawn, seeing it with new eyes—with human eyes and human perceptions, while his inner ears and voice still lay quiescent. And his ability to sense the Core—the unique sensitivity that had driven his family first to come here and then to leave him here—completely silent, even though he knew this area now to be steeped with activity.

Then he returned to the house—to Regan.

She still slept, bright blond hair escaping its braid, one side of her face marked with faint, fresh scars and a fading bruise.

Days, he'd been on the run as lynx—surviving only on instinct, and surviving only because he had so much of it. Days, she'd been under the Core's influence—an influence they probably still didn't expect her to break, never mind suspect that she had.

He felt a spark of surprising pride at what she'd done this past day—finding him, rescuing herself from the Core, facing the hunters…freeing him from the bullet that had trapped him in the working. She looked small beneath the quilt, curled around herself to make herself a landscape of curving hip and shoulder, her waist a valley between.

It was a simple matter to work his belt loose and step out of the loincloth and leggings to slip under the quilt behind her, and irresistible to run his hand along the length of her, even with the protest from his shoulder. Soft skin and smooth curves, toned muscle yielding slightly to the gentle pressure of his touch—a moment of worship, and of disbelief.

That she existed. That she'd come here. That she'd absorbed the nature of who she was after so many years of fearing it—of who *he* was. That she'd given so much of herself to him, abruptly changing his life from that of someone alone to someone who simply *wasn't*. The pride swelled, filling him—blossoming into something else, something with which he had no experience at all.

Possessiveness. Aching. Wanting.

More than something physical, as much as he hardened against her bottom, so tightly rounded and pressed up against him. He sighed along her neck, bringing his hand back up to slip beneath her arm, caressing along the outside of her breast—thinking not of what he'd been taught or how he'd been warned, but simply of what might please her.

She sighed in sleepy pleasure and leaned back against him, offering herself with a murmur of welcome. He let his hand drift over her belly to find the little jewel and play with it, and then lower to cup her, fingers gently working.

"Mmm," she said. "I take it you're feeling better?"

"There are parts of me," he told her, "that feel very fine."

She said, "Uh-huh," in a voice that meant she'd noticed, and then sucked in her breath, lifting her hips to his hand. Somewhat more breathlessly, she asked, "Seriously, you're…?"

"Be gentle with me," he said, smiling against the back of her neck.

She responded with a squirm. He slipped his good arm beneath her, easily lifting her to lie across his body—giving him beautifully unfettered access to everything and everywhere he might want to touch. She arched against him, her hands seeking him—trying to touch, trying to stroke.

He fended her off, absorbing the sensations of her body over his, the way he reflexively lifted to meet her and the building heat she provoked with little more than her presence and her response to him. "Please," she said. "Please be inside—"

As if that didn't test his sanity as much as anything could. A growl slipped out, vibrating between them. "I don't have your protection."

"I know—but I get it now. *You heal fast.* You said you were safe, and that's why, isn't it?"

Safe and never without the wherewithal to prevent conception—even if she hadn't been. So he answered by shifting her to her side, drawing her leg back and up over his hip—sliding into her with a gentle *rightness.* She stiffened and groped for him, finally reaching behind herself to land a hand on his hip—trying to force the pace.

He was having none of it. Instead, he reveled in it—all of it, from the delicious tease of their slow, slow movement to her rising whimper to the golden hair spilling back over his chest and the wash of energies, a cool thrum of earthy color building slowly to the intensity of whirling red and molten fire. He let it feed the deep build of his own pleasure until she dropped her head back and cried out in a rush of climax—taking him right along with her, his pleasure bursting out from startled understanding.

As much as he had done this for her, she had given it *to* him.

Given herself to him.

And when he caught his breath, he would have sighed over the rasp in his throat that spoke of a purr, if he hadn't also understood just that quickly—

The Sentinels would find him, would interfere with them—would take him into what amounted to custody, to make him one of them whether he wanted it or not.

And the Core would hunt them down—would do everything necessary to gain this ground, to keep their plans safe from him.

To keep them safe from a woman who could hear the land.

And he knew nothing of how to stop them.

Chapter 25

Regan slept again, if only briefly. She dozed off with the luxurious sensation of Kai's hand wrapped around her waist, his fingers tickling ever so slightly around the edges of her piercing. She woke to the absence of him, the quilt pulled carefully up over her shoulder but no match for his missing warmth.

When she cracked her eyes open, she found him standing in front of her unfinished painting, his head tipped as he pondered it, the late-morning light shining strongly down on it from above.

The lynx was subtle, but he wouldn't miss it.

"Do you mind it?" she asked him.

He shook his head, a solitary motion. "You *knew,*" he said with a baffled wonder.

"Maybe some part of me did." She crawled out from beneath the covers to sit cross-legged on the bed, patting around for her underwear—not even sure when she'd lost it. Eventually, she gave up and pulled the quilt up to wrap around her shoulders. "Not consciously. Sometimes, I just…paint." Or at least she had done so, once upon a time. She tried to remember if she'd ever gone to that magical painting fugue while working in Boulder, and couldn't. Not that she'd missed it then, working on assignments instead of her own pieces…

But in retrospect, she missed it now.

She thought of her mother, up here in the studio for hours, emerging with tired satisfaction and a certain distant peacefulness.

But Kai turned away from the easel to give her an uncertain look, and she thought she knew why. She didn't shy away from it, either.

"What's a Sentinel?" she asked. "What's the *Core?* How do you do what you do and how do they do what they do and for God's sake, *why?*"

"I said things," he guessed.

"You did. You said the Core had poisoned you. *Arshun,* who calls himself a Realtor, and those men we saw at the dry pool…the men you killed. Not that it seems to have discouraged them."

He turned away from her, looking out the window—the view of tree and rising ground, impossibly blue sky. *His life.* "I was afraid I remembered—"

"You did," she said again. "They called you *Sentinel.* More than once."

He took a deep breath, let it out with something of resignation. "It's not something I should tell."

"You didn't. *They* did. And it's too late, and I'm not going to stop asking." It would have been easier if she hadn't been naked beneath the quilt, but here she was, and she faced the man to whom she'd so completely surrendered her body not long before. Now they were both just as vulnerable—Regan, waiting for the truth…and Kai, guarding his secrets.

The corner of his mouth twitched, a genuine if transitory smile. "As if you didn't already know what you know."

"Lynx," she said.

Something in him relaxed. He rotated his injured shoulder, so carefully, and then stretched, window light gleaming over the play of muscle in his torso, along his shoulders—the complete and utter abandonment of himself to the stretch.

He dropped his arms and returned to the bed, crossing to sit cross-legged behind her—where, to her surprise, he lifted the tangle of her hair from her shoulders and began to finger comb it. *Grooming.*

She sighed deeply and tipped her head back to it, and was about to warn him that he couldn't distract her from her questions when he spoke again.

"It's called 'taking the lynx,'" he said. "Or 'taking the other.' My parents were not strong-blooded—not what they called field Sentinels—but if my father had taken a change, he would have been a gray wolf. My mother would have been a lynx. My sister Holly...I don't know."

The shock of sudden truth hit her just as hard as her initial realization. "Oh, my God," she said. "It's not just you. It's not just the lynx."

"Wolf and bear and big cat," he said by way of agreement, working his fingers through a particularly stubborn knot and then petting the hair down as if soothing it. "Sometimes elk, sometimes deer, sometimes other— but predators, mostly." He picked up another knot. "Many more who can't change than who can. All of them Sentinels."

Them. They. She didn't fail to notice it, but she didn't ask. Not with so many other questions crowding her tongue.

He scraped the hair away from her nape, sending a shiver of pleasure across her skin, and didn't give her time to ask. "It started nearly two thousand years ago," he told her. "Two half brothers, druid and Roman. The son of the druid, trying to protect his land, drew on it to become *other,* and his sons and daughters did the same, and his grandchildren. The son of the Roman called his brother dangerous, and assigned himself to stop those Sentinels, even though he—and his heirs—had to steal power to do it, corrupting its nature in the process."

Regan tried to imagine an unfettered tribe of those like Kai—seeing how easily he had fought his way through overwhelming odds, how hard it had been to take him down at all. "Were they right?" she asked. "The Core? Were those Sentinels dangerous?"

Kai shrugged. "Not by intent," he said. "But who knows what they would have become without the Core to temper them."

This time, she did say it. *"Them."*

His fingers caught in her hair; he kissed her nape in apology and continued working, and she came to understand that the grooming soothed him as much as it did her—for she heard the difficulty in his voice when he said, "I am not one of them."

"Arshun sure thinks you are."

"So will the Sentinels, when they come." Finally, his hands rested. He pulled her back against his chest and she let him, as much as it also pulled her off balance. *In every way.* "They have been in existence for two thousand years," he said. "Maybe they're necessary for one another. But they're not necessary for *me.* I have my own ways."

"So I've seen," she murmured, and she thought how they'd worked together to make the forest uncomfortable for the poachers who shouldn't have been there—and thought, too, about all the ways he'd welcomed her to those same woods. With such skills, he would hardly need to unleash the lynx.

In fact, if he did, he'd threaten his own existence as much as the ones he faced.

"Can they all do what you do?" she asked him, letting her hand drop back to skim along his thigh, where he cradled her against his crossed legs. "With the land?" She felt him growing hard beneath her, but he made no move to act on it and neither did she. It was just what they were, together—just as she felt the satisfying throb of response in her own tender body.

He shrugged. "Some do more, some do less. There are healers and protectors and communicators with their own skills. The thing I do...what no one else can do..."

But he hesitated, and not as if giving up a great secret, but with the reluctance of one who'd so long felt alone. If he told her this thing, and she didn't understand, he would be more alone than ever.

She didn't have to guess. She *knew*.

And she remembered well giving up her own secret to her own one best friend and having it rejected.

She turned within his arms, just enough to glimpse his face—the way he'd shuttered it. "Look at me," she said. "Look at what I do." She gestured at the canvas, at herself—out the window at the woods. "Look at *us*. Do you really think I'm *not* going to get it?"

He made a sound in his throat and kissed the top of her head. "I *hear* them," he finally admitted. "I *taste* them. I know them, no matter how they hide from others."

She studied his face, seeing the echo of distaste there—the stain of what their presence did to him. "Just you?"

"They would kill me for it. And the Sentinels would use me for it. Here, I'm just myself...doing what I'm supposed to be doing." A bitter edge crept into his voice. "What I was born for."

"What, you think I'm going to judge you for that?"

His arms tightened around her. "I think some would.

Because I don't go to the Sentinels and offer myself to them against the Core."

She made a derisive humph. "I'm not sure I like either of them. And it sounds like they get along fine without you, while here..." She took a breath of the pine-scented air drifting in through the window. "This place thrives *because* of you."

But his silence told her it wasn't quite that simple. "What?" she asked warily.

"Things change," he said, resting his cheek against her hair—inhaling the scent of it, not the least bit self-conscious about his pleasure in it; his erection shifted against her. "When my family left, they did it for me—and for them. They had to protect my sister, so the Core didn't try to use her against us to get at me. They had to protect me."

"You were less conspicuous alone," she guessed, and felt him nod.

"We hoped—" He broke off, hunting for words, and she understood him to be far less casual about his family's departure than he tried to sound. "We hoped we would meet again. But we had no contact."

Nothing. She winced, feeling the pain of that. "What about that letter you had—?"

He'd gone so still, she knew she'd asked the right question. "My father wanted me to know that the Core has a new kind of working, a thing so hard to...*taste*...that they consider it undetectable. That mostly, they're right."

She got it. Right away, she got it. "But you can." A little thrill of fear stifled the pleasure of being in his arms, against his chest, tucked in with his cheek against her head. "Just like with the gun and the bullets. So they need you. The Sentinels need what you can do."

He didn't respond right away—and then, his words at first seemed oblique. "A while ago," he said, "maybe a year or so…I woke from a dream. A *nightmare*. A thing so full of death and grief that I knew it meant something… and I never knew what." He released a breath, long and slow…stirring her hair. "Now with my father's letter…I think it was real. I think…they died, that night. That yes, now they need me."

She pulled away from his grasp, twisting so she could regard him more fully—feeling the new tension where her hands rested against his chest, seeing his expression gone shuttered.

"Can you do that?" she asked him bluntly enough. "If you feel the whisper of the Core here in Cloudview when there are only a handful of bullies pushing a few workings around, what would it do to you to be out in the middle of it all? Surrounded by Sentinels and Core and *humanity?*"

He shook his head, not meeting her eyes.

It was answer enough.

"There has to be another way," she said fiercely, feeling the sudden threat to everything she'd just found with him, the things she'd just found in herself that might well be unbearable without him. And no more unbearable to contemplate the way the outside world would crush a wild spirit, a lynx inside a man who lived for his forest. Who she suddenly hoped would live for *her*. "Kai, there *has* to be!"

But he didn't look at her.

He didn't look at her at all.

"The Sentinels are looking for me now," Kai told her eventually—after she'd showered, and made him a lunch of deliberately runny eggs and crisp bacon. She'd diced some fruit into a yogurt and teased one of the bacon slices from his plate on her way by.

He ate standing up, too restless to do otherwise. Looking out the kitchen window to the horse at his hay, staring up the mountain…pacing briefly into the small living room and back out again, and trying to imagine what it would be like in a city full of indoor places and concrete and asphalt between him and the land.

Regan tried for patience, but he saw the strain of it in her brusque movements and occasional gleam in her eye. And if he wanted to sweep her up and hold her close and assure her that all would be well…

Well, he couldn't.

So he watched the flush on her cheeks and neck, the gleam of gold hair spilling out from a high ponytail and remembered the lurking temper in her. He reminded himself of her mettle, coming back through the working that had shuttered her memories—and facing down all her fears in the doing of it.

"They'll probably find me," he told her, coming back into the kitchen with his empty plate and trickling just enough water over it to soak the leftover egg. "When I was in the woods…when I was hurt—"

"You *are* hurt," she said, enough of an edge to her voice that he ducked his head for a brief smile. She was fighting back now—against the preternatural circumstances that had so stunned her not long before. He instantly loved her for it.

Besides, she was right. They'd checked the wound, found it healing fast and well…*Sentinel*. But not healed. Not yet right. "When I thought I would die alone, then," he said, correcting himself, "I reached out to them. They have someone who heard. So they're looking."

She jabbed her spoon into her yogurt mix. "The real question, then," she said, "is whether they'll get here in time to help with Arshun's little gang."

"Posse," Kai said. "They call the small units 'posses,' the ones who attach to a particular leader."

"My dad should be safe for the moment," she said, nodding at the posse remark without commenting. "He signed a power of attorney before the surgery—and Uncle Cal has agreed to stall Arshun if he calls anyway. Besides, Arshun doesn't have any reason to worry about his little scheme. Whatever he did to mess with Dad's head—" She glanced sideways at him, her fury at the thought of Arshun's attacks on her father simmering close to the surface. "Let's just say Dad doesn't have the same incentive to overcome it."

Kai shook his head. "And if others get in their way? Phillip is already in the hospital. What about the sheriff? Or even those poachers?"

"Mary and Bill," Regan said, her hands pressed flat on the table as if she could push the horror of it away. "They know everything in this town." She looked at him in sudden stark misery at the sudden weight of responsibility—at the potential consequences for her friends. "What we do now matters, doesn't it? More than just whether Dad and I lose this place. It matters to everyone here, whether they know it or not. And either way…what happens here changes your life. *Forever.*"

"Forever," he agreed, and felt walls closing in around him. *Between them.*

"What about me?" she asked. "Do we find out who I am in all this? How I even begin to do what I do? Or my mother?"

Kai hesitated on these particular words, knowing she still wanted the truth—and that she'd know if she didn't get it. "Your mother," he said, "is one of the reasons the Sentinels are so careful about their own. She is why the first lesson we learn with maturity is how to keep our seed from taking."

Her eyes widened. "You think I'm—" She shook her head in exaggerated denial. "No, no, no. Look." She lifted her fingers from the table. "Just plain old regular person. These hands are never anything but hands."

He left the restlessness of the window and came to

her, taking those hands. "Not everyone shows what they would be if they can't take the change. Sometimes the blood is remote. How many people do you know with extra intuition, or a special way with animals?"

"I don't *want* to be one of them," she said fiercely. "I don't want any part of them and their secret war and what they've done to your family because of it—what they've done to *you*. You should have been able to live here without hiding yourself!"

He tried to imagine that—his family comfortably interactive with the town, his sister, Holly, going through school there…a background of dating and sports teams and all of them working with the local forest rangers instead of working around them.

"I think I might still be in this life," he said, glancing out the window again. "I think maybe this is who I am."

"But you wouldn't be alone," she told him. "And you would have had a choice."

He pulled her up from the chair—and when she didn't resist, right into his arms. She felt right there, so snug against him he could perceive every line of her body. He ran his hand down alongside her side, letting it span across her ribs, her waist—letting it come to rest just over the rounded curve of her bottom. Not intimate so much as possessive.

She turned her cheek against his chest and rocked slightly within his arms, seeking and sharing the same comfort. Her hair tickled his nose, and he reveled in it. But he told her, "They need never know of you. But…you might find help in them. I have always known what I am—and what I'm for. My family was steeped in it…they gave me what I needed. You have nothing."

"I have you," she said, back to her fierce voice, muffled as it was. She pushed back away from him, eyes gleaming again. "Don't I?"

"Yes," he said without hesitation, giving her fierceness right back to her—all the surge of the wild within him—making it a dare to the world that would try to come between them. "You do."

Chapter 26

They planned to check Phillip's for the gun, and they planned to check the town for the Core, taking advantage of the cover of the Apple Blossom Festival. But they did neither in the broad light of day, much as Kai chafed and Regan fretted.

In the end Kai helped Regan with such mundane things as late-afternoon chores. Regan made a particular point of refilling the mustang's slow feeder and a second water trough—the one from which Bob could drink. She left the dog with an entire wild turkey, pulled from the bottom of the freezer and waiting for just such an occasion, and latched the door ajar so that cat could come in and out.

Because neither of them truly knew what would happen next.

She took a phone call from her uncle Cal—reassurance that her father was recovering well enough and that her uncle had easily put Arshun off, and with the truth at that.

The anesthesia had hit her father hard, and it would be days before he could address mundane matters.

"They did that one to themselves," Regan had told Kai as she hung up the phone. "However they made this all happen…he wouldn't be *recovering* if they hadn't done something he needed to recover *from*. Damn them anyway!"

"My father often said," he told her, "that they had too much liking for intrigue. For manipulating events."

"Yeah," she muttered. "Well, they can manipulate this." For she'd pulled out her father's plinker .22 rifle and left it beside the door with her purse, an incongruous pair.

For Kai and Regan weren't waiting, not for a minute. For while the Core darkness still threaded through Kai's soul, disabling his ability to use his unique perception of them, the Core had a tendency to leave other trails. And soon enough, the Sentinels would be here. They were close. They were looking.

When they got here, Kai would be ready.

He looked at Regan—also ready, also done with having things happen *to* her and the ones she loved, and ready to turn the tables. He warned her, "A hunt can last for days."

"Doesn't matter." She'd dressed in jeans and the red bandanna shirt, a light trail jacket over it all and her ponytail spilling gold over her shoulder. "We've got days. But I don't think it will. I think they're at the festival, trying in Arshun's oily way to become part of the town. I think they'll take one look at you and give the game away."

Because he lived. Because one look at his expression would let them know that the game had changed.

"Also," she added, and not without a possessive pride, "even if they're not there, they'll know you're hunting them soon enough." She eyed him, the faintest smile at her mouth. "Or did you really think you could walk into town like that and *not* have the instant attention of every woman there?"

His leggings. His breechclout. The tunic, long enough for complete modesty but not so long as to obscure the rugged nature of the rest of it. Tough bare feet, about to tread as confidently in town as they did here in the woods.

He'd never brought this part of himself to town. They'd seen, until now, only what he'd wanted them to see.

She'd been right earlier. Whatever happened after this, it would change his life forever.

Maybe it was time.

"Parking," Regan muttered, while Kai shifted uncomfortably in the front seat of the small SUV, flinching as Regan wheeled a tight turn past the boardwalk.

The Apple Blossom Festival had filled the town to bursting with cars nosing out of every spot, decorations fluttering and a clear pattern of foot traffic heading for the long, narrow park at the end of town. The faintest hint of music filtered into the car—no recognizable notes, just a hint of the bass and rhythm. "All that worry about whether we'll find them or whether the Sentinels will find us, and I should have been worried about the parking."

Kai made a noncommittal noise, bracing to protect his shoulder as they went over a pothole. Behind the driver's seat, Regan's purse burst into song.

"My phone," she said. "Normally I'd just let it go to voice mail, but considering...do you mind?"

He gave her a blank look, and only belatedly realized she not only wanted him to rummage for the phone, but to answer it.

In some things, he was more worldly than anyone else could be, in the most basic sense of the word.

In others, he didn't have a clue.

She must have realized it, for she pulled over in a wide

spot in the ill-defined boardwalk asphalt area and reached back to lug the purse into her lap, flipping up a side pocket to pluck the phone out. By then it had stopped ringing.

"I'm sorry," he said. "I don't really think much about phones."

"You don't say." She flipped the thing open with casual efficiency and pressed one of the buttons. "No biggie. I'll call them back." Though she frowned at the display. "I'm not familiar with the number."

"You can't know them all," Kai said, which only seemed sensible.

She laughed. "No. In fact, I can't." She pushed a key-pad and put the phone to her ear. "Hi, this is Regan Adler. Someone at this number just tried to reach me?" And then, in the slanting light from a distant parking lamp, her brows went up. "Kai? Sure. He's right here."

She handed over the phone. "It's for you."

Kai regarded the phone with some hesitation, all the feral certainty of his lynx fled in the face of social caution.

Besides, he might break the thing.

She picked up his hand and pressed the phone into it, putting it to his ear and biting her lip on a smile when he narrowed his eyes in lynx annoyance.

Just like that, his annoyance vanished—completely obliterated by what had just happened. How naturally he'd displayed the part of himself he'd always worked so hard to obscure from others. How naturally she'd reacted. How accepting.

For her, he suddenly realized, he would probably do anything. Including talk on a cell phone.

Even if he did hold it somewhat away from his ear. "This is Kai."

Phillip's voice, distorted as it was by the device, none-theless carried unmistakable relief. "You're all right."

"Phillip," Kai said with that same relief, catching Regan's eye to see her share it, eyes wide and pleased. "Are you well?"

"I will be," Phillip said. "But they told me—they *implied*—that they'd hurt you."

Country music played in the background, tickling Kai with resonance. On an impulse, he cracked the car door—that same music filtered in from the distant park. He said, "They did hurt me. They meant to kill me. They *didn't*."

Phillip's breath gusted unevenly through the phone. "Do you understand what this is about? Any of it?"

Kai glanced at Regan, who unclipped her seat belt and leaned across the seat divider to put her head next to his, her hand on his to tip the phone slightly. "Regan is here," he told Phillip, because he thought that was polite.

"Phillip," Regan said. "Are you here?"

"In the capable care of Mary and Bill," he said. "Kai, do you—?"

"Yes," Kai said. "I have some understanding. Not all. There is a man named Arshun—"

"The Realtor," Phillip said in surprised recognition.

"He is here to acquire certain resources."

Phillip snorted. "I know *evasive* when I hear it, son."

"I'm sorry," Kai said, by which he meant "that's as much as I can say." An experienced field Sentinel might do better—might have an entire list of ways to respond without lying and without telling the whole truth. Kai wasn't experienced...and he was hardly Sentinel at that. Just Kai Faulkes, a man who lived alone and who took the lynx.

Phillip sighed into the phone. "Doesn't matter. I know enough. No one in this town is prepared for a man of his kind—not the sheriff, not the people. Not me, when it came to it."

Kai heard the self-censure in Phillip's voice and hated it. How could any single man have been prepared for a Core posse?

But Phillip considered himself one of those who protected.

Like Kai.

"I'm sorry," he said again. "They were after the gun."

"They didn't get it," Phillip told him. "But aside from the fact that I've been looking for you for days, dammit, that's one of the reasons I called Regan. I hoped—"

"I'm with her," Kai said, and since Phillip had called Regan's phone and knew Regan was listening, he thought Phillip would also understand what those words truly meant. *She is mine.* "We're doing this together."

"Good," Phillip said. "But be careful. I think they're going to go after that gun again. I don't understand its importance, but—"

"The safe," Regan said, interjecting herself into the conversation with an apologetic glance at Kai. "How do we get in?"

Without hesitation, Phillip rattled off a string of numbers. Regan closed her eyes, lashes heavily shadowing her cheeks in the strongly oblique lighting from the streetlamp, her lips moving as she repeated them.

"I didn't know," Kai said into the phone, feeling it so inadequate. "When I left the gun with you, I didn't know they would come for it. I just knew it needed to be closed away."

"They didn't leave in one piece," Phillip said, his grim tone a contrast with the cheerful music in the background. "But I think there are more of them…and you had better be careful."

"More than careful," Kai said. "I will be myself."

And Phillip, even not knowing all the truths of that statement, chuckled. "Then *they* had better watch their step. Take care of it—and come talk to me when you can."

"We will," Regan said, making it into *we* with deliberate words as she added the conventional words of goodbye

and took the phone from Kai, flipping it closed as she sat
back in the driver's seat to regard him with a certain resignation. "Well," she said. "We came to hunt. I guess now
we know where to start."

They left Regan's vehicle where she'd pulled it over, a
blatant use of nonparking space, and walked to Phillip's
building. They might have run, if Kai had felt up to it. But
after a few jogging steps, he'd fallen back to a long-strided
walk, clamping his arm to his side. And they'd gotten here
soon enough at that pace.

It had taken Kai only moments to duck back into the
darkness of the office, seeing as clearly as he ever did and
moving in silence. When he came out, he carried the gun.
More than that, he gave it to her.

Regan stared at it with a mix of dread and revulsion,
seeing more than just a black metal weapon, feeling more
than just the weight of it in her hand—knowing it for a
thing of death.

Kai left her with it to pace the room, barely a hitch in
his stride; Regan followed him with her gaze, taking in
the damaged interior of the dojang.

There wasn't much here to break, but Arshun's men
had left their mark. Photographs knocked from the walls,
blood smeared across white-painted block, the door half-
off its hinges and closed only in a token fashion. Kai
moved through it in evident frustration, his expression
intent and his head slightly tipped and his movement in-
fused with stalking grace.

Until he looked at her with that frustration and shook
his head. "The bullet is out," he said. "But the working
lingers. I can't *hear*—" He shook his head again. "*Hear*
isn't the right word. *Sense*. I should be able to sense them.
To *know* them—or to track them."

"If I was better at this…" She made a face, filled with

inadequacy, and with the sudden folly of having believed she could help him at all.

That stopped him short. "No," he said. "We each have our own skills. This is different from being able to touch the land." He looked at the gun with some disdain. "Another could shield these workings from detection, even by the Core—I can't. Another could deactivate the workings—I can't. We work with what we have."

"Then what?" She held the gun out. "Carry it around until they find us?"

He grinned a fierce expression at her, and she suddenly realized that was exactly his intent. He stood a little taller, a little straighter...the gleam of a blue eye in shadow, the lynx brimming out from beneath.

"Okay," she said, just a little breathlessly. "That's one way to run a hunt."

He took a step toward her; it did nothing to dispel the aura of the *other* he'd suddenly brought into the room with him. "In most ways," he said, "I'm not Sentinel at all. Their concerns aren't my concerns. But in other ways—"

"No," she said, her voice low with the wondering realization of it. "You're *more* Sentinel than any of them. Because you're here on your own...just doing what you were born to do."

Understanding widened his eyes. "Protect this place."

He didn't add "at all costs." But then, he'd already proved that.

And Regan found herself saying, "But not alone."

He startled her by stalking right up to her—close enough to push the gun up against her body, where she imagined that the cold metal had a burn to it. "Yes," he told her, the rasp in his voice gone hard. "Alone."

Her temper spiked in an instant, and she forgot to be in awe of his strength and his beauty and even his nature. "If you think I'm just going to stand by and..."

He shook his head, an impatient gesture, though Regan had pretty much sputtered herself out of words on her own.

"Not standing, no." He wrapped his hand over hers on the gun. "Making sure this goes to the right people. The ones who are already looking for me."

She looked stupidly at the gun—at its undefined parts and side buttons, hint of protruding sights and low-profile hammer. "Kai, no—"

"Go meet them," he said. "Away from this place. Hide this along the way if you can—deep in concrete or metal. Arshun didn't come to this place because he could tell it was here—he came because he realized it was where *I* would go. I should have known—"

But Regan was stuck on what he asked of her. "Kai, *no*—"

He squeezed his hand over hers, hard enough so the gun's metal features pressed into her skin. "The gun itself doesn't matter so much," he told her, inexorable. "The bullets do. They carry the silent workings—small amulets. I don't know how—my father told me they require a certain kind of metal."

"Like we saw at the dry pool," she said numbly, drawn into the conversation in spite of her turmoil.

"So this is new. This is something the Sentinels need to know, so they can learn how to defend against them."

"Fine." She pulled her hand from his, and the gun with it. "Then come with me. We can meet them together. And they don't get the gun until they make sure Arshun is gone from Cloudview."

Regret speared through his expression. He closed his eyes, shuttering it—and opened them to a distant sort of determination. "We have no idea how close the Sentinels are…and once Arshun realizes you're gone with the gun, his people will come after you. Unless I distract them."

She stared at him with more dread than she'd thought

she could feel. "Then I should stay! They're not threatened by me—they don't even know I've remembered the truth about them. I can run to them, tell them you've gone all scary rogue—that's what they believe about Sentinels in the first place, isn't it?" Her voice went up in pitch with her desperation—and with the refusal in Kai's expression, the lift of his chin and the implacable nature of his stance. "I can promise them the gun, take them out into the woods...get us lost!"

He shook his head. "You have no protection from their workings. Once they realize...they'll make you one of theirs again."

"They won't, because I'm ready for them," she said fiercely. "Even if they do, you'll get me back again. I'm no *threat* to them, that's the point! But you—"

He turned on her, pushing her back a step with his presence alone. "Can't do what you can do!"

Stunned by the pain she felt in those words, she stood unresisting as he closed on her, threading his fingers through her hair at the nape and pulling her close for a kiss that consumed her with its ferocity. Nothing gentle about it, the way his mouth worked against hers, full of passion as much emotional as physical—full of the lynx, with nip and clash and play. And even while her body flared to life beneath it, her chest clenched in a reactive sorrow, something deeper than conscious thought and understanding.

He pulled away, kissed her brow and her cheek and then wrapped her close—no longer protecting his injury as he held her, his face buried against the side of her neck... drawing her up so her toes just touched the floor.

And then he let her go, and stepped away—*turning* away. "I can't call the Sentinels to me," he said, and his voice held the low rasp she suddenly recognized as lynx. "Not anymore."

"What makes you think I can?" she demanded, still reeling and still just as determined.

He sent her a crooked sort of grin, not quite turning back to her. "Because you have," he said. "How do you think you drove the poachers away?"

She moved around to face him, glaring. "*We* did that."

"And now you know how." He looked down at her, and his expression reflected the same sorrow still lurking hot and tight inside her. "But you always did. You just didn't know what you were doing. When you found my home… It's all the same."

"It's *not!*" she snapped at him, so suddenly angry she didn't even know what to do with herself, from one high emotion to the other, all centered around *Kai.* "It's not the same at all! I wasn't doing any of that on purpose! I was only *loving*—"

She clapped a hand over her mouth with a startled sound.

Loving you.

Because, of course, she did.

He swept her up again, held her close—just held her this time, his breathing a broken-sounding rasp in his chest. This time when he would have stepped back, she stopped him—snagging his tunic, the gun still between them, to capture him for a kiss. Her own kind of ferocity, gentler than his but just as insistent—and he didn't hesitate to offer her the same. Offering her, if not words, a response so heartfelt it felt tangible.

Loving you back.

But he did, eventually, lift his head. And she didn't stop him.

"Drive down to Alamogordo," he said. "Find a place for the gun. Under stone, under asphalt. Call for help. The Sentinels are looking. It won't take long."

"How long," she asked him, "will be too long?"

He only shook his head, lifting his shoulder in a hint of a shrug.

"What," she asked him, feeling the scrape of her own voice in her throat, "are you going to do?"

His smile was more a lift of lip than a curve of mouth; his eyes held a dark, dry humor. "Be myself," he said and left her there.

Chapter 27

Regan found herself back in her car, utterly unprepared to drive away from Cloudview—struggling with the impulse to turn around and find Kai.

But this was his world. His people, whether he claimed them or not. His *life*.

What did she know of any of it, except what she saw of it through him?

So she did as he asked. She stuck the gun inside the armrest console and started up her little SUV, wheeling it around in the darkness and knowing that Kai headed in the opposite direction on foot—being seen at the final hours of the Apple Blossom Festival. And being himself. Not the lynx—she knew better than that. But not quite as anyone here had ever seen him before, either.

She drove the steep, winding road out of town, past the arching canyon trestle, and then past the vista parking, both hands clutching the wheel and her speed a little reckless for both the road and the circumstances. She made herself slow down, becoming more thoughtful. Already looking for that spot in her mind that meant "reaching out," and finding it through memories of Kai—of looking for him, of her desperate, emotional efforts to understand herself and what she felt and what she could do.

At the time she'd taken that final step—*reaching, looking*—it had all seemed the hardest thing she had ever done. Now those memories came tinged with a sweet flavor, a satisfaction. She'd found what she'd needed—she'd found him, and she'd found herself.

Now she could find these Sentinels and bring them back to Kai before it was too late.

Beware...

Her foot eased off the gas before she even realized it, her shoulders stiffening.

That subtle hum of thought came not from around her, but from behind her. Not in response to her own initial attempts to send out to the Sentinels, but a totally unexpected thing.

BEWARE!

She cursed, holding herself together until she could ride the outside edge of the looming hairpin curve to the rugged canyon road it held. She pulled across the delta of that road entry, breathing hard. "What is your *problem?*" she snapped back at the land. "You're going to get me killed, and then where will Kai be?"

Flashes of music, flashes of danger. Not so much tasting of Kai as they did of Cloudview itself, of unsuspecting laughter so familiar as to go back to her childhood, the tang of elk jerky on her tongue, the gentle hum of an electric wheelchair in movement, a broad, round face with its pug nose and wide smile.

Mary. And Bill. And with them, Phillip.

"No," she said, a baffled protest into the silence of the car. "How does that do Arshun any good at all? They have

nothing to do with this. They *know* nothing." Not even
Phillip. Not really.

But Kai cared about them.

And she saw darkness all around them.

Kai walked the long stretch of Cloudview's single main
street, avoiding the streetlamps simply because of his comfort with the night. The occasional family-packed car swept
past, slowing at the sight of him…slowing a little more to
take him in, then accelerating onward.

Good. The more people who saw him, the better chance
he had to keep Arshun's focus here in Cloudview.

He made it past the long string of home-grown shops
fronting the road to the left, and the more recent, imper-
sonal services on the other side—gas station, water co-
op, post office. The music from the park swelled and then
faded into applause; the festival lighting grew to take over
the night sky.

Someone here might know how to find Arshun in his
Realtor guise, even if the man hadn't joined the cheery
little festival activities. And if Kai looked hard enough,
then Arshun would know he was here.

He encountered small groups walking in the opposite direction, bumping shoulders and laughing a little
too loudly, carrying the scent of alcohol. They didn't spot
him until he was nearly past—their laughter broke off
into startled silence, eyes unanimously wide as they took
in his clothing, his bare feet…the nature of his movement.

Then they burst back into laughter, staggering along
their way.

Kai found himself smiling grimly in the wake of them.
They'd seen what he'd hidden from these people for so
long, even if they wouldn't quite remember it in the morning. And this night, they wouldn't be the first.

He moved through the edges of the milling crowd—

threading the closing vendor booths and the small family clusters singing along with the country favorites, toddlers draped over their shoulders and young children drooping at their sides.

The singing invariably stopped as he passed, and that was okay, too.

"Kai?"

He almost didn't recognize her—a tidy woman not so much older than he was, her short brown hair clipped loosely back, her expression startled as she turned and found him beside her, her blazer and slacks casual but smart. And then he caught the scent of her and the scent of old books and abruptly felt stupid. *Miss Laura.* Of course, Laura from the library.

"It *is* you," she said, dropping her voice to a normal volume as the music fell briefly silent and the lead singer offered the crowd some patter while the others changed instruments. "Why—" But she stopped herself, looked him up and down and smiled. "Of course," she said. "This is the real you, isn't it? Not the face you show the rest of us."

"This is me," he agreed, unaccountably relieved at her easy acceptance. "I thought I would find Mary and Bill here…and Phillip."

"They were here," she agreed. "But they might have left early—Phillip probably shouldn't have tried to make it out tonight, even if he is in Bill's old push wheelchair." She shook her head in dismay. "Terrible thing, what happened—and to Phillip of all of us!"

Because of me. Because, unlike a true Sentinel, he had no real idea what he was doing, or who he was dealing with.

"I'm looking for a man named Matt Arshun," he said. "Do you know of him?"

She wrinkled her nose in reservation. "I know of him,"

she said. "Don't think much of him—he acts like a man who can buy his way into town."

"If you see Bill or Mary, let them know I'm here. If you see Arshun—"

He'd forgotten to keep his reaction to the man hidden; he'd forgotten to keep the lynx fully sheathed. Her mouth never quite closed on her words unfinished, her expression faintly stunned. She nodded so faintly he doubted she knew she'd done it. "You're worried," she said, coming to conclusions. "I'll look for them."

And he didn't bother to hide himself now, not when it was too late, and not when it would stick in her mind, driving her to seek out Mary, or to ask about Arshun. She saw it in him clearly enough, reflecting it with the uncertainty in her eyes. He left her that way, making no effort to smooth over what he'd done.

It was what he'd come for after all.

A car swept by where Regan sat blocking the canyon turnoff; then another.

She tried reaching out to him...found him. Just the hint of his presence, strong but faintly uneasy...out of his element. Determined. Carrying that undertone of the lynx.

And with no sense that he could perceive her, or that he'd made any effort to respond. Still blinded by the working that lingered in his blood, after too many days of sitting hard in his flesh.

It crossed her mind to wonder if he'd ever be whole again, and she bit her lip on the sorrow of that thought— the very real understanding, as no one else could understand, what a tragedy it would be for him if not.

For her, should it ever happen to her.

This thing she'd feared for so long, that she'd evaded for so long...had suddenly now become an irrevocably important part of her.

Just like Kai.

And Arshun was there, at the festival—not only aware of Kai, but waiting for him. Setting the stage to make him choose between his friends and himself.

The man who didn't call himself Sentinel, but who lived the ideals of one.

"Better than *you*," she said out loud, bitter words spoken to the unaware team now theoretically closing in on them. "You should have been looking out for this area. And you should have been the kind of people Kai's family felt safe with."

Or her family, for that matter. Whoever it had been, back in the family tree, who'd given her this faint tracing of Sentinel blood, and more than a little connection to this land. Her hands tightened on the steering wheel, hard enough to hurt. "You people *suck*."

And when she said it, she sent it out. A message by land, sent with all the fervent emotion behind it—rippling on through the trees and stone and precious underground layers of water.

She felt the startled reverberation as it slammed home nearby. As someone *heard*. And she heard it well enough in return—*Who?*

Not a query so much as a demand, and one that felt strangely entitled, at that. As if she didn't have a right to be there at all.

"Come and find me," she told the unknown, putting a snarl into it. A lynx snarl, the essence of what she'd come to feel from Kai.

And then she wheeled the SUV around in a tight, reckless U-turn and headed back up the mountain. Back to Kai.

Chapter 28

The park sat at the far edge of Cloudview's narrow ribbon of level ground. Behind it rose a sloped area threaded with narrow gravel lanes and vacation cottage clusters, all studded with mature pines and mossy-green undergrowth.

Kai stood on the bank just above the park and swept his gaze over the very human assembly of sound and motion, conversation and light and shiny things.

It wasn't a big park, but it had its dark corners. They weren't places Bill would go for any casual reason, not in the chair. But it was time to check them—to turn this excursion of *being seen* into a hunt.

Kai headed back down the bank with purpose, skirting the edges of the festival lights if not quite the dispersing crowd. Slipping into who he was, what he was—not whole, with his shoulder damp and throbbing, but whole enough for this. His leg, bearing his weight with only an ache of complaint.

He spotted the empty wheelchair just as Miss Laura

also reached it—and just as three men came on him from the side, casual and joking and falling into startled silence as they recognized him…and he, them.

They'd dressed in jeans and Western-styled button-downs for the festival, their heads bare and—until that moment—their expressions congenial. At the sight of him they stopped short, but it didn't take long for the nominal leader to snort and gesture with the oversize plastic drink cup in his hand. "You really *do* think you're Grizzly Adams."

"Gentlemen," Miss Laura said by way of protest, frowning at them.

"My name is Kai Faulkes," Kai told him, grim from his discovery and in no mood to deal gently with these men. "Do you know anything about this?"

"What? No," the man said, more or less automatically, and then looked down at the wheelchair and said, "I mean, *no*. About what?"

"Look," said the youngest of them, jamming his hands into his front pockets and giving Kai a wary look. "We don't want any trouble. Your girlfriend has that photo, and we know it. So whatever your deal is—"

The third guy interrupted. "Don't get your panties in a twist, Randy. He's already run into someone tougher than he thinks he is." He nodded at Kai's shoulder, where enough blood had soaked through the bandage to feel chilled against his skin.

Too much activity too soon. As if he'd had a choice. But he ignored the third man, responding directly only to the other two. "Have you seen the man who was using this?"

Their leader shrugged. "Earlier this evening, sure. Hard to miss that crew—the fat lady and the crippled guy from the store, and the guy in this chair. Beat to hell, he was. I heard there was a break-in at his place. I guess he wasn't as good with his kung fu as he thought he was, eh?"

"Gentlemen," Laura said again, drawing herself up. They had the grace to look abashed—but Kai was focused in on the hunt, shifting his attention to the youngest of them with question in his gaze.

"No, man," the guy said and glanced at the chair. "Hard to imagine he walked away from this thing. He looked pretty messed up."

"If you see him—"

"Yeah, yeah," the third guy said. "We'll tell him you're looking. Sure we will."

"If you see him," Kai said, a tone so flatly implacable that the guy stepped back, hands raised in exaggerated innocence, "*help* him. And if you won't help him, get someone who will."

Laura said, "He can't be far. He could hardly walk."

"Yeah, good luck with that," the leader said.

Laura put a hand on Kai's arm—it was enough to restrain him, but not to keep him from bristling. "It's a very small town," she told the men. "I hope you're planning to leave tomorrow, because I doubt you'll find service here after tonight."

The man snorted and lobbed his half-full cup into the nearest of the festival trash cans. The others followed him out of the park, although the youngest of them looked over his shoulder. "Hey," he said to his friends, undoubtedly thinking himself out of earshot, "isn't Kai the name of the hotshot hunt guide? The one Martin Sperry said he'd book for us this fall?"

"We'll find someone else," the leader of them muttered.

"Probably not," Miss Laura said, apparently keener of ear than most. She glanced around the thinning crowd. The music still played, the lights still bloomed over the artist's canopies, but Cloudview was never a late-night town and this family-oriented festival was no exception. "I'm getting worried. This doesn't make any sense."

No. It didn't. Not unless the Core had decided to push the boundaries of the conditions of détente between the Core and the Sentinels in the quest to recover their weapon—unless they'd again broken cover to reach Phillip.

In which case, the last thing he needed was the help of a kind woman who knew nothing of this world outside her own. Because he, too, knew not nearly enough—only what his family had taught him, and nothing of how a Core posse truly behaved in the field.

"Maybe the sheriff is here," he suggested to her.

"I'll just bet he is—or not far away. And, oh—" her expression brightened with determination "—I bet the band would make an announcement!"

Kai nodded, already crouching to eye the ground around the wheelchair—hints of his blued night vision overlaying the shadows, a lifetime of living and hunting in the forest at his fingertips as he brushed them over a gouge in the tough, flat native grass.

"Kai," she said, and he stiffened under the tentative hand she pressed to his shoulder. "Are you all right? Those men were right—you don't look well. And…we've been worried." She smiled wryly at his surprised look. "All of us. About you and Regan both. Things just haven't seemed right over this past week."

"Things aren't right," he told her. "But I'm about to do something about it."

This night, the lynx was on the hunt.

The far edge of the park petered out into darkness, a cluster of bear-proof garbage bins, a concrete well house and mature pines making the transition into private property forest.

There should have been a light over the bins; there wasn't.

Kai did little more than establish a brief pattern of sign

toward the bins before he quit tracking and started stalking. Not a true stalk, slinking and gliding and freezing in place, but a steady pace with intent behind it and his night vision kicking in to show the way. Up to the cluster of bins within the trees, past them to the well house—hearing nothing, seeing nothing…

The land silent around him.

"Kai, get out!" The truncated shout came from close by, muffled into a grunt of frustration. *Bill's voice. Mary's cry of dismay.*

But he had no time to step back and assess the danger. Light flooded the area, blinding him. He snarled in protest and warning, backing a few quick steps until he thumped up against the tree he'd just passed, one arm in front of his eyes and the other up as a ward.

Someone came on anyway, slamming reinforced knuckles into his shoulder and a quick patter of blows to his torso when he snarled and twisted away from that sudden renewed agony.

But the man had made a mistake, standing in that single spot to mete out punishment, arrogant with Kai's blindness. Kai blocked one blow, then another—and then, cornered too close to his attacker to launch a decent offensive, he sprang up for what would have been a resounding snap-kick to the head and instead used his knee—more agile, more limber than ever expected. The man went down hard from a blow to the temple, and Kai landed on his feet, crouched for action and blinking hard into the light.

"Kai!" Mary gasped, sounding more like admonishment than relief—and when his vision cleared, he saw it was just as much astonishment as anything else. Saw the same on Bill's face, along with the unvoiced curse lingering on his lips.

But Phillip sat on the ground with the wryest of smiles on his battered face, his arm clasped around his ribs and pride evident above all. "Kai," he said with an out-of-place calm that said Kai had only just confirmed what Phillip had suspected all along.

And the man sprawled at Kai's feet said nothing, but he didn't have to. He was Core, and he wasn't alone.

Chapter 29

Regan drove back into Cloudview against a stream of departing cars, and through the family and friend clusters still heading to their scattered parking spots. She quite rudely pulled right onto the winter-brown grass, helping herself to a parking spot that didn't exist. She yanked the gun from the center console to slip it into her jacket pocket where it barely fit.

The lights still blazed over the park, but the musicians were packing up and only a few vendors lingered. She ran to one of the food vendors, panting up with enough purpose that the man behind the window shook his head ruefully before she even got there. "Sorry, we're closed—we've got nothing on the grill."

"How about leftovers?" she asked him, too desperate to pay heed to his hiking brow. "Anything in aluminum foil?"

It didn't quite make enough sense; he only frowned at her.

"I don't care if the food is still good," she said, hands

wrapped around the blunt lip of the little sill. "I just need the foil!"

"I can't sell you old food!" But he took another look at her face and reached for a shelf just barely within sight of the window. "For Pete's sake…have you some tin foil." He tore off a sheet and shoved it through the payment slot.

She snatched it up, not caring so much about his doubtful expression. "Thank you! Thank you so much!"

"It's just foil," he muttered, barely audible as she ran back for the car and then nearly ran into a woman she instantly recognized as Miss Laura, there on the edge of a pool of light.

"Regan!" Laura sounded as desperate as Regan felt. "Have you seen Kai? He was just *here*—and Bill and Mary and Phillip *aren't*."

Regan supposed she should have pretended not to understand that fractured statement.

The problem was, she did. She understood completely.

She dropped to her knees, tugging the gun from her pocket and ignoring Laura's gasp. "Where did you last see him?"

"My God, Regan, what are you doing?"

"I have very little idea." Regan didn't hide the grim note in her voice as she fumbled with the gun, finally ejecting the magazine. *"Where?"*

"Just outside the vendor area—Phillip's wheelchair is there, and I don't know if you've seen him, but the man can barely walk—" Laura interrupted herself, straightening. "Regan Adler, what's going on?"

Regan glanced up, pushing bullets from the magazine and onto the foil. She still couldn't feel whatever had affected Kai, but she supposed that's what made these little missile-size amulets so dangerous—no one but Kai could.

No wonder his family had hidden him. No wonder the Core wanted him dead, now that they'd found him—now that he'd given himself away, coming to the defense of the land. Regan had felt the land cry out, that first day at the dry pool. But Kai had felt the silent amulets.

"Miss Laura," Regan said, deliberately giving her the respectful address she'd used as a child, "that voice worked on me once. Not so much now."

"Damn," Laura said. She pressed her lips together in pure exasperation—and in worry. "It was worth a try."

Regan balled the foil up around the cartridges, making sure it was plenty crumpled to create baffles of insulation. Such as they were. "Look," she said. "It's a long, long story, and it doesn't have an ending yet." She replaced the magazine into the pistol, fumbling a little with it until she heard it click into place. One cartridge in the gun now, sitting right in the chamber.

Not for long.

She stood, jamming the gun back into her pocket. "If I don't find them *right now,* the ending we get isn't going to be a happy one." *Hide it in earth, in metal, in concrete...* She had metal, more or less. She glanced around the park. *Concrete.*

Sure, under the pavilion. But she could hardly pry it up and—

There. The permanent park garbage can, set in its formed concrete container. Surely the two of them...

"Help me," she told Laura, no part of it a request.

"But what—?"

She turned on the woman, letting her new *fierce* come out. "Just do it! If I can ever explain, I will—but this is for Kai! For Bill and Mary and Phillip!"

And for all of Cloudview, even if they never knew it.

She ran for the garbage receptacle, and Laura did follow—if not at a run, then briskly enough.

"Push," Regan said. "I just need to tip it up a little—"

For a moment, as Laura awkwardly crouched to join

her, she thought they wouldn't do it—that they couldn't. And then it slid a few inches, caught on the lip of the uneven ground, and started to tip.

Hastily, she jammed the crumpled foil beneath it, up into the crack between the concrete base and the trash can it held. She jerked her fingers away. "I'm clear!"

The receptacle thumped down into place, and Laura backed away, brushing at her salmon-colored blazer.

Regan couldn't help but do the same, brusquely slapping at her jacket. "Thank you. I swear, if I can ever explain—"

Laura frowned at her. "I don't know if it's bad luck that Jaime Nez is off dealing with some guys who couldn't hold their beer or if you're better off."

"Neither do I," Regan said, more frank than she'd meant to be. How could she hide what was happening from a town still awake from a festival—or from this woman who was already searching for their missing friends?

She couldn't, that's how. And she wouldn't waste time trying. She had to find…

Laura said, "I've been all around this place looking for them, and they're not at the store or answering their phones. We even made an announcement."

Then Regan would start with Kai—and Kai would find the others.

If he hadn't already done it.

And if the Core hadn't found *him*.

Arshun. Arshun and three of his men—two replacement musclemen and Marat. Waiting for Kai…*counting* on him.

Arshun nudged his minion with a pointy-toed shoe. "Get up," he said. "I'd dock you for that sad display, but I think everyone here knew it was inevitable." He bestowed a condescending smile on Mary and Bill, who tightly held one another's hand. "Well, perhaps not quite everyone."

Kai put his back against the tree, his ribs aching and

his shoulder full of shards of pain; he couldn't quite stand up straight. "I'm here. Isn't that what you wanted? Let them go."

"It's not quite what I wanted," Arshun told him as the downed man struggled to his feet and stood without any assurance in himself. His partner loomed in lurking mode, while Marat stood behind Bill, a small man looming with menace. "But don't worry. If I complete my business here, I'll release them. After all, you've already seen what I can do with memory—they're no threat."

"I've seen you're not as good as you think you are," Kai told him. "You couldn't control Regan for long."

"I *knew* it!" Mary burst out. "I knew there was something wrong with that girl!"

Arshun lifted one shoulder. "She was more than she first seemed," he said. "I would have handled that differently if I'd known."

"You shouldn't have *handled* her at all." Something inside Kai went darker, just a little less controlled. "You shouldn't have touched anyone in this town."

"Town," Arshun scoffed. "It's barely an ugly spot on the map."

"Funny," Phillip said. "I definitely feel the same way about you, whoever you are."

"You'll never have the chance to figure it out." Arshun's words came a little less casually.

"Tell him, then," Kai said, finally managing to straighten himself, pressing his shoulders against the tree—remembering how the land had lent him strength and warmth in those hours he would have died without it, and narrowing his eyes at the reminder of its loss. The sensation of darkness still threaded through him—leaving him to bleed, leaving him blind. "Tell him," Kai repeated, "how you've come looking for a safe place to hide your evil, and that you don't care how you get it."

"Evil." Arshun regarded him with annoyance. "That's just rude."

"Tell them all," Kai said, "that you want the Adler land, and when you didn't get it, you arranged for Frank's injury—and then you went after Regan. Tell them how this situation has grown so big in your hands, and the trouble you're in from it."

"Certainly," Arshun said. "Shall I also tell them how you've managed to stop me so far? Or that your little Regan takes after her mother, seeing and hearing things that should get her committed? If she is, do you suppose she'll last any longer than her mother did, once the doctors did their worst?" He made a *tsk*ing noise. "Doctors just don't understand your kind very well, do they?"

"Kai," Mary said, her voice trembling, "what is he talking about? What are *you* talking about?"

"You see?" Arshun indicated the three hostages. "Now you've upset them."

Never facile with words, Kai found himself without them now. He growled deeply, leaving no doubt about that threat.

"Actually," Arshun said, looking satisfied, "*no one* truly understands your kind. Including you, apparently. Do you think we don't know you're up here alone?"

Kai saw her the instant before he heard her. *Regan.* Arshun had no warning at all.

She stepped out from behind the brick well house and into the light, the gun clasped in an inexpert hand, her posture defiant. "You're wrong," she said, determination in her voice and stance and definitely in her eye. "He's not alone. And you have no idea what we can do together."

"Regan…" Kai couldn't hide his dismay. *Regan and the gun both.* Why had she come here into danger? Why had she brought the gun straight to the Core?

She didn't need a translation—or even a connection to

him—to understand his reaction. "I had to," she told him. "I—I heard the warning." She lifted her head, encompassing Mary and Bill and Phillip...and Kai himself. Her expression held determination; her uncertain voice revealed her fear. "I couldn't just leave this to happen."

No. Of course not. Because he'd taught her who and what she was. Because he'd shown her who and what *he* was.

Or what he was supposed to be.

"Sentinels," Arshun said with disgust pushing through his satisfaction, one hand up to still his two musclemen when they would have moved for Regan. "You just can't help yourselves." He gestured at the gun, snapping, "Marat!"

The least imposing of his men—the one who had managed the amulet cleansing—stepped out from behind Bill's chair. "Yes," he said. "It's not as strong as it should be— but that's our prototype."

"*That's* why you want it back so badly," Regan said, looking down at the gun. "It's not just about taking my dad's place for your secret hideaway. You can't afford for the Sentinels to find *this*." She narrowed her eyes at Arshun, a quick glance to his men and back. "I bet you can't even afford for your own people to know it's here, can you?"

Arshun showed no concern. "We're a small team, dealing with a rather large task. Stubborn people, unexpected Sentinels...life just isn't fair sometimes." He smiled at her, showing teeth. "Give me the gun, little Sentinel girl, or I'll start hurting people."

"Regan," Bill said, his voice full of unspoken words. A little bit "get this bastard" and a little bit "you're the one with the gun—use it!" and a whole lot "don't let them hurt Mary."

"*Regan,*" Kai said, his voice full of unspoken words,

his body warning him that it couldn't be relied upon. *Be careful* and *I'm furious* and *I love you.*

"Regan," Arshun said, his voice full only of a mocking satisfaction.

Regan lifted the gun just enough to clear her foot. "Let them go," she said, "and I won't bury this bullet in the ground where you'll have to waste your precious time hunting for it while everyone out there comes running. Let them go, and I'll tell you where the rest of the bullets are hidden. Let them go, and you *might* have the chance to get out of this place with your secrets."

Arshun fixed her with a hard look as Marat said, "That would explain its weakness. She's unloaded it."

"I've mostly unloaded it," Regan agreed. She looked at Kai, a glance of purpose that he couldn't quite interpret.

It did nothing to quell his turmoil of emotion—the need to snarl his fury conflicting with his impulse to wrap his arms around her and never let her go—or the impulse to shove himself between her and Arshun, as little good as it would do.

Regan lifted her chin. "Let them all go. We'll walk back out into the park, I'll put this gun down and we'll go our separate ways."

Arshun barked laughter. "And then what? We start our little game all over again? Or have you forgotten your father?"

"My father signed a power of attorney before the surgery," Regan said, shrugging, and Kai tried to hide his surprise just as he hid what the short fight had taken out of him, pushing himself back against the tree.

It didn't matter. Like everyone else, Arshun had eyes only for Regan. "That simplifies things, but doesn't stop me from using him."

"It *is* simple." She gestured slightly with the gun. "Let them go. Let *me* go. And get what you want."

Arshun seemed to consider it. Actually seemed to consider it...

Kai felt the swell of warning from within himself, knowing they couldn't trust this man even for this moment. His amulet expert had a hand in his pocket, a knowing look on his face...if he so much as brushed against Regan on the way back out into the park, she would be theirs again.

And it wouldn't matter for how long, because it would be long enough. She'd never break free in time to stop them from regaining all the advantage they'd ever had. They'd kill Kai, they'd bury problematic memories from Phillip, Mary and Bill and they'd run roughshod over this little town.

You should have done as I asked. Taken the gun, found the Sentinels...

Been safe.

"You won't fire it," Arshun decided, taking a step toward her; his men gravitated toward Kai. "You won't draw attention to us this way."

Regan laughed, utterly without humor. "They aren't my secrets," she said. "and you're the one who started stomping around up here."

Arshun glanced at Kai, a knowing look. She might not have secrets, but Kai...

It doesn't matter, he thought at her, grabbing her gaze just long enough for that. And it didn't. The Core knew he was here. The Sentinels knew he was here. His friends already knew he was more than they'd ever thought, if not exactly why.

Regan's eyes reflected pale in the overhead light, flashing with the faint lift of her head. She might not understand his exact message, not with the land severed between them. But she understood the reassurance behind it, and the intent—and she sent him back one of her own. *Apology. Determination.*

Arshun should have paid attention.

"You won't," he said again, and made a sudden grab for her.

She shot him in the foot.

Someone cried out in surprise from behind her, and Phillip made an aborted, protective lurch for Bill and Mary, unable to do more than crumple beside Bill's chair, and Kai—

Kai moved.

With Arshun's shout of anger and pain in his ears, and the man himself sprawled back on the ground in awkward surprise, groping for some weapon of his own, Kai moved.

He went for Arshun first, pushing off the tree and into action—releasing the lynx just enough to swell fury over his weakness, to reach for the unerring swiftness of his other—to bring his hand slapping down at Arshun and bat the emerging pistol from his hands and skittering away into the trees.

He rolled aside, bounded up and drove all that energy into a stiff-armed blow against the solar plexus of the next man, the one he'd already taken down once—and then planted his hands on the man's shoulders, using him as a pivot and ignoring the scream of pain in his own shoulder as he kicked out to catch the second muscleman against the side of his face, a cracking blow to his jaw.

Kai landed in a crouch, a snarl on his lips and already targeting Marat—but Regan cried out in surprise, dropping to her knees and ignoring her proximity to Arshun. Not just ignoring him, but shoving his foot aside as she ran her hands over the dirt. "Help me!" she shouted—distinctly over her shoulder. "We have to find it!"

Kai caught a brief hesitation of movement from behind the well house, and Regan looked back again. "Miss Laura—!"

Laura. Still here, making herself part of this. She

emerged—at first with hesitation, and then with more purpose—and dropped to her knees beside Regan, running
her hands over the hard dirt.

The earth trembled; the trees groaned around them.

Mary clutched at Bill from behind the wheelchair, new
fear on her face. He grabbed her hands, clutching back.
Phillip cursed in astonishment—his attention, once riveted
on Kai with eyes narrowed and assessing, jerked away—
went to the ground, went to the woods.

Marat cast a wild glance at Kai, at Regan—at Arshun,
who snapped something that Kai made no attempt to understand. Not so far into the lynx, not fighting so hard
against the darkness that clutched him anew, and not when
he already knew what he needed to do.

When Marat darted for Regan, Kai went for him—
slamming into him, one hand at his throat and one drawn
back into clawed fingers, ready to strike—ready to tear,
as any wild thing would tear at its prey.

Regan screamed at him. *"Kai, NO!"* Even Phillip
shouted out in warning, as if it was so obvious to them all
that Kai had lost something of himself—to the darkness,
to the anger...to the lynx.

"Kai," Regan said again, no longer scrabbling at the
ground but scrambling closer to him—and if one part of
him strained for the touch of her, the other snarled vi-
ciously at her encroachment.

But he stayed his hand, fingers still clawed and trembling with restraint.

"You—" Regan said to Marat, stumbling over quick
words. "You're the one who does these amulet things. Turn
it *off.*"

The man didn't take his eyes from Kai—barely seemed
able to talk at all, frozen with fear and his lips hardly moving. "Can't."

Kai understood it as a refusal and snarled, eyes narrowed…lynx rising. He gathered himself—

"Kai!" Regan said sharply, a sound that barely penetrated the swirling darkness, the taste of old blood in his mouth, the deep, ancient anger that swelled in him—pushing up from a wounded earth and right through him because he'd been wide-open, hunting connection, missing it…yearning for it. It mixed with protective fury. *Injured. Cornered. Dangerous.*

Regan spoke; he shook her off in rejection. She persisted, her voice in his ear; her hand closed over his in midair, where it had no impact on the terrible, stiff weapon he'd made of it. Still she twined her fingers around his, applying gentle pressure—and with her touch came new sensations.

Warmth. Comfort. A tingle of soothing presence. A hint of liquid arousal.

Love.

"Kai," she whispered, coming close to his ear as he suddenly became aware of how hard he trembled with tension and battle, how much he hurt, how appallingly easy it would have been to turn the weapon of his body against her. "Not this. Not as man, not as lynx. Not as *mine*."

Mine.

He'd been afraid of hurting her. He'd been afraid of loving her—so long warned against what his unfettered strength might do to her.

Please, Kai. Stay mine.

Her fear pressed against him. Not fear for her body, but fear for that which she'd already given him. Fear for her heart—fear for his.

The greater harm.

He took a deep and sudden breath, a sharp sound on a gulp of air. He thought of them together…of the gentle beauty of the control he'd maintained in her bed. Of his ease in it. Of *reveling* in it.

Stay. Mine... "Yes," she whispered, her hand squeezing his. "Please."

And dazed, he let her pull him away.

Dazed, he found and met her gaze. *Yes. Yours.*

She wrapped one arm around him, resting her cheek briefly against his shoulder. And then the relief and pride in her expression changed to something else. She flattened a hand against the rumbling ground and came up with the gun.

Marat froze from where he'd been inching away, more walleyed at the groan of the surrounding trees than he was about Kai—but gave the unloaded gun a second look and relaxed again.

Regan said, "It'll still hurt if I hit you with it. And I'm really, really angry, so I'll hit you with it *hard.*"

"You won't have to," Phillip said, and Kai found him close, his stylish cane coming to hover over Marat's face. "I may be beat to hell, but I can still hook this cane up his nostril and rip."

Kai gave a weak snort of laughter, the lynx easing back to give him thinking space.

Marat braced against the quaking earth. "I *can't stop it.*"

"He's telling the truth," Arshun said through gritted teeth. He sat on one haunch, clutching his ankle; blood poured from his shoe. "The workings aren't *stopped.* They run their course."

Wood cracked not far away, then again—with ominous grace, a tree gave way, groaning all the way down—they all froze, hearing it but unable to discern exactly where it stood or where it would land.

A sudden final rush of breaking branches, the springy bounce of the crown landing—

Regan glanced at Laura, who'd stopped searching to

stare wide-eyed at Kai, at Regan—at the two of them, and what they were together. "Better dig, then. That bullet can't be buried too deeply." She lay down the gun to reach for Kai again, this time withdrawing the knife the lynx had forgotten he had, tossing it toward Laura.

"I don't understand a single moment of this," Laura muttered. She stabbed at the dirt, fingers pushing in behind to feel for metal. A sudden flurry of shouts rose from the park interior, along with the sound of ripping cloth and twisting metal. *Something giving way.*

"Why the hell did you even shoot the ground?" Arshun snapped at Regan, abandoning his own pain to yank keys from his pocket and join Laura's efforts.

"I shot *you*," she snapped back at him. "Why the hell did you bring your poison to this town in the first place?"

The new voice came without warning and without apology. "That's what I'd like to know."

The two figures coming around the well house moved with grace and authority and power—the man taller than Kai with an impressive breadth of shoulder and strong build beneath work jeans and the rolled sleeves of an untucked flannel shirt.

More than that…

Sentinel.

Big cat, with tawny hair gone dark at the temples, shadowed eyes full of intent—power, riding beneath a deceptively easygoing stance.

The petite woman at his side looked even smaller in comparison, her presence more contained—her dark hair scraped back into a neat ponytail and her eyes big and smoky, carrying the same natural kohl effect as Kai's, only more so. Also cat of some kind. Also Sentinel.

The lynx raised a growl at them.

"God," said the woman. "What a mess."

Arshun swore, falling back from his efforts. Marat

swore, closing his eyes and flipping a faint wave at Phillip and his cane. Giving up.

Kai crouched in warning. *Sentinels.* Just as much of a threat as the Core in their way. Here, on his turf—

"That," said the woman, dealing him a dark look, "is the first thing we'll deal with."

"You leave him alone," Regan said, and her spiking concern came through Kai, clear and jarring. "I didn't bring you here for him!"

But the man ignored them both, his head angled as if to catch a sound on the wind. He strode right up beside Laura, and she fell away in no small alarm—giving him all the considerable space he needed to crouch and place his hand flat over the earth. He closed his eyes, his face quiet but for a few faint flickers of effort.

More shouting from the park presaged the *pow* of an exploding light, then another—

And then the world seemed to take a breath, a deep and momentary silence. It was followed hard on by an even deeper rumble, one that growled around them like water spiraling in on a drain.

Regan's grip on Kai's hand grew even tighter, a desperately frightened note in the land—and Kai battled what it roused in him, battled darkness and territorial fury and the lynx coming out to protect it all.

Leaning on her heart to stay himself.

The earth beneath the man's hand popped, the sound of it sharp and startling. He let out a long sigh into the following silence and opened his eyes, shifting back to sit on one heel, his wrist resting over an upraised knee. "Sorry," he told Arshun, a shrug in his voice. "I broke it."

But the earth's wound still rippled with darkness— rippling right through Regan and Kai. The man knew it; he shook his head at the woman. "I can try to do something with the leftovers, but I think we're better off letting it heal on its own."

"That's fine," she said tightly, her gaze pinned on Kai. "We've got other things to handle."

Kai knew threat when he saw it. He snarled, felt it well up out of him along with the lingering darkness right along with Regan's sharp fear—radiating through the rush of bloody warmth from a wound just as reactive to the Core working as the land.

"Hey," Regan said, starting a little as she turned to him.

From such beautiful eyes, the woman's expression turned hard. She glanced at the gathering—Kai's friends, so suddenly exposed to worlds they never should have seen—and her mouth flattened. "Joe, we need to take him and the minions and go. *Now*. Before—"

Before nothing. Kai gathered himself—

But even as he pushed away from the ground, Regan jumped up before him—her back to him, her arms outspread to keep him—blocking him, blocking them. And where Kai growled deeply, his body vibrating with all the forces trying to shred him from within, Regan's voice came sharp and hard.

"No," she said. "You may not take him!"

"You," said the man named Joe, shaking his head, "are something else we have to figure out."

"You can't take either of us!"

Her panic hit Kai's fragile control like a blow. He wrapped his arm around her, as if pulling them so closely together might somehow save them both.

And maybe it did.

Regan steadied. "You want to protect? Then *protect*. That includes what's best for your people. If that was ever true, then Kai wouldn't have been alone against these people—and he wouldn't have had to hide from you in the first place!" In her steadiness, she reached out—to Kai, to the land. Soothing. Shepherding.

And gathering. Finding the roiling dark ripples…pulling them in, and then pushing the accumulated darkness back out at the Sentinels who had come not just to help save the day, but to turn on one of their own.

"Lyn," said the man, looking suddenly wary.

"I feel it," she said, putting out a hand as if that would make a difference. Flinching. "*Stop* her."

But Laura had seen enough, and she scrambled to her feet, coming up beside Kai—shaking with fear and reaction, but holding her ground. "Kai and Regan are ours," she said. "I don't care why you're here!"

Mary said, "You can't just *take* them."

Phillip pulled himself to his feet, unsteady—putting a hand on Kai's shoulder to anchor himself and letting his very presence speak for him.

"He's *mine,*" Regan said, and her touch on the land came through to Kai as firmer, calmer—and tasting of his own lynx, as if she'd drawn on that, too. "And I'm his, and neither of us belong to *you.*"

With some desperation, the small woman said, "Joe Ryan, if ever there was someone going dark—"

But Joe Ryan reached out to touch the side of her face and said, "This is defensive, sweetheart, not aggression. And bullying the land isn't what I do." He looked at Regan, wincing at the ongoing push of the lingering pain and darkness and then held Kai's gaze. "Bullying our own people, Lyn…it isn't what we *should* do. Even with all of this."

"God," she said again, pressing the fingertips of both hands against her brows—partly in pain, partly in obvious defeat. "What a *mess.*" She turned away from them, tucking herself up against her partner and welcoming the arm that came around her. "Yes. All right. We'll work it out. Now *stop.*"

And Kai let his legs go out from beneath him as Regan released the land, turning to throw her arms around him—with Phillip's hand on his shoulder and Laura's hand on his arm and Mary's hand on his back and Bill's wheelchair humming up to close in behind.

"We belong to *us*," Regan said, and he rested his forehead against her shoulder and let the lynx breathe in of her.

Chapter 30

"Do you think they can find us here?" Regan lay on a blanket over flat rock, her bare skin soaking up the high altitude sensation of cool air and tingling hot sunshine. She let herself float in it, still replete with her response to Kai's love—her body still sensitive from his fingers, still pulsing intimately from the moments she'd twined her legs around him, her heels digging into the hard curve of his low back and lean flanks, his name on her lips.

His breath gusted out, not quite so much sigh as the expression of a frown. He rolled smoothly to his feet and moved a few steps away, stretching with languid grace.

She didn't open her eyes; she knew where he was. That he stood on the edge of the outcrop, looking out on the land from the very same place she'd stood not so long ago— the place from which she'd finally found him…and in the process, found herself.

Eventually, he said, "Now that they know of me, they can find me anywhere. They can find us."

She took a moment to absorb the truth of that.

Not that she hadn't known it. Joe Ryan and Lyn Maines were more than just reasonably local Southwest Sentinels. Joe Ryan spent his time in Flagstaff, Arizona, monitoring the San Francisco Mountains…*shepherding* them. As Kai did, he spoke to the land…if not its essence so much as its power flows, and on an entirely different level.

A much bigger and louder level.

It was hard for him to hear what Kai could do; it was impossible for him to perceive the Core as Kai did. But given purpose, he could and would track them down.

Whereas Lyn Maines would never lose them. Not the woman who could taste the merest hint of a Sentinel's personal trace.

Regan wrinkled her nose under the sunshine. If there were two individuals *more* capable of tracking them down, she couldn't imagine it.

"I guess I knew that," she said, brushing a hand across her stomach in reminiscence of his recent touch.

"If they were going to follow us, they would be here by now." His voice sounded distant; her mind's eye filled in his expression—eyes half-closed, his face a thing of wild beauty, hair glinting black and the lines of his cheek and jaw strong beneath the sunshine, hard muscle strong beneath gleaming skin.

"I guess I knew that, too. I just can't help…" Restless, she sat, wrapping her arms around upraised knees.

They'd been nonplussed, Joe Ryan and Lyn Maines—and a man named Nick Carter, who was their Southwest consul boss, and who spoke to them from Tucson through an equally bemused woman named Annorah, whose communication skills made her the hub for the entire region.

Brevis, they called that.

Regan had a lot to learn. And so did Kai.

But it seemed that they would, for now, learn it right here.

Lyn Maines hadn't liked it. "One *hell* of a mess," she'd said, there in the long-distance conversation that everyone but Regan could hear—even Kai, now that he'd been found and included, had a sense of Annorah's mind voice. "Not one but *two* of them. And one of them a fully blooded field Sentinel."

By then, they'd all retreated to Phillip's dojang, having delivered Bill and Mary to their home and Phillip along with them.

They'd left behind them the shaken remnants of the festival, the damaged trees and damaged vendor booths, and the festival organizers rushing to wrap things up so cleanup from the inexplicable earthquake could be tended during daylight.

They'd also left behind the poachers, who'd come rushing out of their cabin in response to the gunshot and the earthquake, loaded for bear and instantly understanding that they'd stumbled into something bigger than they were—deciding, on the spot, that they'd help with the next day's cleanup and save their hunting for the moments when it became legal.

They'd left Miss Laura at the library, where so many of the books had fallen from the shelves—and she'd assured them that she was fine, and that reshelving the books would offer her time to absorb what she'd seen. She and Phillip and Bill and Mary had perceptibly made the decision to accept the token flash of badge from Lyn and Joe, leaving questions unspoken.

To Regan's surprise, they'd left Arshun in the care of his men—such as remained. "We each police our own," Joe had said simply. They'd retrieved the hidden cartridges and headed out with the gun and its invaluable ammunition in hand.

At the dojang, things hadn't gone so smoothly. "A hell of a mess," Lyn Maines muttered, pacing the padded floor with all the energy Regan didn't have. She'd stabbed a sharp look at Kai, and by now Regan knew to expect that from her. "You need training. It's not optional. You need protection while you get that training. You need to be in the field—a Sentinel who can trace the silent amulets! Do you even know how many lives you could have saved over the past eighteen months? Do you even know what's been *happening* with us over that time?"

Kai—exhausted and hurting and reeling—had said nothing.

Regan understood, better than Lyn Maines, better than Joe Ryan, that he had gone to a place within himself where he was likely to say nothing.

Joe sat on one of the spectator benches, elbows propped over his knees, wrists relaxed. *All* of him relaxed, for that matter. Easygoing, even in the middle of it all. "Lyn," he said, "we all have reasons for the secrets we hide."

That had brought her up short—but not without a scowl aimed his way.

"He's got to have training," Joe agreed. "*She's* got to have training. But this isn't one of those times when being a hard-ass is going to work." At her narrowed eyes, he smiled—just there, around his eyes—and added, "As much as I love the ass in question."

"Not," she ground out, "appropriate."

But Regan found herself smiling for the first time, and Joe had seen it and nodded and said, "Don't worry. We can see how it is. We'll make it work."

A funny, wistful look crossed Lyn's face. "They do love him here," she said, looking at Kai. "They have no idea what just happened, and if I have anything to say about it, they never will…but…"

They do love him, Regan had finished for her. Just for who he was. And so did she.

In the two days since, while Regan and Kai reassured

Frank Adler and holed up at the cabin and healed, the Sentinels had done little more than leave updates on Regan's voice mail—brief words concerning the arrangements being made, the discussions of the incoming tutor… their attempts to locate Kai's family, who no longer had any reason to hide.

Regan thought she'd meet them soon. And she could only hope she passed muster, because she wasn't going anywhere. Sentinels aside, her life had changed irrevocably; she could never leave this land again.

She never wanted to.

She took a deep breath of the pine-scented air, lifting her head to focus on the here and now. Kai still stood where he'd been, his head slightly turned in response to her—the sun gilding his naked back, his stance everything that was primal and wild and *other*.

"I'm going to paint you like this," Regan said without even thinking. Her painting would go on—so would her career. Maybe it would even take a turn for the better, given this new inspiration. "Big, broad strokes, all insinuation and implication. Wild. Like you."

He turned his head a little bit more, sharing his smile. "I think it's time to go down," he said. "To them. To see what happens next."

She rose to her feet—never as graceful as he was, but comfortable in her nudity, comfortable with the woods, comfortable with him. "All right," she said, sliding her arms around his waist, pressing up against his warmth. "Let's go, then. Together."

The lynx purred.

* * * * *

Special Offers

Every month we put together collections and longer reads written by your favourite authors.

Here are some of next month's highlights— and don't miss our fabulous discount online!

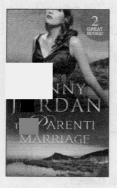

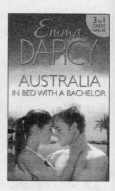

On sale 21st February   On sale 28th February   On sale 21st February

Save 20%
on all Special Releases

Join the Mills & Boon Book Club

Want to read more **Nocturne**™ books?
We're offering you **1** more absolutely **FREE!**

We'll also treat you to these fabulous extras:

- 🌹 Exclusive offers and much more!

- 🌹 FREE home delivery

- 🌹 FREE books and gifts with our special rewards scheme

Get your free books now!

visit www.millsandboon.co.uk/bookclub
or call Customer Relations on 020 8288 2888

FREE BOOK OFFER TERMS & CONDITIONS

Accepting your free books places you under no obligation to buy anything and you may cancel at any time. If we do not hear from you we will send you 2 stories a month which you may purchase or return to us—the choice is yours. Offer valid in the UK only and is not available to current Mills & Boon subscribers to this series. We reserve the right to refuse an application and applicants must be aged 18 years or over. Only one application per household. Terms and prices are subject to change without notice. As a result of this application you may receive further offers from other carefully selected companies. If you do not wish to share in this opportunity please write to the Data Manager at PO BOX 676, Richmond, TW9 1WU.

The World of Mills & Boon®

There's a Mills & Boon® series that's perfect for you. We publish ten series and, with new titles every month, you never have to wait long for your favourite to come along.

By Request

Relive the romance with the best of the best
12 stories every month

Cherish™

Experience the ultimate rush of falling in love
12 new stories every month

Desire™

Passionate and dramatic love stories
6 new stories every month

nocturne™

An exhilarating underworld of dark desires
Up to 3 new stories every month